HOLE IN THE WORLD

HOLE IN THE WORLD

A NOVEL OF THE LOST LEVEL

BRIAN KEENE

ISBN 978-1-937009-72-4 (TPB)

Apex Publications, LLC
PO Box 24323
Lexington, KY 40524

Also available as a DRM-free eBook.

Visit us at www.apexbookcompany.com.

This one is for Paul Campion, through thick and thin.

[1]
RIDERS ON THE STORM

At least they're not talking much, Lucinda Hawkins thought as she eased the airport shuttle bus through the blizzard. Lucinda had been awake for seventeen hours straight, was well into overtime, and had a vicious migraine forming behind her temples. The coffee cup in the drink holder beside her was cold, the coffee inside it was even colder, and the bus's heater was lethargic at best. It wheezed like an asthmatic robot, belching out pitiful, lukewarm drafts of air. Lucinda gripped the steering wheel and stared straight ahead into the storm. She couldn't see more than a few feet ahead of her, and although the plows had gone through only moments before, the road was already covered again with drifting, blowing snow. Lucinda was tense, tired, and pissed off. Yattering passengers, angry over their flight cancellations, would have only added to her stress levels. A few of them murmured into their cell phones, but for the most part, they sat in uneasy silence, watching the snow fall.

As often happened while she was driving, Lucinda's thoughts turned to her granddaughter, Mikya. Her mother, Lucinda's daughter, had passed away two years ago after a quick and unexpected battle with ovarian cancer. The girl's father was currently serving twenty-five to thirty years at the Maryland Correctional Institution in Jessup. He was allowed two visits per week, but had expressed no interest in seeing his daughter, and indeed, hadn't even added Mikya or Lucinda to his approved visitor list. Lucinda was raising the five-year-old on her own, something she hadn't expected to be doing at this stage of her life. Raising children was hard enough when you were in your twenties or thirties. To be doing it again at age forty-eight? That was exhausting.

Mikya was with a neighbor tonight, one that Lucinda trusted, but she also knew that the little girl would be upset about spending the night there. Since the loss of both parents, she'd clung even tighter to her grandmother. Lucinda hadn't minded, though. After two ex-husbands and the death of her only daughter, Mikya was pretty much all she had. Mikya was Lucinda's whole world, along with her few friends from church, and this stupid job.

A snapshot of the little girl was taped to Lucinda's dashboard. Next to it, tucked into the console, was a paperback copy of *And Then There Were None* by Agatha Christie. Lucinda had checked it out of the library last week, and read it during her lunch breaks. Judging by the weather, she'd be lucky to get a lunch break tonight.

A passenger seated behind her raised his voice, apparently losing his cell phone signal. "Buzz? Buzz, are you there? Oh, you stupid fucking cock-sucking phone!"

Lucinda frowned. She debated asking the man to watch his language, but she didn't want to start an altercation. He already seemed wound up. If he became any more belligerent, it could distract her from the road. The storm seemed to be growing worse.

Across from Lucinda, beneath a blue handicapped sign, a bespectacled man in a wheelchair stared at the angry caller, his expression impassive. Seated next to him was a short, thin man, who was nodding off and apparently oblivious to the commotion. Lucinda glanced at them and then turned her attention back to the road. She wondered how anyone could be sleepy in the midst of a blizzard. Then she remembered that she had heard him speak when they first boarded the shuttle. He'd had an Australian accent. The time zone difference was probably catching up with him. Poor thing.

"Buzz?" The irate passenger's voice grew louder. "Shannon? Are you there? Goddamn it! This fucking phone ..."

Sighing, Lucinda focused on guiding them safely through the storm, and tried to tune the man out.

The snow fell harder.

———

PAUL LEGERSKI STARED at his phone in annoyance. He had three bars of coverage, yet the call had dropped. Noticing that the screen was smudged, he wiped it off on his San Jose Sharks jersey, and then tried redialing Shannon again. He watched as the signal bars rose to five, then dipped to one, before finally settling on three again. It looked like the call was connecting, so he brought the phone to his ear.

"Buzz," he said, calling Shannon by her nickname. "You there?"

"I'm here, Paul," she replied, "but I can barely hear you over the noise."

"What noise?"

"There's a weird background noise. It was there before the call dropped, and now it's back again. Don't you hear it?"

"No."

"You sound like you're in a wind tunnel."

"More like a blizzard," Paul said. "Listen, let me tell you

what's going on in case the call drops again. They've cancelled all flights out of Baltimore. The airport is shut down. I tried to get a flight out of Washington-Dulles, but apparently they're closed down, too. The airline is putting us up in a hotel tonight, at least. I'm on the shuttle now, heading to it."

"That sucks."

"Tell me about it. What's the weather like back there in Corona?"

"Sunny and warm. You know how it is. Typical California day."

"Wish I was back home."

"I wish you were, too. Oh, and I forgot to tell you! Guess wh—"

Shannon's voice was suddenly replaced by another, as if their call had intersected with someone else's. The new speaker was male, his tone gravely and harsh. It reminded Paul of the Klingon's on *Star Trek*. Paul frowned as the voice overrode Shannon's. The language was like nothing he recognized.

"Garblish farhtuk! Diaber thunkinct!"

"Buzz," Paul said into the phone, "if you can still hear me, I'll call you back when I get to the hotel."

"Manush klepti! Sinkavitch ganuk!"

"Yeah, fuck you, too, buddy. Cocksucker ..."

Paul disconnected the call and stuffed his phone in his pocket. Then he glanced across the aisle and noticed a paralyzed man in a wheelchair staring at him.

"Phone," Paul said with a shrug. "Bad connection. Must be the storm. I've got a signal but the fucking call keeps dropping."

The man smiled, indicating what Paul assumed was sympathy. For a moment, Paul imagined pushing the man out into traffic, or straddling his wheelchair and slowly strangling him to death. His penis began to stir and twitch in his pants.

Careful, he thought. *You keep daydreaming about shit like that, you'll get a hard on right here in the shuttle. That wouldn't do. That would attract the wrong kind of attention, and you can't afford that ...*

Paul looked out the window, watching the snow fall. He'd never seen anything like this. Snow, yes. As the owner of his own environmental consulting service since 1997, he'd travelled all over the world, and seen plenty of snow. But he'd never experienced a storm like this one. It felt almost apocalyptic. He marveled at the size of the drifts along the road and idly wondered how his Tesla Model S would perform in such conditions. Probably not very well.

He considered the flask of Maker's Mark in his suitcase—checked with his luggage so it wouldn't get pulled by security when he was boarding—and debated having a drink. Then the bus slid to the right, jolting all of the passengers before it lurched back into the lane. A few passengers gasped in alarm, and murmured among themselves. Paul decided against standing up and rummaging through his suitcase. There would be time enough for a nightcap when they reached the hotel.

No time for killing, but time for a drink.

<hr/>

WHEN GREGORIO LOPEZ overheard the man seated next to him mention Corona, California during an apparently ill-fated phone call, he felt an immediate and overwhelming wave of homesickness. Gregorio wasn't from Corona. He lived much further north, in San Francisco. But just the mention of his home state filled him with a deep sense of sadness and longing. He'd been due to arrive back there in the morning, and had been looking forward to seeing his wife, Tania, and their beautiful fifteen-year-old daughter, Maricela, soon after landing.

Instead, because of the blizzard, he now found himself

stranded on the other side of the country in Maryland, packed into an overcrowded shuttle bus, with no idea of when he'd be able to catch another flight. The harried ticket agent at the airport had told him to check back with the airline in the morning. Before Gregorio could get further clarification, another passenger had begun arguing with the ticket agent. The exchange quickly grew heated. He'd slumped away, dejected and confused, and boarded the shuttle with a large group of disgruntled passengers.

Outside, the snow swirled, obscuring everything—buildings, trees, even the road signs. It looked like they were driving through a desert of white. Indeed, the only thing not white was the darkness beyond the snow.

The bus suddenly slid again, lurching to one side. Several of the passengers gasped aloud. Gregorio clutched his seat, holding his breath and waiting for the skid to subside. He heard gears grinding, as the driver reduced their speed. Then, the moment passed and they continued on as if everything was normal. He exhaled slowly.

His thoughts returned to his family once again. He missed Tania and Maricela. It felt as if they were a million miles away. He found himself wondering if he had been a good husband and a good father. Had he done everything for them that he should? Did they know he loved them?

What the hell is wrong with me? Why would I think that?

Gregorio frowned, disturbed by these sudden self-doubts. Where were they coming from? He chalked it up to fatigue and the overall uncertainty of his current travel plans. Of course his family knew that he loved them. It was ridiculous to think otherwise.

Trying to shrug off the sadness, he pulled a graphic novel from his carry-on bag—*The Infinity Gauntlet* by Jim Starlin. He was looking forward to the eventual—seemingly inevitable— Marvel Studios film adaptation, but nothing would ever compare to the actual comic. He'd read the series many times before, but there was comfort in the familiarity of it. Except that when he opened the book, Gregorio realized that it was far too dark inside the bus to actually read it. He could barely see the small print in the word balloons. He'd just have to wait until he got checked in to his room at the hotel.

Gregorio sighed, and his thoughts once again returned to his family.

◻▭

PARKED ACROSS THE AISLE, Chris Hansen sat in his wheelchair and thought about how fucked up things had quickly become. Cities, airports—any place where there were a lot of people—had always made him claustrophobic and tense, especially nowadays that he was a self-imposed, housebound hermit. A resident of Cashmere, Washington, it took Chris a considerable amount of willpower just to venture into a city like downtown Wenatchee, let alone one as big as Baltimore. He'd come here under protest, ultimately giving in to the insistence of his wife, Francesca, and his friends, H Michael Casper, Paul Goblirsch, Mark Sylva, and Leigh Haig.

Chris smiled. He referred to them as friends, although—before the last few days—none of them had ever met in person. Their friendship had been limited to online interactions. They'd all just attended a book collector's convention together—BiblioCon XVII. Leigh had even flown from his home in Australia to Chris and Francesca's home in Washington state in order to accompany Chris on the trip, since Francesca was unable to go.

Chris had been hesitant, reticent, and (in truth) fearful about the excursion, but in hindsight, he was truly glad he'd come. It was well worth it. He'd had a good time. Yes, there was too much noise and too many people, some of whom had gawked at him ("Look, Mommy," one child had shouted. "It's Professor X!"), but the time spent enjoying real-life camaraderie with the others had made it all worthwhile.

Until now. Now, everything was fucked.

It wasn't the blizzard that worried Chris. It was the delays the blizzard had caused. As a quadriplegic who couldn't walk and couldn't feel from his armpits down to his feet, travel was always a nuisance for Chris. His catheter and colostomy bag were always a consideration. The catheter went through a suprapubic cystostomy—a hole midway between his navel and pubic bone, and then plugged into a longer tube that ran along the outside of his leg and attached to a bag that was strapped to his lower leg by a strip of Velcro. His colostomy pouch hung on the left side of his abdomen, just below his ribcage. Sores from inactivity were also always a concern, and even more so when traveling long distances. He had to constantly be vigilant of them, and often relieved the pressure on his bottom and the back of his legs by leaning side-to-side or leveraging on his elbow and raising his ass up off the chair. Luckily, Leigh and the others had been under-standing and accommodating, and had helped him with these tasks as best they could. Chris had been grateful for the assistance, and was reminded once again of just how much he appreciated Francesca—and how much he loved her.

But the potential delays caused by this storm were of more serious concern to him. Although he hated to admit it, Chris was in decline. His spinal cord was a mess, with a bulging disc at the C5-6, a certain amount of unraveling as liquid built up over time, bone spurs, and arthritis. He was losing wrist flexion, along with his left triceps, as his C7 nerve slowly grew strangled and pinched. As a result, he took a lot of medication—Baclofen for muscle spasticity, Vicodin for pain, Gabapentin for neuropathic pain, Vitamin D, and amitriptyline. Francesca had packed enough to last him for the trip, plus spares enough for three days. If their delay took longer than that, he'd be in serious trouble.

As if on cue, he felt a burning cramp, similar in sensation to a low-voltage electric shock, as his intestines did their normal job. This was neuropathic pain. His nerves sent pain signals to his brain from stimuli that weren't necessarily pain causing. Grimacing, he sighed.

"You okay, mate?" asked Leigh, seated beside him and stirring from his half-asleep state.

Chris did his best to smile. "Yeah, I'm okay. I just hope we get to the hotel soon."

"It sucks that Macker couldn't make the trip."

"I know," Chris agreed. Macker was another of their online friends, and had been unable to attend the convention. "But then again, he's at home and we're not. Hopefully, it's not much farther to the hotel."

━━━

LEIGH HAIG ECHOED his friend's wish. Not only was he exhausted, but his ass and back were sore from sitting. It occurred to him that over the last week, he'd done more sitting than at any other time in his life. He'd sat on a plane from Australia to Los Angeles, and then another plane from there to Washington state. He'd sat in Chris's home while Francesca had helped familiarize him with everything Chris would need. Then the two of them had sat on yet another plane as they flew across the United States on their way to Baltimore. There had been several nights of sitting in the hotel bar, sitting in the hotel restaurant, sitting in conference rooms listening to panelists, and sitting in their shared hotel suite, talking late into the night. And now, here he was, sitting on an airport shuttle bus as it lurched and bounced and slid through steadily worsening road conditions. Each jolt sent a new wave of pain coursing up his spine.

He thought about how good a massage would feel, which in turn, led him to think about his wife, Penny. She was back home in Victoria, watching their daughter, Erin. He missed them both terribly. Leigh had always loved to travel, and he and Penny had done quite a bit of it together, with trips to China, Japan, and America. They'd only managed one great trip since Erin was born, but now that she was getting older, they intended to start again, taking a few weeks off every couple of years and visiting overseas, with Canada and more of the United States being prominent destinations. Journeying by himself was certainly different than traveling with Penny. Despite the excellent company of his friends, Leigh was lonely. Without his wife and daughter, he felt incomplete.

At least the book convention had been a success. Even if it had sucked, he would have enjoyed it just for the opportunity to meet Chris, H, Paul, and Mark in person. But it hadn't sucked, and he now had an extra suitcase—one he had purchased at a shopping mall across from the convention center—packed full of books he'd bought during the event. Most of them were signed, limited, collectible editions. Soon, they would join his collection of three thousand other books back home.

If I ever make it home, he thought, and then frowned. *Where the hell did that come from? I must be more tired than I thought.*

Yes, he decided. That was probably it. He glanced toward the back of the shuttle, where Paul, H, and Mark were sitting. It had been fun, sharing a suite with his friends, but maybe he needed some down time to himself. Some peace and quiet. Leigh decided that after they got to the hotel, and checked in, he'd help Chris get situated and then relax with a book. Maybe a bit of reading would ease his mind. If he could stay awake that long, of course. He smiled in anticipation.

But when he looked back out the window, and saw the snow falling harder, his sense of foreboding returned.

———

COLINDA CARROLL WATCHED the thin man sitting next to her shift uneasily. She'd heard him speak moments ago to his companion—a middle-aged man in a wheelchair—and she was pretty sure he was from Australia, judging by his accent.

Colinda hated winter, preferring summer and the beach instead, and the storm outside was making her nervous. She needed something to take her mind off it. Colinda considered initiating small talk with the Australian, pointing out that he wasn't the only foreigner on the shuttle, as she hailed from Canada, but then decided against it. She was an introvert, and striking up conversations with complete strangers wasn't something that came easy. Her dog, a springer spaniel named Bender, was the same way. He loved to cuddle, but was anti-social and had no idea how to behave or what to do around other dogs.

And besides, what could she possibly say to the guy? "Hey, I overheard your accent. You must be from Australia. I'm from Kingston, Ontario—the Limestone City! Ever heard of it? I know we just met, but can you talk to me for a while and take my mind off the storm outside?"

No, that wouldn't work.

It would have been different if her fellow passenger had been a customer in her shop. Then she would have felt comfortable talking. Colinda owned a hair salon called Envy. There, in her element, she could make small talk. At Envy, she was comfortable. But not here on a shuttle bus in the middle of a blizzard and far from home. There was nothing comforting about this current situation.

Colinda had traveled to Baltimore to attend an international hair show. This had been her second such trade event, the former having taken place in Berlin. While she had enjoyed herself, she was anxious to get home. Her thirteen-year-old daughter, a provincial gymnast, was competing in two days, and Colinda had promised she'd be home in time to see it.

The bus rumbled and bounced again, jostling the passengers. Colinda's feet throbbed. She always wore heels, because at five feet, two inches tall, they gave her some extra height, but she couldn't wait to get to the hotel and take them off. Brushing a piece of lint from her pink blouse, she decided to call home and check on her daughter and Bender.

She pulled her cell phone from her purse. The screensaver showed a picture of Charleston, South Carolina—one of her favorite places in the world. She'd spent a delightful week there several summers ago, touring old houses and antiquing. The cell had two bars of service. She searched through the phone's contacts and called her daughter.

JESSE CARROLL JUMPED when his cell phone rang. He'd almost been asleep, lulled by the combination of the engine's hum, the wind whistling outside, and a deep fatigue brought about from traveling. So, when his ringtone—the first few bars of his band EverSay's first hit single—blasted out of his jacket pocket, it startled him.

As he fumbled for the phone, he wondered who could be calling him. His father would be asleep this time of night, and his mother had passed back in 2006. He was single, and currently unattached, so it probably wasn't a woman. It was unlikely to be work-related either. He'd previously worked as a tour manager for several different rock bands and hip-hop artists, including stints with Prosper Johnson and the Gangsta Disciples,

Retribution Incorporated, Your Kid's On Fire, and Suicide Run, but had given that up a year ago to play guitar for EverSay. Maybe it was one of his bandmates, Harvey or John Summer, calling.

The phone rang again. Embarrassed, he smiled nervously at the passengers seated next to him—a heavy-set guy who appeared happy despite the situation with their cancelled flights (and also appeared to be quite possibly drunk) and a gorgeous blonde in a pink blouse who was making a phone call of her own.

Pulling the cell phone from his pocket, he glanced at the screen. The number wasn't one he recognized. He brought the phone to his ear and answered.

"Hello."

There was a pause.

"Who's this?" The person on the other end was female.

"This is Jesse. Who's this?"

"Jesse who?"

"Jesse Carroll. Who are—?"

He trailed off, realizing that the woman on the other end of the call was the long-haired blonde in the pink blouse sitting across from him. She must have come to the realization at the same time, because he saw her gape at him.

"I'm sorry ..."

He watched her say it even as her voice came from his phone.

"Stereo sound," he said, with a goofy grin.

"I'm sorry," she apologized again. She still held the phone to her ear.

"That's okay," he replied.

Frowning, the woman glanced at her phone and ended the call. Jesse did the same.

"That was weird," he said.

"I don't understand." The woman stared at her screen. "I was trying to call my daughter. Look at the screen. It says that I dialed my daughter. So how did it get your phone instead?"

Shrugging, Jesse smiled. "I don't know. It must be fate."

The woman seemed too perplexed to notice his attempt at humor. She glanced back down at the phone, and then up at him.

"Did you say your last name was Carroll?"

Jesse nodded. "Yeah. Jesse Carroll."

"That's my last name, too ..."

"Hey, maybe we're related! Long lost cousins or something."

The blonde shook her head in confusion. "This doesn't make any sense."

"I'm betting it had something to do with the storm," Jesse suggested. "Maybe the cell signals got all mixed up. Try calling your daughter again. Let's see what happens."

Nodding, the woman once more turned her attention to her phone. Her frown increased. "Well, now it says I don't have any service at all."

Jesse checked his cell phone and found the same.

Outside, the snow grew thicker, further obscuring the road.

DAVE RODEHEAVER WATCHED the man and woman as they lapsed back into silence again. He thought about commenting on the strange occurrence, but the woman already seemed uncomfortable, and besides, he couldn't think of anything useful to contribute to the conversation. "Hey, that's really weird how your calls got crossed" didn't seem particularly helpful. Everyone on the bus was already stressed enough, whether they showed it or not. It was probably better for him to just stay quiet and not add to the confusion.

Earlier, he'd caught glimpses of several aircraft stranded on the runway, but now, the snow fell so thickly that he couldn't see anything at all. The weather and his proximity to aircraft brought back memories of his three tours of duty in Afghanistan. As a sixteen-year Air Force veteran who'd served as an Aircraft Maintainer, Dave had worked on F-117s, F-16s, F15s, B-52s, and C-130s. He'd taken early retirement just a few months ago, although, in hindsight, he had misgivings about doing so. He and Summer had been married for a decade, and the military had kept them living apart for most of that time. To be discharged now, and finally home, only to find himself going through a divorce ...

Dave shook his head and sighed.

He pulled out his phone and stared at the screensaver, a picture of himself, Summer, their eight-year-old daughter Autumn, and his fourteen-year-old step-son, Bryant.

"How about you?" The speaker was the guy who'd said his name was Jesse Carroll. "You got a signal?"

"No," Dave said, looking up from the phone. "No service at all."

He slipped the phone back into his pocket and shivered, noticing that the temperature on the bus seemed to be dropping. Had it been this cold in Pittsburgh? He couldn't be sure, but it hadn't seemed like it. Dave had flown out of there earlier in the afternoon. He was supposed to have had a two-hour layover in Baltimore before heading home to Ida, Louisiana. Obviously, he'd be here longer than two hours.

Dave wondered how long it would be before he saw Autumn again. He'd try to call her from the hotel.

And maybe—just maybe—he'd try talking to Summer about working things out.

Still shivering, he closed his eyes so that the passengers around him wouldn't see the tears welling up in them.

JAMIE LA CHANCE was busy trying not to go insane. His biggest fear was claustrophobia. A few months ago, he'd had to be pulled out of an MRI tube twice because he couldn't handle the confinement. Being packed onto this overcrowded shuttle bus wasn't quite that bad, but it certainly wasn't pleasant.

At age fifty-eight, Jamie was a successful attorney who mostly defended other lawyers and doctors against malpractice claims. He also acted as defense in lawsuits against product manufacturers and distributors when people got hurt using those products (such as amusement park rides), lawsuits against directors and officers of corporations for alleged misconduct ranging from theft of assets to abuse of power, lawsuits against famous people when they crashed their cars into others, long-haul truckers who ran over and killed people, and desert road race promoters when their racing vehicles flew into the crowd and killed or injured spectators.

He'd flown from his home in Lomita, California a month ago to assist as part of the counsel for a Rockville, Maryland Little League baseball team whose owners were being sued over a fight in their parking lot that had resulted in death. The trial had wrapped up yesterday, and Jamie had been looking forward to getting home tonight and possibly seeing his girlfriend, Lisa. He'd heard from his daughter, Leslie, and his son, Travis, but not from Lisa for a few days. She'd known how busy he was, how absorbed in the case he had been. He missed her, and was anticipating doing all the little, simple things they did when they were together.

Jamie had a motto, articulated by Robert Brault—enjoy the little things, for one day you may look back and realize they were the big things. But this snowstorm was no little thing, and he was definitely not enjoying this bus ride. He wished, not for the first time on this trip, that he had some marijuana. He preferred edibles these days. It was strange to come from California, a state where it was legal, to a place where it wasn't.

He glanced down at the floor, trying to soothe his nerves, and spotted something glittering beneath the seat across the aisle. The man seated there had his eyes shut, but Jamie didn't think he was asleep. The shiny item was behind the man's feet. Jamie peered closer, and realized that it was a watch. He glanced back up at the man. Judging by his haircut and posture, Jamie guessed he was probably ex-military, and perhaps only recently released from duty, or possibly still a reservist.

Clearing his throat, Jamie leaned forward and tapped the guy on the knee. The man opened his eyes. Jamie saw tears glistening there.

"Sorry to bother you," Jamie said, "but I think you dropped your watch."

He pointed at the floor. Frowning, the man bent over and searched. He picked the watch up and studied it.

"It's not mine," the man replied. "Nice one, though."

"Oh. Somebody must have dropped it before we boarded, maybe? Is anyone else missing a watch?"

The passengers seated nearby shook their heads. Another shrugged and then turned back to the window, watching the storm.

The man held it out to Jamie. "Finders keepers, Mr. ...?"

"La Chance. Jamie La Chance."

"I'm Dave Rodeheaver. And keep it. It's yours."

"Are you sure?"

"Yeah, absolutely. You found it first."

Dave smiled, and while there was a hint of sadness to the expression, Jamie noticed that the man's tears had dried.

"Thanks," Jamie said, accepting the watch. He turned it over in his hand, admiring the fancy band. It was a woman's watch. Maybe he'd give it to Lisa or Leslie. But when he checked the watch's face, he realized that it was broken. Then he noticed something else. "Huh. I've never seen anything like that before."

"What's that?" Dave asked. "Is it broken?"

"I guess so." Jamie grunted. "Maybe. It's ... it's running backwards."

He held the watch up so that Dave could see it. As the two of them stared, the hands on the watch spun counter-clockwise, and much faster than a normal timekeeper would. Minutes flew by in seconds, and seconds ... they seemed not to exist at all. Then, while they were still staring, the hands reversed and began spinning in the right direction. They slowed. Sped up again. And then reversed once more.

"It's definitely broken." Dave shrugged. "That must be why the person didn't come back for it."

Jamie nodded. "I'll give it to the driver when we stop, just in case somebody wants to claim it."

They lapsed into silence. Dave closed his eyes once again, and Jamie stared at the spinning hands, rotating one way and then the other.

Little things, he thought. *Seconds are little things, but they add up to big things.*

━━━

BENN MARTIN WATCHED the two guys near him discuss the watch they'd found, while everyone else around him messed with their cell phones. He considered checking his own phone, but Benn was a big dude, and the seats on the shuttle bus were small. There was no way he could rummage through his coat pocket and pull out his phone without disturbing and jostling his seat mates—especially the older guy with the grey and white beard, pony tail, and stingy brimmed fedora seated to his immediate right. The man was probably fifty, and almost as big as Benn.

Between the two of them, there wasn't much space.

Good thing I wore deodorant, Benn thought. *And good thing this guy did, too.*

Benn was all-too-aware of what an imposing figure he must represent to some of these people. At well over six feet, dressed in black jeans and a black Killing Joke T-shirt (the band rather than the comic book), and sporting tattoos of a David Bowie skull, the ravens Huginn and Muninn, a wolf's head with "Carpe Jugulum" beneath it, and a goat's head with "Ad Finem Metallicus" (which translated to Metal to the End), he probably looked more like a roadie for Tool or OPETH rather than what he really was—a qualified electrician and engineer who worked on Hydro Power stations and high voltage sub-stations.

It was that occupation which had brought him from his home in Dunalley, Tasmania to here in the States for the last two months. Benn had been working at a hydro plant in Peachbottom, Pennsylvania, just downriver from the more-infamous Three Mile Island. The stint had been a good, if somewhat challenging job, and the pay had been excellent, and he'd enjoyed seeing a little bit of the U.S. (including trips on his days off to Philadelphia, New York City, and Pennsylvania's Amish Country, as well as a sojourn to The York Emporium, one of the East Coast's biggest used bookstores, where Benn, an avid bibliophile, had spent a wonderful few hours and a lot of money). He'd been nervous about visiting the States at first. He was no fan of Donald Trump, and had heard horror stories about travelers getting hassled at the airport. Granted, things were just as bad in his country. They'd elected Tony Abbot and got Pauline Hanson (who made Trump look like David Suzuki) and her party, into the Senate.

Despite all that, he was ready to go home. He'd heard the thin guy near the front of the shuttle talking earlier. His accent had made Benn even more homesick than he already was. He loved the States, but he was anxious to get back to a place where his accent didn't mark him as "not from around here." He wasn't looking forward to another night spent in another hotel room, searching through Netflix for a decent horror movie—something they never seemed to have. Last night, instead of going to sleep, he'd spent the evening looking at the length of current movies compared to classics. He'd found himself wondering why modern movies were getting longer, yet had less stuff in them. Dune was only two hours and fifteen minutes long, but was a massive, culture-defining space opera. Conversely, the latest James Bond film was nearly half an hour longer, and had no plot whatsoever.

Yes, this was how he'd been spending his evenings. It would be good to get home again. He hoped flights would be cleared to leave again in the morning, once the storm had passed. At this rate, the books and souvenirs he'd purchased and subsequently packaged up and mailed home, would get there before he did.

The thought struck him funny, and Benn smiled at the image in his head of two forlorn cardboard boxes sitting in front of his door, waiting for him to return.

▭

Scott Berke wanted a cigar.

He was stressed, tense, and angry. A cigar would go a long way toward alleviating all three. It wasn't the blizzard or the travel delays that had soured his mood. Scott was used to both. As the Sales Manager for a prominent biotech company—a division of the Globe Corporation—who also handled global support and training, Scott had been all over the world and had experienced every type of weather system imaginable. He'd been through blizzards, droughts, hurricanes, typhoons, heat waves, tropical storms, and even nice sunny days on every continent except Antarctica. A snowstorm in Baltimore and an overnight delay were minor nuisances. Indeed, Scott considered such delays to be nothing more than part of the job. Not as important as, say, selling beneficial bacteria for water quality control to city planners in India, or similar bacteria for soil enhancement to farmers in Kenya. Not as meaningful as helping Beijing clean up a polluted river or assisting the Russians with waste water spill-off from Chernobyl. And certainly, not as fun or interesting as helping cannabis growers in Colorado or Mexico set up their hydroponics and aquaponic systems. But a part of the job, nevertheless. Scott had a home in Port Charlotte, Florida, but it was really just a place to keep his stuff. He lived in airports and hotels. The world was his home.

No, it wasn't the storm or the delay that had him stressed out. It was the people around him. They were crammed into the shuttle bus like sardines in a can, and he was fairly certain the vehicle was well over capacity. Scott didn't like people he didn't know. In truth, he didn't like most of the people he did know, either. He could fake it when on the job. Put him in a sales or training situation, and you'd think he was extroverted and naturally outgoing. "The nicest guy in the world" his co-workers and clients would have said. But he wasn't. He could be a dick.

And he was fighting the urge to be so now, as the big roadie-looking guy seated to his left fidgeted restlessly. The man was probably twenty years Scott's junior, but he had several inches and pounds on Scott. After turning fifty, Scott had managed to lose a decent amount of weight. He was currently down to 209 pounds, although a layer of stubborn body fat hid the muscles beneath. There wasn't a spare inch on the seat between him and the guy in the Killing Joke T-shirt, and he squirmed self-consciously every time their thighs rubbed together.

At least we're both wearing our deodorant, Scott thought.

The same couldn't be said of some of their other fellow travelers. Body odor, perfume, and cologne clashed in the air. Some of the passengers were visibly upset by their current situation. Others sat quietly, expressions of acceptance, reluctant surrender, or desperation on their faces. Most were quiet, except for three guys sitting near the back of the bus. They talked among themselves, and it was clear from their demeanor that they were traveling together, or at least knew each other. Scott couldn't make out what they were saying. He was hard of hearing, and usually only understood about seventy-percent of what people said to him. The rest he pieced together from the context of the conversation. Sometimes he got it right. Other times, what he surmised was embarrassingly wrong.

Scott desperately wished he could stretch. While he wasn't running any marathons, he was in decent shape for a man his age, except for his knees and shoulders, all four of which ached right now. Worse, he felt the distant stirrings of what he feared might be a headache. Scott suffered from severe migraines that made it difficult for him to function for several hours—and even for days, on occasion—without a sumatriptan injection.

Maybe it won't be a migraine, he thought. *Maybe it will pass once we get to the hotel and I lay down.*

But first, he was going to have a goddamned cigar.

⊏━⊐

TOD CLARK WAS SEATED across the aisle from both Scott Berke and Benn Martin. At 360 pounds, he dwarfed both of them. He watched with bemusement as the two men kept shifting, trying to get comfortable without bumping into each other. Tod was grateful that the pretty auburn-haired woman seated next to him and her daughter (who was currently slumped to one side and asleep against her mother's shoulder) were both tiny. It gave him the ability to stretch out a bit, something he desperately needed to do after being cooped up in coach seats on airplanes all day long.

Tod lived in El Paso and worked at the local high school in dual capacity—as the head football coach and an alternative classroom teacher, working with troubled students and disciplinary cases. He loved his job, especially the coaching. He was good at it. The faculty, supervisors, school board, and parents all had one requirement of him—win games. It was an edict he'd had no trouble meeting.

Unfortunately, hard economic times had come to El Paso, just like the rest of the world. Tod's hours had been cut. He was still serving as the coach, but his classroom time had been eliminated. His wife, Suzin, had retired the year before, and while her pension was substantial, the hit on their monthly income was severe. He'd flown to Baltimore to interview at another high school. He didn't particularly relish the idea of living on the East Coast. He'd spent all his life out west, growing up in Oregon and living his adult life in Texas. Plus, he and Suzin had recently purchased a small ranch that served both as a weekend getaway, and as a physical location for Suzin's new, official non-profit organization—HELP MEOWT C.A.R.E.S. (which stood for Cat Adoption Rescue Eternal Sanctuary). He'd hate to give that up, as well.

But the job, if he got it, was too good to pass up.

And got it he had. Tod had thought before flying out to the East Coast that his chances must be pretty good. This was his second interview. The first had taken place online via Skype. A week later, they'd asked him to fly out for a face to face. They had even paid for his travel and lodging. That had been a good sign, but Tod hadn't truly relaxed until they'd shaken his hand and welcomed him to the team.

He'd called Suzin after the meeting, but had gotten her voicemail. He'd left a message telling her the good news, and promising to call back once he'd checked in for his flight. Tod decided to try her again, and let her know about the flight cancellation. So far, she'd been supportive of the idea of moving. They didn't have anything to tie them to Texas, other than the ranch and the cat sanctuary. Suzin's brother, Robert, could maintain those for the two years Tod needed before he could retire. They had no kids, and their dog, Apache, had passed the year before. There was a feral cat named Milli that hung around the ranch, as sort of an unofficial mascot to the sanctuary, but Milli had been there before them, and would survive without them, especially if Robert were there to care for her.

Tod shrugged. Maybe a change of scenery would do them both good.

He pulled out his cell phone and dialed Suzin. When he brought it to his ear, he heard a strange, soft hissing sound, like static, but muted.

"Hello?" Tod frowned, puzzled.

"... cannot see land. We seem to be off-course."

The speaker wasn't his wife. It was a man, and he sounded as if he were far away.

Tod asked, "Who is this?"

"Lieutenant Charles Taylor. Identify yourself, tower."

"Um ... I'm not the tower. I'm Tod. We must have gotten our calls crossed."

"We cannot be sure where we are. Repeat—cannot see land. Tower, do you copy?"

"I think you have the wrong number," Tod replied.

If the man on the other end heard him, he gave no indication. "We can't find west. Everything is wrong. The equipment ..."

"Hey?" Tod raised his voice. "Can you hear me?"

"We can't be sure of any direction. Everything looks strange, even the ocean."

The hissing sound grew louder. The strange man said something else, but Tod couldn't understand him. Then, the call dropped and the phone went dead. When Tod glanced at the screen again, he saw that there was no service. He frowned.

As he slipped the phone back into his pocket, he realized that the auburn-haired woman was staring at him.

"Must be the storm," he said, shrugging. "Sorry. Hope I didn't wake your daughter."

The woman smiled. "You didn't. It's okay."

It is *okay,* Tod thought. *Why wouldn't it be? It's just a snowstorm.*

PAULA BEAUCHAMP GLANCED down at her daughter Erin, who was currently sound asleep on Paula's shoulder, and smiled. She envied Erin's ability to sleep in the midst of this mess, and wished that she could do the same.

They'd been due to fly back to their home in Dearborn, Michigan tonight, but like everyone else, had instead been stranded here in Baltimore. Paula had so far been unable to reach her husband, Mark, and update him on the situation, and her phone's battery was dead due to both her and Erin using it to play games and surf Facebook while they'd waited in the terminal.

Paula's neck and shoulder muscles were growing stiff, but she didn't want to disturb Erin. She leaned her head back against the bus window, and felt the cold and dampness seep through to her scalp. Paula closed her eyes for a moment, and was surprised to discover that she could hear the wind blowing outside along with the hum of the bus's tires and the drone of the engine. She shivered. Erin stirred in her sleep, and her brow creased. It sounded brutal out there, the howling wind more akin to a hurricane than a blizzard. Then, beneath that, Paula heard another sound. She couldn't identify it, but it seemed ... unnatural—a white noise stew of throbbing pops, crackling hisses, and monotonous, possibly electronic tones. It was almost musical in its dissonance, reminding her of the ambient drone songs of Andrew Coltrane.

Paula felt static electricity moving through her hair. She pulled her head away from the window, and the sounds ceased. Erin moaned in her sleep. With her free hand, Paula reached out and stroked the girl's hair. The lines on Erin's troubled brow smoothed. She sighed and nuzzled closer.

It was hard for Paula to believe that Erin had just turned nine years old. It seemed like just a few months ago that she'd been learning to crawl and to talk. Of course, it had seemed that way with all of Paula's children. Jim was now twenty-nine, and Laura and Jenna were both twenty-three. Where had the time gone?

Time, Paula mused. What she wouldn't give to be able to control it or pause it just for one day. To have the ability to step outside of time's stream ...

Paula's eyes closed. Her head nodded back against the window again. As she fell asleep, the weird noise outside grew louder.

⊏⊐

BOB LEWIS, of Aurora, Colorado, was also asleep, and though he could hear the noise, he thought it was just part of his dream.

Most of Bob's dreams were like everyone else's, but occasionally, he had a series of lucid dreams during which he was conscious and aware. The location was always the same—some sort of ancient labyrinth, with rough-hewn stone corridors lit by flickering torchlight, and myriad branching passageways and doors. Sometimes, he traversed the maze alone. Other times, there was a figure there with him. He thought of it as a figure because despite being shaped like a human, he was certain that it wasn't. Its voice was odd and full of echoes, and it had a face and hands like those of a porcelain doll. The rest of its body was concealed in flowing black robes, and although Bob had never seen its feet, he heard the figure's footfalls on the stone, despite the fact that it seemed to glide rather than walk.

The figure was not with him this time, and for that, Bob was glad. The last few times he'd dreamed of his companion, the mime-faced entity had told Bob that he was to be a sacrifice. When Bob demanded to know more, the figure had merely stated that Bob would provide an exit. Bob didn't know what that meant, but he didn't like the sound of it. He wished that his subconscious would just state things clearly.

Bob realized that he'd been down this passageway several times before. While he'd always been able to open the labyrinth's doors in his dreams, there was one door that had always remained locked, no matter how many times he willed it to open in his lucid state. He saw the door again now, and approached it. As he reached for the knob, the torchlight seemed to flicker and swell, growing brighter. The walls around him shimmered, as if composed of a heat haze rather than solid matter.

And then, he heard the voice of his sometimes-companion, echoing from far away.

"NO. THAT IS NOT AN EXIT. THAT IS ..."

Bob opened the door.

And woke up.

Or, at least, he thought he'd woken up. But then he realized that he must still be half-asleep, because as he glanced out the window at the swirling snow, he thought he glimpsed a pterodactyl taking flight.

He blinked, and it was gone.

Bob glanced around at his fellow travelers, but none of them had seemed to notice.

Bob shivered. It was cold on the bus. Rubbing his arms to warm himself, he pondered the dream. What had his subconscious been trying to tell him? Why had he been able to open the sealed door this time, when all other previous attempts had failed? And why had his dream companion sounded so panicked by his successful effort?

And what the hell was the dinosaur all about? What had that represented?

Shrugging, he pulled out his phone, opened his chess app, and played a turn of his current game, moving his queen diagonally to the edge, and trapping the black king.

"Checkmate."

The game paused, and then the app crashed, closing without saving his move. When Bob checked the home screen, he saw that his phone no longer had any service. That wasn't unusual, given the weather conditions outside.

No, the unusual part was that the clock on his home screen now read 00:00.

———

GEOFF GUTHRIE WAS THINKING about the period of his life where he had followed the Grateful Dead on tour—from age fifteen to twenty-seven, the year Jerry Garcia died. Geoff had seen nearly 150 Dead concerts, including San Francisco, Las Vegas, New York City, Philadelphia, and elsewhere. He was trying to remember if he had ever seen one in Baltimore, which was where his flight from Buffalo, New York, where he'd been attending a training class for his job as a programmer, to his home in Palm Beach County, Florida had been redirected to after the blizzard had shut down air travel across the Mid-Atlantic region.

He heard the guy next to him mutter "Checkmate." Geoff glanced in his direction. His seatmate was now staring at the phone, frowning. Then something else caught Geoff's attention outside—a flash of bright light that seemed to cut through the darkness and obscuring snow. The guy next to him must have noticed it, too, because he turned his phone off and looked out the window, as well.

Both of them stared in silence as more flashes of white light followed. Then, the sporadic bursts seemed to coalesce into a widening spiral, like a horizontal whirlpool of sorts which the bus seemed to be driving through the center of.

Geoff leaned forward. "What the hell?"

"Now I know I'm not dreaming," his seatmate said.

Geoff barely heard him. His attention was focused on the bizarre display. The spiral increased in speed and size, surrounding them on both sides. Geoff turned to the window behind him and stared down, trying to catch a glimpse of the road. Instead, there was only darkness, and something that looked like flickering pinpoints of light beneath it. If he hadn't known better, he'd have thought they were stars.

The other passengers had now noticed the vortex, as well. Some of them exclaimed aloud. Others watched silently, their faces registering puzzlement and—in a few cases—fear. One woman and a girl whom Geoff assumed was her daughter were still asleep. He thought that somebody should wake them up. The only passengers who seemed oblivious to what was happening were the three guys at the back of the bus. They were huddled together and so absorbed in their own conversation, that they missed all of it.

Then, the snow disappeared, along with everything else, and the bus shuddered and jolted hard, flinging people from their seats.

Geoff had time to scream, before the darkness outside seemed to fill his head, and then he knew no more.

———

PAUL GOBLIRSCH, H Michael Casper, and Mark Sylva—from Arizona, Minnesota, and Ohio, respectively, and the friends of Chris Hansen and Leigh Haig, who were seated at the front of the bus—had no idea anything was wrong until the bus crashed and the screams began.

And by then, it was too late.

Paul was thrown forward into the aisle as the vehicle slammed into what felt like a brick wall. He wondered if they'd hit a tractor trailer or something. Then he was sliding up the aisle, and the rough, porous, black surface scraped the skin off his outstretched palms and the side of his face. He howled in pain.

The bus flipped over on its side, tossing passengers and luggage like they were rag dolls. The people's screams turned to shrieks.

Wailing, H was smashed against the window. He heard the glass shatter, but couldn't tell if it was broken or not, because his vision blurred from pain and shock. He tasted blood in his mouth, and the side of his head felt warm and wet. Then his vision blurred.

Mark was tossed forward, as well, but instead of sliding down the aisle like Paul had done, he landed on another passenger, a younger man with long hair who seemed terrified and bewildered.

"Sorry ..." Mark winced. "Are you okay, pal?"

"It was the dinosaur," the man gasped. "We must have hit it."

Then the younger man passed out.

Mark slowly clambered to his feet as the shuttle rocked back and forth. His jaw hurt, and when he probed his teeth experimentally with his tongue, he discovered that one of them was loose.

Then he looked up, saw what was outside, and joined in the screaming.

"Shit."

Paul Goblirsch winced as he clambered to his feet. Standing upright was harder than he had anticipated, given that the shuttle bus had come to a stop on its side. He glanced down at his hands and groaned. His bleeding palms looked like raw hamburger, glistening and pink. The pain hadn't set in yet, but he knew it would soon. Already they were tingling. His knees began to quiver. The trembling spread throughout his body.

Shock, he thought. *I must be in shock.*

As predicted, his knees tingled. He looked down at them and saw more hamburger. Paul was wearing shorts. He wore them ninety-nine percent of the time, even during the winter at his home in Arizona. Unfortunately, they hadn't offered him much protection during the crash. Blood trickled down his pale legs.

He tried to clear his head, and recall what had happened. There had been a terrible jolt. The bus had shaken and rumbled, and everyone screamed. Those sounds seemed to have abated now, replaced with distressed cries of pain and bewilderment.

"Paul?"

"H?" Paul desperately looked around. "H? Is that you? Where are you?"

Amidst the moans, sobbing, and screams from the other passengers, Paul heard glass falling from close by. Then H appeared, pulling himself up to stand atop one of the seats. His face was covered in blood, and bits of broken glass sparkled in his hair. H leaned against the bus aisle for support. The visual made Paul's stomach lurch. He felt like he was on an amusement park ride, and that any minute now, the world would right itself again.

"H," Paul said, making his way toward him, "you've got a cut on your head."

"I do? Shit. I thought my face felt warm. Is it bad?"

Paul shook his head. "No. Maybe a few stitches, but that's all. It's still bleeding, though. And there's glass in your hair, too, so be careful."

H bent over and gently shook the glass fragments from his scalp. He swayed back and forth on his feet when he righted himself again. Then he lifted his shirt and dabbed at the injury, sucking air through his clenched teeth as the fabric touched the wound.

"Do you need help?" Paul asked, concerned.

"No, I'm good. You got scraped up pretty bad yourself."

"Never mind me," Paul said. "You look a little wobbly."

H waved him away. "I'll be okay. Check on the others ..."

Paul turned around, looking for Mark. To his surprise, their friend was right behind him. He hadn't spoken to either of them. Instead, he stood, unmoving, and stared at the top of the bus. Paul followed his gaze. Where there had been roof before, there were now windows, several of which were broken.

"Mark?" Paul asked. "Are you okay?"

Mark Sylva didn't answer. Indeed, he didn't acknowledge Paul at all. Paul was about to try again, when another passenger groaned. Paul turned his attention in that direction, and saw a man with brown hair and grey eyes struggling to stand in the off-kilter wreckage. Paul stuck out his hand. The man glanced at his bloody palm, but then took it. Paul helped the guy to his feet. He had to strain to do so, and the pain in his hand was intense. He guessed the passenger stood about six feet five inches. The man was thin but very muscular. He appeared to be in his early forties.

"Thanks," the man said after regaining his balance. "Geoff Guthrie."

"Paul Goblirsch. And no problem. You must lift weights?"

"Yeah," Geoff said, wiping Paul's blood onto his pants. "I do Olympic lifting. I can deadlift 575 pounds. How did you know?"

"I think I threw my back out helping you up."

Geoff laughed, and Paul grinned. H joined them with another groan.

They heard a thump behind them. When they turned around, H was sitting down, leaning against the exit door. The color had drained from his face, and his forehead was bathed in sweat. His pupils appeared to be dilated.

"You okay?" Paul asked.

"My blood ..." H's voice was weak. "I get lightheaded."

"Are you going to pass out?"

"No, I'll be okay. Just need to catch my breath."

"We must have wrecked," Geoff said, looking around. Then his expression turned sheepish. "Sorry. Guess that's an understatement, huh? I mean, of course we wrecked."

"No." Mark still didn't look at them. His attention remained focused on the broken windows above. "We didn't wreck. Not exactly. I mean, maybe we did, but that's the least of our problems."

"Chris and Leigh," Paul said. "We've got to check on them. Can you see them at the front of the bus?"

"I'm not talking about them," Mark replied.

"He must have hit his head," H muttered. "Come over here and sit down with me, Mark. You're not making any sense. You might have a concussion."

Mark finally turned to face them, albeit slowly. Paul noticed that his eyes were wide, and his hair was plastered to his head with sweat, but otherwise, he seemed unharmed. There was no blood on him and his pupils didn't appear to be dilated.

"Look outside," he said, and pointed. "And tell me I got a concussion, pally. You see what I see?"

One by one, they turned their heads up to the windows. Paul realized that the sun was shining. He saw green treetops swaying in the breeze. It appeared peaceful and serene, a jarring counterpoint to the cries and shouts of his fellow passengers.

"Um, guys ..." Paul wiped his hands nervously on his pants, forgetting too late about his injuries. He bit down a scream. "Where's the snow?"

"Fuck the snow," H exclaimed. "Where the hell's the airport? And the road? And how the fuck is it daylight?"

"This can't be real," Geoff said. "It's some kind of trick, right?"

Paul stared at the streaming sunlight and wondered the same thing.

"I need a doctor," somebody shouted from the middle of the bus.

"I'm gonna sue these motherfuckers," another passenger replied.

"Can somebody open the rear exits?" Paul recognized the speaker's voice. It was Leigh. "The front is all smashed up, and this lady is hurt bad."

"Leigh," Paul yelled. "Are you guys okay?"

Leigh hollered back a response, but everyone else began shouting, as well, and Paul couldn't understand him. He turned back to Geoff.

"My hands are pretty bad. Can you help with the emergency exit?"

"Sure."

They clambered to the rear, stepping over misplaced luggage and spilled snack food. Mark followed, seeming to come out of his daze now that there was an objective. H stood to one side and watched, keeping the bloody shirt pressed against his head. His color had returned, but he still appeared weak and unsteady. Geoff, Paul, and Mark managed to get the doors open after three tries. Paul chewed his lip, trying to ignore the pain in his hands. The metal screeched and shuddered. The doors had been damaged, though apparently not as bad as at the front of the bus. When they opened, it was onto a sunny, warm, lush, tropical forest. There was no sign of the road, and certainly no mounds of snow.

"How is this ...?" Paul gaped. "This just ..."

"Let's not think about it right now," Mark said. "Obviously, we're not in Kansas anymore."

Geoff snorted.

"Just focus instead on getting everyone off the bus," Mark advised. "See if anybody is hurt bad, and then we'll figure out what the fuck happened. Alright?"

Nodding, Paul climbed out onto the ground. Then he held the top door open while Geoff, Mark, and H followed. The pain in his hands was quickly growing unbearable. He groaned. Noticing that Paul was struggling with the effort, Geoff took over, bracing the door so it wouldn't slam back down as the passengers escaped.

"Okay, folks," Paul called, "this way. Single file, please. Everybody try to stay calm."

Their fellow travelers began to make their way toward the emergency exit door.

"Stay calm?" H whispered. "How long do you think that's going to last, once they get a load of our situation?"

"Be quiet and pass out," Paul whispered back.

And then H did.

———

PAULA'S first scattered thought upon waking up was that the house was on fire. She smelled smoke. Worse, she heard Erin crying. She couldn't see, and when she tried to sit up, she realized something heavy was laying on top of her.

"Mommy!"

Erin's voice was panicked and terrified. Paula's pulse throbbed in her temples. Grunting, she tried to sit up again. The weight shifted, but didn't move. Her vision cleared, but was still blurry. Everything seemed ... liquid, somehow, as if she had opened her eyes at the bottom of a murky swimming pool.

Someone moaned in her ear. A man. Paula cringed as something soft brushed against her head. She realized that it was hair. A moment later, the weight on her chest shifted again. Then it spoke.

"Oh God, I'm sorry. Are you okay?"

The weight disappeared. Paula realized it had belonged to someone, and that someone had been lying atop her.

"I can't see," she gasped. "My daughter! Where's my daughter?"

"Mommy?"

Something else brushed against Paula's face—a cloth of some kind. She jumped, startled.

"Relax," the man said. "You can't see because there's blood in your eyes. I'm just wiping it away."

"Oh God ..."

"Don't worry. It's not your blood. It's mine. My nose is bleeding. I must have hit it when we crashed."

A few strokes with the cloth and sure enough, Paula could see again. The cloth had been a shirttail, and it belonged to a tall, slightly overweight young man whose long brown hair and beard immediately reminded her of Jesus—except for his nose, which was swollen to about twice its size and still leaking blood. Above his shoulders, she saw the seats she and Erin had been asleep in. A tree branch had punched through the side of the bus, only inches from where they'd been sitting. Erin stood to the young man's left. She seemed unharmed but was obviously distressed. Paula bolted upright and then fell back down, realizing too late that the shuttle bus was on its side.

"Erin," she called. "It's okay. I'm okay. See? I'm right here, baby. Are you hurt?"

"I skinned my knee," the girl sobbed.

"Here," the man said. "Let me see it."

He turned to her and Erin shrank away.

"It's okay, sweetie," Paula said. "He's going to help."

The young man smiled. "I get it. You don't like strangers. Can I tell you a secret?"

Erin nodded, and the young man leaned closer.

"I don't like them much either," he whispered.

Despite her fears, Erin smiled. It was slight, but it was a start. Relaxing a bit, Paula sat up.

"My name is Bob Lewis. And your name is Erin, right?"

The girl nodded again.

"Well, now we're not strangers anymore. How old are you Erin?"

"N-nine."

"Nine years old? Well, I've got something here for you. Hang on."

Bob reached into his pants pocket, fumbled around, and then

produced a shiny quarter. He held it up and showed it to them both. His expression was very serious. Then, suddenly, the quarter disappeared. Erin gasped and Paula grinned.

"Where did it go?" Erin asked.

"Well," Bob said, "let's take a look."

He reached for her knee, and this time, Erin didn't back away from him. He did a quick, cursory examination and then—pop— the quarter appeared in his fingers again, as if he'd pulled it from the scrape on her knee. Erin laughed with delight.

"Here you go." Bob handed Erin the quarter. "You keep that. And your knee is going to be fine. It's not even bleeding. A bandage and maybe a kiss from your Mom, and it will be good as new."

"Thank you," Paula said. "Erin, what do we say?"

"Thank you," Erin echoed. "How did you do that?"

"Magic."

"Are there any more quarters?"

Bob smiled. "Let's get out of this bus, and we'll see."

Bob helped the two of them maneuver toward the back, where some other men had managed to force open the rear exit doors.

"Are you okay?" he asked Paula. "I hope I didn't squash you or anything?"

"I think I'm alright. How's your nose?"

"It hurts," he said. "A lot. But I don't think it's broken, and I can still breathe through it. At least I ..."

His voice faded. Paula noticed that he was staring at the open doors. A tattooed man with glasses and a thick shock of black hair motioned at them to keep coming.

"What's wrong?" Paula asked.

"Look outside," Bob whispered. "Notice anything different?"

Paula did. Gone was the snow and highway and airport

buildings. They'd been replaced with trees and foliage and sunshine.

"B-but ..." she stammered. "How is that ... what ...?"

"Magic?" Bob shrugged. "That's what I'm going to tell myself until we figure out the real explanation."

━━

Tod Clark, Scott Berke, and Benn Martin had been tossed into each other during the crash. Tod had escaped injury, and Scott was okay except for the twinges of pain that rippled through his back every time he moved. Benn, however, had a jagged shard of metal sticking out of his forearm. It was about the length and width of a baton. When he tried to crawl forward, he shivered in pain and collapsed, sweating.

"I need a doctor," he shouted. "Somebody ...?"

"I'm gonna sue these motherfuckers," another passenger replied from closer to the front of the bus.

"Here," Tod said, reaching for Benn. "We'll give you a hand."

"Thanks."

Tod turned to Scott. "Can you help us?"

"Absolutely." Scott nodded.

"Thanks," Benn gasped. He twitched, shuddering with pain. "Aw fuck, that hurts."

"You'll be okay," Tod said. "We'll get you outside. I'm sure somebody already called 911. I'm Tod, by the way."

"Benn."

They both turned to Scott.

"I'm Scott. Hang on just a second. Let me get my bag."

"The bag can wait," Tod suggested. "Let's get him out of here first. Not to mention we're kind of blocking the aisle."

Shrugging, Scott assisted Tod in helping Benn to the exit.

"My tattoos," Benn asked. "Are they okay? Did it cut through them?"

"Your ink is fine," Tod assured him. "Now hang on. We're going to lift you down out of the bus."

"You might be going into shock," Scott advised. "Just try to stay calm."

Benn gritted his teeth, shivering as Tod and Scott helped him. All three of them were sweating, but it wasn't until they'd gotten outside and noticed the change in the weather that they understood why.

———

DAVE UNTANGLED himself from a pile of suitcases and carry-on bags. When he tried to stand, a jolt of pain shot through his foot. Hissing, he tried it again, but slower. This time, he remained upright.

"Are you hurt?" Jamie asked.

"I twisted my ankle, but I'll manage."

"Are you sure?"

"Positive. I've seen and had worse, believe me. How about you?"

"I think I'm okay." Jamie patted himself from head to toe, as if to confirm. "Just shaken up."

A giant of a man in front of them mentioned calling 911. Dave pulled out his cell phone and was relieved to see that it was undamaged. But when he tried to dial, he noticed that there was no service, nor were there 4G or wireless signals. That wasn't so weird, in and of itself. There were still places in the world without cell phone coverage. He'd encountered it himself in Afghanistan, from time to time. What struck Dave as strange was the cell phone's time and date feature. Every time he turned the phone on, the time and date were prominently displayed on the screen. They even automatically adjusted for time zones when he traveled. The time showed 00:00 and the date was missing altogether.

"You said your name was Jamie, right?"

"That's right. Jamie La Chance."

"Do you still have that watch you found?"

"Let's move up there," someone shouted from behind them. "What's the hold up?"

"I must have dropped it," Jamie said. "Why?"

Instead of answering, Dave searched around them. He spotted the watch sticking out from under a suitcase. Bending over, he reached for it.

"Hey," the impatient person yelled. "That's my suitcase. What the hell are you doing?"

Ignoring him, Dave picked up the watch. He stared at it, frowned, and then showed it to Jamie.

The watch had stopped.

———

"Hey," Paul Legerski shouted again. "What the fuck did you do to my suitcase?"

Ahead of him were two men studying a watch. The younger man turned around and stared at him.

"Relax, asshole. I didn't touch your suitcase."

"Well, then, how about moving it along? You think I want to stay in here all night?"

The younger man muttered something. Paul couldn't be sure what. It sounded like "waiting for you outside." Before he could respond, the man next to him said something.

"I think you mean day."

Paul turned to the speaker. He was a man about five feet, nine inches tall, with brown hair and eyes.

"Excuse me?"

"You said you didn't want to spend all night on the bus. It's daylight out there."

"That's ridiculous." But when Paul turned, he saw sunlight streaming through the broken windows. "That's ... that's ..."

"Weird," the man said. "I'm Greg, by the way. It's short for Gregorio, but nobody calls me that. Everybody either calls me Greg or Sarge."

Greg stuck out his hand, but Paul declined to take it. Instead he bent over and lifted his suitcase from the wreckage.

"No offense, Greg," he said, "but I'm not interested in making friends right now. The only thing I want to do is get off this fucking bus so I can call an attorney and sue the fuck out of the airline, the airport, the shuttle service, and everybody else. Fuck off."

Greg stared at him for a moment, and then pulled his hand away.

"On second thought, you can call me Gregorio, asshole."

━━━

AT FIRST, Leigh was certain that Chris must be dead. The impact had sent him flying from his wheelchair and on top of the bus driver. He lay there, unmoving and covered in blood. Something that looked like a wet, uncooked sausage lay across his belly, glistening. Leigh's gorge rose as he realized it was a length of intestine. The entire front of the shuttle had been smashed in and driven back into the bus itself. Parts of the engine block were sticking out of the dashboard, and the hood had crumpled up through the windshield. Blood spatters covered the front seats and glistened on an unopened bag of potato chips that he supposed had fallen from somebody's carry-on bag.

"Chris?"

His friend didn't respond. Behind them, a woman sobbed. Leigh turned around, and saw the pretty blonde who had been sitting next to him. He remembered her telling the guy across the aisle that her name was Colinda. His name was ... Jesse? Yes, Leigh thought that was right. They'd had that weird crossed call thing happen, right before ...

What had happened, exactly? They'd crashed, of course. But what had caused it? Sitting up front had provided Leigh with a clear view of the highway. The road had been clear, other than the snow drifts. No other vehicles had been on it. He remembered seeing some strange lights, and the bus driver slowing down as they appeared. And then ...?

And then Chris had gone flying.

Leigh crawled over to his friend. He reached out with one tentative hand, hesitated for a moment, and then touched him. Chris was still warm. Leigh leaned closer and choked with relief. Chris was still breathing.

"Hang in there, buddy. I'm going to get you out of here."

He patted Chris, trying to reassure him, and then Chris stirred. His eyes fluttered.

"Leigh?"

"It's okay. You just keep still."

Chris blinked. "I can't move. I think I might be paralyzed."

Leigh's breath caught in his throat. After a moment, he realized that Chris was grinning. Then he remembered, and realized how stupid he must have sounded telling Chris not to move.

"You asshole," Leigh said. "That's not funny."

"Yes, it is."

Leigh shrugged. "Okay, yeah it is."

"Is that a piece of intestine?" Chris asked.

Leigh nodded.

"Whose intestine is it?"

"I thought it was ... yours."

Colinda moved up behind them. "Is he okay?"

Leigh nodded. "I think so."

Jesse joined them, shaking his head when he saw the damage to the front of the vehicle. "Jesus, we're lucky to be alive. Where's the bus driver?"

Frowning, Leigh realized that he was kneeling in blood. Slowly, he turned Chris over on one side. Both he, Colinda, and Jesse gasped. The driver—most of her anyway— was beneath Chris, and it was obvious from her wounds that the intestine had belonged to her.

Leigh took a deep breath. "Can somebody open the rear exits? The front is all smashed up, and this lady is hurt bad."

He heard Paul yell from the back of the bus. "Leigh? Are you guys okay?"

"Yeah," Leigh shouted, "but we need some help up here."

He couldn't tell if Paul had heard him or not, because there was too much commotion. Leigh turned his attention back to Chris.

"Listen, mate, are you hurt?"

"I don't think so, but it's hard to say for sure. Do you see any obvious injuries on me?"

"No." Leigh looked him over carefully. "No, I don't see anything on the outside. But you could have internal injuries. I don't want to move you, but you're lying on top of the driver, and she's hurt bad."

"Where's my chair?"

Leigh, Colinda, and Jesse looked around, and found the wheelchair amidst the wreckage.

"Did it survive?" Chris asked.

Leigh nodded. "It doesn't look damaged. It's covered in broken glass, though."

"Put me in it."

"The glass?"

"The chair," Chris groaned in exasperation.

"But if you've got internal bleeding, or a broken rib or something ..."

"Judging by the looks on your faces, the driver is in a lot worse shape. I'm guessing it was her guts on me. So, stop arguing and move me."

"Okay." Leigh turned to Jesse. "Can you give me a hand, mate?

"Sure, man."

Colinda righted the chair and brushed all the glass fragments off while Jesse and Leigh struggled to move Chris. Both the chair and its occupant were heavier than they looked. When they had gotten him situated, they turned their attention back to the driver, and saw that it had all been for nothing. The steering wheel had been driven back into her chest, pulping her mid-section, and half of her face had been sheared off by a shard of metal. Just to be certain, Leigh knelt in the gore and checked her pulse, trying hard not to vomit. He found nothing.

"Is she ...?" Colinda asked.

Swallowing his gorge, Leigh nodded.

Leigh waited with Chris until all of the other passengers had safely filed out of the bus. Then Mark and Paul made their way toward them.

"I'm glad you guys are okay," Paul said. "I'd shake your hand, but ..."

He held up his bleeding palms. Leigh winced at the sight.

"Jesus, mate. That looks painful."

Paul nodded.

"Where's H?"

"He's outside." Mark motioned to the rear of the shuttle. "Banged his head up a little bit, but we think he'll be alright. Apparently, he faints if he sees his own blood."

With some effort, the three of them managed to wheel Chris through the wreckage and out into the sunlight.

"What the hell is happening?" Leigh murmured. "Where are we?"

Nobody answered him.

The passengers all stood near the shuttle, some in groups, and others alone. Many checked their cell phones, expressing dismay over the lack of signals, and missing dates and times. Some tended to the injured. Others milled about in shock, staring in bewilderment at their surroundings.

Leigh sank down on his haunches, nearly collapsing. He felt as if all the strength had suddenly drained from his body. The lenses of his eyeglasses steamed over with condensation.

Paul stared down at him in concern. "You okay, man?"

Leigh shook his head. "It's like we fell through a hole in the world."

"If so," Paul said, glancing up at the trees, "then where did we land? Where did that rabbit hole lead?"

"Sit down on the grass," Scott told Benn, "and let me take a look at your arm."

As Benn—with some assistance from Tod—walked over to the grass, Scott closed his eyes for a moment, and shuddered. His headache was getting worse—definitely the early stages of a developing migraine.

"Are you a doctor?" Tod asked him, breathless.

"No," Scott said, opening his eyes again, "but I can clean and dress wounds, even stitch them if need be. I have treated a few of my own over the years."

Tod persisted. "So, you're like a CIA guy or something? Military?"

Scott shook his head. "Nothing like that, I'm afraid."

"Stuntman?"

"No."

Benn winced, clutching his arm. "You just get hurt a lot?"

Scott shrugged. "I can be accident prone. I also raise reptiles and amphibians, so I've been bit a time or two. I've stitched myself up before, and treated myself with antibiotics and supplies from the pet store. Good enough?"

Nodding, Benn sank to the ground. "Fuck yeah. At this point, anything will do. I can't believe this. Right at the end of the trip and this happens?"

Scott and Tod knelt next to him.

"It's not as bad as it looks, Benn." Tod smiled reassuringly.

"Maybe," Benn grunted, "but it hurts like hell."

"How about you," Scott asked Tod. "Do you have any medical training?"

"I'm a football coach. I've seen a few broken bones. Lots of sprains. Never anything like this, though." Tod turned to look at the other passengers and called out, "Is anyone here a doctor?"

An older man with blood on his face stepped forward, swaying unsteadily on his feet. "I'm not a doctor, but I taught high school biology, anatomy, and general wellness for thirty-two years. Maybe I can help?"

Scott shrugged. "Do you faint at the sight of blood?"

"Just his own," said another man. This one had nasty abrasions on his palms and knees. "I'm Paul Goblirsch. My bleeding friend is H."

"What's the H stand for?" Scott asked.

"It doesn't stand for anything," H said. "It's just H."

"Back there," Paul continued, "are Leigh, Mark, and Chris. And our new friend Geoff."

Scott turned and saw a skinny guy, a stocky guy, a guy in a wheelchair, and a guy who looked like a bodybuilder. He nodded at them, then returned his attention to Benn's wound. The metal stuck out of his forearm like a broken bone. Blood seeped around the edges. He knew there was going to be much more of it as soon as they removed the shard.

"Okay," he said. "Benn, I want you to lie down. We're going

to elevate your arm. Tod, you're going to hold his shoulder. Geoff, can you take his legs?"

Nodding, Tod and the bodybuilder moved into position.

"I heard you talking earlier," Benn said to the skinny guy. "Where are you from, mate?"

"Melbourne. How about you?"

"Tasmania."

The skinny man grinned. "Nice! I'm Leigh Haig."

"Benn Martin." He tried to raise his arm to shake hands, but then groaned in pain.

"You guys can catch up later," Scott insisted. "Right now, I need you to lie still."

"What are you going to do?" Benn asked, licking his lips. His eyes were wide.

"In a minute, I'm going to pull this metal out of your arm, and when I do, I don't want you thrashing around. You do that, and you could make it worse. Nick an artery or something."

"We wouldn't want that," Benn moaned.

"No," Scott agreed. "We wouldn't. But first, we'll need a tourniquet, some antiseptic, bandages, and probably something to help seal the wound. Can the rest of you start checking with the other passengers and see what we can come up with? We need clean cloth, alcohol, painkillers—stuff like that. Try not to get aspirin or Ibuprofen. They'll just make his bleeding worse. Tylenol would be great. Superglue or something similar would be awesome. The quicker we can get it all, the better, of course."

Leigh frowned. "Superglue? Isn't that for, like, gluing broken toys and such together?"

"It's for gluing flesh back together, too." Scott positioned Benn's arm by his side and checked the injured man's pupils. "It was invented for use on the battlefield."

Benn coughed, his jaw clenching with pain. "I don't care if you guys use Elmer's glue. Could we just do something?"

"Sorry," Scott apologized. "You're right. Get to it, guys. And try to hurry. Benn, you just lay there and rest. As long as the metal stays where it is, you won't bleed to death anytime soon. Mr. H, you stay here with me. I want to take a look at your head."

"Okay," H replied.

"H passed out a few minutes ago," Paul said, "but he seems better now."

"I am," H insisted.

"I'd still like to take a look at you," Scott said. "And Paul, your hands and knees are scraped up pretty badly. Your face, too, though not as bad. You want me to look at those, as well?"

"I'll be okay. Benn is our priority. I just need some disinfectant."

"That you do," Scott confirmed. "Last thing you want are those to get infected. Okay, you help the others with their scavenger hunt. H, you stay here."

Paul, Chris, Leigh, and Mark headed off. Scott noticed that Chris's wheelchair was maneuvering with some slight difficulty on the terrain.

Benn moaned. His fingers clawed at the grass, clutching it. Tod and Geoff tried their best to soothe him.

"You're going to be okay," Scott said. "We'll have you fixed up in no time."

"I just want to get home," Benn whispered.

Scott glanced up at their surroundings, studied them for a moment, and then frowned.

"What's wrong?" Benn asked.

"Nothing," Scott replied. "I was just trying to figure out where we are."

Benn licked his lips again. "What do you mean?"

"It's not important. Are you thirsty?"

Benn nodded. "Yes. Very much ..."

"Okay, as soon as someone else comes over, I'll have them find you some water."

"Maybe I should go look," H suggested.

"No," Scott insisted. "I want you to stay right here for now. Are you seeing double? Have a headache? Anything like that?"

"My head hurts, but I think that's because I banged it when we crashed. Otherwise, no."

"And the H really doesn't stand for anything?"

"It really doesn't. H is my name."

"I believe you," Scott admitted. "In truth, I just wanted to check your memory. Listen to your speech. Make sure you weren't slurring your words."

H grinned. "You're pretty good at taking charge, Mr. Berke."

"You can call me Scott. And thanks. To be honest, I'm sort of a loner, but I have to work with people all the time for my job."

"It shows," H replied. "You got these guys into action pretty quick."

"Well," Scott said, turning H's head from side to side and examining his wound, "I guess somebody has to be in charge until help arrives."

H looked up at the sun, shining bright overhead. "If help arrives."

⸻

GREG, Dave, and Jamie stood near the bus, gawking at their surroundings. Paul Legerski stood away from them, alone, angrily trying to get his cell phone to work. His suitcase sat on the ground between his feet.

"How's your ankle?" Greg asked Jamie.

"I can stand on it," Jamie confirmed, "but I'm not going to be running sprints anytime soon. At least, not without wincing. But

I can walk. I'll be okay. Looks like there's some people hurt much worse than me over there."

They glanced at where Jamie was pointing, and saw several passengers huddled over a bloody man. Then their attention returned to the landscape.

"I don't understand," Dave said. "I mean, how is this possible? It was night."

"Not to mention the blizzard," Greg agreed. "And now it's sunny."

"And hot." Jamie unbuttoned his sleeves and began rolling them up. "It must be eighty, maybe ninety degrees out here. It feels like back home in California."

"Except we're not in California," Greg said. "And I don't think we're in Maryland, either."

"Then where the hell are we?" Dave motioned at the trees. "I recognize most of those—pines, oaks, palm trees, but have you guys ever seen them growing together like this in the same place? And there are also trees that I swear I've never seen before. And the wildlife! I saw a crow up on a limb when we first came out of the bus, but I also saw a butterfly that was neon green. It's like home, but it isn't. So, where are we?"

"Did either of you actually see us crash?" Jamie asked.

Dave nodded. "Sure. I mean, we all saw it, right?"

"No," Jamie said. "We all felt something happen, but we didn't actually see a crash. Or, at least I didn't."

Dave shook his head. "The front of the bus is all smashed up. The driver got speared by the steering column. I'd say that indicates a crash. We crashed into a tree."

"Did we?" Jamie motioned at the wreckage. "Or did the tree crash into us?"

"I saw some weird lights," Dave volunteered. "Right before everything went to shit."

"I did, too," Jamie said. "I assumed they were from a plane

taking off or landing. We were near the airport, after all."

"Maybe we got transported somewhere else," Greg suggested.

Dave chuckled. "What? You mean time travel? Another dimension? Little green men?"

"Maybe it sounds unbelievable," Greg admitted, "but how else do you explain what's happened? It makes sense to me."

Dave turned to Jamie. "What do you think?"

Jamie shrugged. "I believe it is the height of arrogance to think that we are alone in the universe. I don't know about little green men, but of course there are aliens. As for time travel, I absolutely love the concept, but I am totally clueless as to whether it is a possibility. I do believe in alternate worlds, as it simply makes sense for there to be multiple dimensions."

"So, then, you believe that's what's happened to us?" Dave asked.

Jamie paused. "I don't know. I believe that something strange has happened. Obviously. But we don't have all the facts yet, and until we have all the data, the only thing I'm sure of is that we're in trouble."

Dave stared off into the forest. "Somebody will come. They have to."

Greg and Jamie thought it sounded like he was trying to convince himself.

⸻

"Excuse me, sir?"

Paul Legerski stuffed his useless cell phone in his pocket and glanced up. Standing before him were three passengers from the bus. He recognized the first two—the guy in the wheelchair and his skinny friend with the Australian accent. They'd been sitting near him on the shuttle. The third passenger was one he didn't recognize—a short man with black hair, black glasses, tattoos, and

a strange hybrid accent that Paul thought might be Boston and ...
Ohio, maybe? The third passenger spoke again.

"Sorry to bother you, but I noticed you have your luggage
already. We've got an injured guy over there. There's a piece of
metal sticking out of his arm. It's pretty bad. We were wondering
if you might have any Tylenol?"

"You're going to treat him with Tylenol?"

"Or liquor," the Australian piped up. "Maybe you have a
whiskey flask, eh? And we need bandages and such, or clean
cloth that we can turn into bandages."

"Anything at all would help," the man in the wheelchair
added.

"Sorry." Legerski shrugged. "I can't help you."

The Australian frowned. "Mr. ...?"

"Legerski. Paul Legerski."

"I'm Leigh. These are my mates Chris and Mark. Listen, you
might not have noticed, but we've got a bit of a situation here."

Legerski laughed. "That's the understatement of the year!
You think we've got a situation? Yeah, I'd say we've got a fucking
situation."

"I-I didn't mean any o-offense," Leigh stammered. "It's
just that—"

"Look," Legerski interrupted, "I need to get in touch with my
attorney, and I need to walk somewhere until I find a signal
because I'm not getting anything here."

Leigh blinked. "Your attorney?"

"Yeah, that's right. I'm going to sue the airline, and everybody
else connected with this epic cluster-fuck. We crashed, what, ten
minutes ago? Where the hell are the emergency responders?
They should be here by now, but I don't even hear any fucking
sirens. This is unacceptable. So, if you don't mind—"

Mark stepped past Leigh and shoved Legerski backward
a step.

"Actually, asshole, we do mind."

Legerski shoved back, glowering down at him. "Listen, you little cocksucker ..."

"No, you listen!" Mark grabbed him by the front of his Sharks jersey with both fists. "Now, maybe you didn't hear us before, but we've got an injured person over there. Do you have anything in your bag that might help us or not?"

"No. And you've got two seconds to let go of me."

"Or what?"

"Both of you knock it the fuck off."

Chris's voice was soft, yet it held an undeniable edge. Legerski and Mark both paused, and glanced at him. Then, they released each other. Mark smoothed his hair with his hand. Legerski stood as still as a statue.

"Come on," Leigh said. "Let's go ask somebody else."

They turned away from him and began to walk away, but not before Chris ran over Legerski's toe with his wheelchair.

"Ouch! Goddamn it, watch where you're going."

"Oops," Chris replied. "Sorry."

Toe throbbing, Legerski watched them approach another group—a woman, a young girl, and a kid with long hair and a beard. Before they could reach the other group, they were approached by a fourth man. Paul overheard them call this newcomer Paul, as well.

Two Pauls, he thought. *That won't do. This place isn't big enough for two Pauls.*

Grinning, he stared at the middle of Mark's back.

Right there, he thought. *Right there is where I'll stick the knife. You wanted to know what I'd do if you didn't let go of me? Well, you'll find out. You're going to be number thirty-eight, fuck-wad. At first, I thought it might be that other guy from the bus, but now you'll have the honor. I'll wait until they get us out of here, and settled in at the hotel, and then I'll fucking find you and make you bleed. You, and then you're little faggot buddy from down under, and then that crippled fuck in the wheelchair. And anybody else who wants to fuck with me.*

Legerski knew that killing someone—let alone three people—this far from home was risky. If they found some type of evidence that matched up with his victims on the West Coast, and they began searching passenger manifests and travel records, they might discover a clue to his identity. But on the other hand, Maryland was so far away from the locations of his thirty-seven previous victims (the ones that had been discovered, at least) that authorities might not connect the two at all.

He turned his head to the sky, squinting against the sun's glare. Legerski had to admit, this didn't much look like Maryland. And where the hell had all the snow gone? All the white had been replaced with green.

No matter. White. Green.

Soon, he'd turn it red.

He stalked off toward the trees, holding his phone out in front of him, searching for a signal.

"Hmmm ..."

Jesse stared at the forest surrounding them. His expression was concerned.

"What's wrong?" Colinda asked, trying to get her cell phone to work.

"The forest," Jesse said. "There were birds singing before. Now, there's nothing. It's gone quiet."

"Maybe the birds are scared of us?"

"Maybe." Jesse nodded, his expression still pensive. "Or maybe they're afraid of something else."

"Like what?"

Jesse shrugged. He opened his mouth to respond, but then just shrugged again.

⊏====⊐

"FOLKS!" Paul Goblirsch moved to the center of the crash site and held up his hands, signaling everyone. "If I could have your attention for a minute? Please?"

"Good job," Mark whispered. "Way to take charge, Paul."

Paul glanced over his shoulder at Mark, Leigh, and Chris, and couldn't help but grin. Despite the bizarre situation, he was glad his friends were with him. Realizing that the other passengers were all staring at him, he turned his attention back to the crowd.

"Thank you," he said, speaking loudly so that everyone would hear. "My name is Paul Goblirsch. As you probably noticed, we're all in a bit of a situation here. Now, I know everybody is scared. I'm scared, too. I don't think any of us are sure what happened ... or where we are."

"Our phones aren't working," said a woman. "Did the driver radio for help?"

"I'm sorry, ma'am. I didn't get your name?"

"Colinda."

"Well, Colinda ..." Paul took a deep breath. "The driver is dead."

The crowd murmured. A few people gasped.

"I'm positive help is coming," he said, raising his voice again. "Someone is sure to notice that we're missing. But it might take a while. I think we can all agree that we might not be where they expect to find us, right?"

Some of the passengers nodded. Paul noticed their expressions ranging from bewilderment to terror. They mirrored his own feelings. He thought about his wife, Janet, and their two daughters. Even if the authorities weren't aware that they had crashed, Janet would hit the panic button when she didn't hear from him.

"All we have to do is sit tight," Paul said. "I'm sure most of you have people waiting at home. They'll be worried about us. Someone will come. But in the meantime, we've got a few injured people over there. One of them is fairly serious. Is there anybody else here who needs medical assistance?"

He waited for a show of hands. When there was none, he continued.

"Okay. Mr. Berke over there knows first aid. He's going to help the injured. But we need your assistance with that. We need medical supplies. We're looking for ..."

Paul's voice trailed off as he realized nobody was listening to him any longer. All of their attention was focused on the tree line behind him. He turned slowly, and looked. A few of the treetops shook violently, but there was no wind. There was no sound, either, except for the rustling branches and leaves. Then, they stopped trembling. Seconds later, some treetops closer to the clearing began to tremble. Whatever was disturbing them was coming closer.

———

ERIN WASN'T PAYING attention to the grown-ups. She sat in her mother's lap. Mr. Bob was sitting next to them on the grass. She liked Mr. Bob. He was funny and kind, and did neat magic tricks. But right now, Mr. Bob and her Mommy were both listening to the man with the bloody knees and hands. Erin didn't want to look at the bloody man, because he reminded her of her own scraped knee.

Instead, she focused on a tiny butterfly with a wingspan of only a few inches. It was orange and red and pink in color, and it quickly flitted between the flowers growing in the clearing, alighting on a different plant every few seconds. Erin thought it was one of the prettiest things she'd ever seen, and its movements delighted her. She continued to watch the butterfly as it flew closer to the forest, hovering right at the edge of the tree line. As a result, she was the first one in the group to actually see the dinosaur as it pushed through the trees and emerged into the clearing.

Then, all of the adults started screaming.

BENN STARED OVER TOD, Geoff, and Scott's shoulders, mouth gaping in mid-moan. He forgot his pain, forgot his fears that he was dying, and forgot the nauseating feeling of his own blood leaking from his body. Instead, his thoughts were consumed with the impossible thing looming over them. Benn was so paralyzed with fear that he couldn't even scream.

H, seated nearby, did it for him.

Benn had once taken a boat cruise on the Adelaide River in Darwin, near the Kakadu National Park. During the trip, he'd been a mere arm's length away from a twenty-foot long crocodile. He remembered how imposing it had looked—how absolutely solid. He remembered the sound it had made, and even how it had smelled. The thing emerging into the clearing reminded him of the crocodile in some ways. It sounded similar, and smelled exactly the same, albeit stronger. And just like the crocodile, it looked solid and imposing. Heavy.

But that was where all similarities ended.

Benn was fairly certain that the creature erupting from the forest was an Allosaurus. It stood about sixteen feet high, and he guessed it was probably thirty feet long, from its massive head to its long, heavily muscled tail. A pair of horns sat above and in front of its eyes, and small ridges ran from its nose up to the base of the horns. It tottered over them on large hind legs.

The dinosaur's head swiveled from left to right, perched oddly atop its tiny neck, as it surveyed them. Then, it opened its mouth, revealing dozens of knife-sized, sharp teeth, and made a sound—not a roar, as Benn expected, but more of a rumbling hiss. Again, he was reminded of the crocodile at Kakadu National Park.

"There goes the neighborhood," Benn whispered.

Screaming and shouting, the passengers abandoned the crash site and fled, running in all directions toward the shelter of the surrounding foliage.

"Help me with him." Scott jumped to his feet and grabbed Benn's uninjured arm.

"Oh fuck," Benn wheezed as the Allosaurus focused its attention on them.

Tod and Geoff moved quickly. Tod grabbed Benn's other arm. Benn bit down a scream as pain coursed through the limb. Geoff held his legs. Next to them, H stumbled to his feet, seeming disoriented.

Shock, Benn thought. *He's in shock. If that blow to the head didn't do it, then this sure did.*

"I'm sorry, Benn," Scott said. "This is going to hurt."

"It's okay," he moaned. "Let's just get the hell out of here."

"Pick him up, guys."

Grunting and snorting, the Allosaurus lumbered toward them.

"Hurry," Scott urged, his voice thick with barely controlled panic.

They lifted Benn off the ground, and he shrieked. The pain was so intense that his vision blacked out for a second. When he could see again, he realized that they were carrying him across the clearing, casting terrified glances back at their pursuer. With another throaty hiss, the dinosaur plodded after them, deceptively fast despite its enormous bulk. With three quick strides, it closed the distance between itself and its prey, ignoring the bewildered H and bearing down directly atop them. Its small, three-fingered forearms thrashed with excitement, the curved and pointed claws clacking together with a loud clicking sound. Then it darted forward, head lowered, mouth wide. Drool dripped from its maw.

"Look out," Benn yelled.

With a yelp, Geoff let go of Benn's legs and leapt aside. Scott and Tod held firm. The Allosaurus's jaws clamped shut on Benn's legs, just below his waist. He shrieked as the teeth shredded his flesh and splintered his bones. His vision turned white for a second as a wave of excruciating pain washed over him.

Scott and Tod pulled on his arms, but the dinosaur jerked its head, refusing to release him. Then, with a vicious yank, it tore Benn free of their grip and stood to its full height. Screaming, Benn could only flail helplessly as he dangled from the creature's mouth. It swung its head from side to side and then opened its jaws, tossing Benn into the air. He crashed to the ground at the dinosaur's feet, knocking the air from his lungs. He heard his ribs snap as gouts of blood spewed from his mouth, ears, and nose. The impact pushed the metal shard further into his arm. He tried to scream again, but only managed a wheeze.

Somewhere behind him, Benn heard Scott and Tod shouting. Their words were lost beneath the creature's roar. A large glob of saliva dripped from its slavering jaws and splattered his face.

Mewling, Benn tried to roll over and crawl away, but his body wouldn't respond. He willed himself to move and found that he couldn't. With a great effort, Benn managed to raise his head. He glanced down at his lower half, and found it in ruin.

Where's my leg, he thought, *and what's that thing sticking out of me? That can't be my bone ...*

The dinosaur loomed over him, seeming to grin.

I'm sinking, Benn thought. *I'm sinking in the quicksand of my own thought, and I ain't got the power anymore.*

The dinosaur hissed again. Before Benn could react, the beast pinned him to the dirt with one massive foot and then, with a satisfied grunt, lowered its head to feed.

Benn's last, confused thought was of the two boxes of books he'd shipped home. He wondered who would sign for them.

The jaws closed over him.

SCOTT, Tod, and Geoff fled for the safety of the trees while the dinosaur began to feed. The terrible sounds the creature made while it was eating echoed behind them.

"We should go back to help," Scott said.

"Fuck that," Geoff exclaimed. "It's already got him! There's nothing we can do."

Tod tried to respond, but neither of them could understand him. He panted and wheezed, his face a deep shade of red. His skin was slick with sweat.

He's going to have a heart attack, Scott thought as they plunged into a thicket of tall, green ferns. *And where did that H guy go?*

LOOKING for a safe spot to hide, Leigh, Mark, and Paul Goblirsch ran for a stand of bamboo on the edge of the clearing. Chris raced along behind them in his wheelchair. As the terrain grew rougher, his speed slowed, and the chair's motor and gears began to whine.

"Come on," he urged. "Come on, goddamn it."

The others stopped at the bamboo grove and turned around. They shouted in dismay when they saw he had fallen behind.

"It's too rocky." Chris waved. "Go on without me."

"Fuck that," Mark replied. "Let's help him, guys. Hurry up!"

They ran back to Chris and tried pushing the chair, but it was heavier than it looked.

"How much do you fucking weigh, dude?" Mark asked.

"It's not me. It's the chair."

Mark grunted, gritting his teeth and pushing.

"Go on without me," Chris said again. "I'm going to slow you guys down. The chair will never make it."

"Then we'll leave the chair," Leigh said.

Leigh and Mark lifted Chris out of the chair, while Paul cast a terrified glance back at the dinosaur. The others did the same. The creature was still on the other side of the clearing, taking its time tearing Benn apart piece by piece. Its jaws and forearms were stained with his blood. Most of the passengers had disappeared, but one lone figure was still stumbling about the clearing, seemingly disoriented.

"It's H," Chris said.

Paul cupped his hands around his mouth and shouted. "H! Over here. Hurry!"

If their injured friend heard them, he gave no indication. Instead, he turned and headed toward the bus in a strange, wobbling gait.

"He must have hit his head harder than we thought," Mark said.

"Either that or he's in shock," Leigh suggested.

They tried shouting for him again, but H continued to ignore them. He hunkered down behind the crashed shuttle, and pulled his knees up tight against his chest, cowering.

"He's fucking out of it," Mark said.

"You guys hide," Paul told the others. "I'll go get him."

Mark grabbed for Paul's arm. Leigh grunted, struggling to hold Chris up by himself.

"Hey," Leigh said. "He's not a sack of groceries!"

"Sorry," Mark apologized, and then turned to Paul. "Think about this, pal. You've got a wife. A daughter."

"And you've got a wife and son." Paul stared at each of them. "We've all got people at home. And H is our friend."

"You don't have to do this," Chris pleaded. "Put me in the chair. I'll distract that thing while you guys get H and hide."

Paul shook his head. "Francesca would never forgive us. We promised her we'd get you home safe, didn't we?"

Chris studied Paul's expression, and saw that his mind was made up.

"Be careful," he whispered.

"I will," Paul said. "Believe me, I want to get home safe, too."

As Leigh and Mark carried him into the bamboo, Chris watched Paul dash across the clearing. The last thing he saw before the reeds closed around them was the sunlight glinting off his abandoned wheelchair.

———

H WONDERED why his ears were full of bees. They had to be, he reasoned. Why else would they be buzzing? He didn't understand how the bees could have gotten inside his ears, but then again, he hadn't understood much of what had happened since the shuttle crashed. Some of it made sense—the gash on his forehead, the young man with the injured arm. But other things, like the environment and the dinosaur, simply couldn't be real. H decided that perhaps Scott was right. Perhaps he should just rest until he stopped hallucinating.

Except that, if the dinosaur was a hallucination, then how

come everyone else could apparently see it, too? They must have been able to see it, after all, given that they'd all run away when it appeared.

He glanced back at the spot where they'd abandoned Benn. H had to admit, for a hallucination, it all seemed very real. He could smell Benn's blood and innards, and could hear—even over the buzzing in his ears—the sounds the monster made as it chewed and swallowed. Worse, he could smell the dinosaur, as well. It reminded him of the stench inside the reptile house at the zoo, except stronger. Fresher.

"Okay," H mumbled. "Hallucinations don't have scents, but that doesn't mean this is real. Maybe it's a test."

Yes, that was it. This whole situation was just an experiment of some sort. Maybe they'd been abducted by a clandestine government agency, or that Black Lodge group people talked about on the Internet. Or maybe they'd all been dosed with LSD or some other type of hallucinogenic drug. Maybe terrorists had released something at the airport that was causing all of them to suffer from very realistic hallucinations.

Far off in the distance, as if at the other end of a long train tunnel, he thought he heard Paul calling his name. He glanced in that direction, and saw Paul, Leigh, Mark, and Chris waving at him. As he watched, Paul cupped his hands around his mouth and called H's name again.

Maybe he's a hallucination, too, H thought. *Maybe they all are. Well, I refuse to participate in this test. I'd better hide.*

He lurched toward the wreckage of the shuttle bus, only to discover that he was having difficulty walking in a straight line. His tongue felt thick and his mouth was dry. H decided that this was further proof he was under the influence of some unknown drug. He glanced over at the dinosaur. It kept the scraps of Benn's corpse pressed against the ground with one massive foot, and lowered its head to tear off pieces. Benn's remains weren't really recognizable as human any longer. What remained was a red, glistening pile of meat. Insects were already crawling on it.

Reaching the shuttle bus, H ducked behind the wreckage, out of the monster's sight, and sat down. He drew his knees up against his chest, hugged his legs, lowered his head, and closed his eyes tightly. The buzzing in his ears began to fade, but now he was aware that he could also hear and feel his heart beating. It seemed unusually loud and rapid.

It won't find me here, he thought. *I'll just hide here. I'll stay here and keep my eyes shut until it goes away.*

His heart rate slowly returned to normal. H sighed, eyes still closed, hoping that when he opened them again, he'd be somewhere else, and this would all be proven to have been a bad dream.

Something clamped down on his shoulder.

Screaming, H leaped to his feet, nearly knocking Paul Goblirsch over.

"Jesus, H!"

"Paul? What are you doing here?"

"I've been shouting. Didn't you hear me?"

"No ... there were bees ..."

Paul frowned. "H, you're not well. We've got to get you out of here, buddy. Come with me."

H shook his head. "There's nowhere to go. Don't you see? This is all just some sort of fucking test. We're rats in a maze."

Paul turned away from him and peeked over the edge of the wreckage, checking on the dinosaur's whereabouts. Then he turned back to H.

"H, listen to me. You're freaking out. You took a blow to the head, and I think you're in shock. Hell, I think we're *all* in shock. But right now, I need you to focus for me. You see that bamboo grove over there?"

H stared at where Paul was pointing and then slowly nodded.

"Good," Paul said. "We need to make a run for that, while the dinosaur is still busy. You think you can make it?"

"Yeah," H whispered. "I think so. I'm sorry, Paul. I don't know what's wrong with me."

Paul gave his shoulder another squeeze. This time, H was comforted by the gesture rather than frightened.

"You're scared, H. I am, too. I don't know what's happened. I don't know how any of this is possible. But we can figure it out later. Right now, we just need to get somewhere safe. Okay?"

H nodded, more certain this time. "Okay."

Paul helped him to his feet, wincing as H squeezed his injured hand. They peered around the shuttle bus. The dinosaur was nearly finished with Benn. Growling and snorting, it rooted through the bloody smear of his remains as if seeking more choice bits.

"Here we go," Paul whispered. "Head straight for the bamboo, just beyond Chris's wheelchair. Fast as you can."

Then he shoved H forward. The two of them raced across the clearing. H's pulse began to pound again, but the buzzing in his ears was gone now, and his head felt clearer. Behind them, the Allosaurus grunted, seemingly surprised. H ignored it, resisting the urge to turn around and look. Instead, he focused on Chris's abandoned wheelchair. He wondered where Chris was and why the chair was unoccupied. Had something happened to him? He didn't ask, because doing so would have wasted precious air, and he needed every breath to keep up the pace. His lungs felt like they were on fire, and his heart rate got faster, thundering in his chest.

Then, with a roar, the dinosaur rumbled after them, and H wasted his breath by screaming. It felt to him as if the earth itself was bucking under their feet.

"Keep going," Paul shouted. "I'll lead it away and then circle around to you guys."

H tried to respond, but could only manage a frightened gasp.

"Mark, Chris, and Leigh are in there, H. Inside the bamboo. They'll see you coming. Just run!"

Then, without another word, he turned around and ran toward the pursuing Allosaurus.

Wheezing, H stumbled and almost fell. The pain in his chest grew worse, and his knees throbbed from exertion. Behind him, he heard Paul shouting at the dinosaur, trying to attract its attention. H paused, wondering if he should run after Paul. Then he saw Mark emerge from the bamboo, frantically waving his arms. H blinked sweat from his eyes and ran on.

———

PAUL GOBLIRSCH's thoughts didn't turn to his wife, Janet, or their daughters as the dinosaur pursued him across the clearing. Nor did they turn to his friends. He didn't glance backward to see if H had successfully escaped. The only thing he focused on was running. He was too terrified to think about anything else.

"Stay ahead ... stay ahead ..."

He made several sharp turns, veering from side to side, trying to throw the voracious beast off-track. At one point, the creature got close enough that he could smell it, but for the most part, he managed to keep out of its reach. He was amazed how fast something that size could be.

Reaching the far side of the clearing, he plunged into some tall grass and spotted a stand of trees straight ahead of him. One tree looked particularly sturdy, with a thick, solid trunk and several low-hanging limbs. He made a beeline for it, all-too-aware that the dinosaur hadn't given up its pursuit. That was good. It meant that his friends were safe.

Now all he had to do was ensure the same for himself.

Gasping for breath, Paul rounded the tree, intent on scurrying up the backside of it. He hoped he could climb to a height above the dinosaur before it reached him. Given the number of branches, he was sure at the very least that this refuge would slow the creature down. He reached for the lowest branch, a limb about the thickness of his arm, and wrapped both of his hands around it. The bark felt extremely sticky with sap. Paul pulled himself up and wrapped his legs around the branch. He felt the sap pull at his bare legs and shorts. Worse, it stung the open cuts on his palms.

When he tried to pull himself up the rest of the way and reach for the next limb, he found that he couldn't. His palms and legs were stuck fast to the tree.

"What the hell ...?"

Whimpering, he tried to free one hand, but it remained fastened to the limb. Worse, his exposed skin was starting to tingle. Unlike the initial sting, the sensation wasn't painful. Indeed, a strange sense of calmness overcame him. He craned his neck to see around the tree trunk and spotted the dinosaur stomping through the high grass toward him.

"Okay," he muttered. "No worries. I can climb higher, soon as I'm unstuck. Just have to pull really, really hard ..."

Gritting his teeth, he flexed his right arm and tried to pull his hand free. Pain rocketed through him like an electric charge as the skin of his palm tore. He felt his blood running down his wrist. It dripped into his face. But his hand was still stuck.

The more he struggled, the stronger the tingling sensation grew, and the calmer he became. By the time the dinosaur reached him, Paul simply dangled there, smiling, his arms and legs encircling the limb. His scraped hands and knees no longer hurt.

The calm sensation vanished when the dinosaur's teeth tore into him.

[4]
WELCOME TO THE JUNGLE

G regorio fled through the jungle, too panicked to even consider which direction he was running. Vines and tree branches whipped at him, tangling his hair and tugging at his clothes. Thorns pricked his flesh, drawing little beads of blood. He ignored them all and stumbled on, oblivious to the damage and pain. The vegetation grew thicker as he plunged ahead, and at times he had to push and fight to clear a path. He flailed wildly with his arms, driven by fear. Above him, birds screeched, hidden in the treetops. Behind him, the dinosaur's roars echoed. Sometimes, the creature sounded far away. Other times, he swore it must be right on top of him. At one point, he heard another of the passengers cry out, but it was impossible to tell which direction the sound had come from or who the person was.

By the time he finally halted, panting and out of breath, Gregorio was covered in dozens of welts and scratches, and bathed in sweat. He bent over in a stand of tall ferns, hands on his knees, gasping for breath, and debated what to do next. The birds grew silent again, and the dinosaur's cries faded.

A curtain of blue-leaved creeper vines rustled nearby.

Gregorio straightened up, intent on running away again, but then the foliage parted and Paul Legerski stepped out. He didn't notice Gregorio right away, as his attention was focused on his cell phone.

I should hide, Gregorio thought. *Let him walk on by. That guy is weird ...*

But no. That wasn't the right thing to do. Legerski was trapped here, just like he was. The man was scared. That fear probably accounted for his behavior back on the shuttle bus. And besides, Gregorio was frightened, too. Having a companion out here in this jungle, even if that companion was an asshole like Legerski, was better than facing things alone.

Gregorio waited until he was at arm's length, and when Legerski still didn't look up from his phone, he called out in a stage whisper.

"Hey, Mr. Legerski!"

Startled, Legerski yelped, dropping his phone.

Gregorio stepped back two paces into the ferns.

"You asshole," Legerski said, stooping over to retrieve the phone. "What the fuck is wrong with you? You scared the hell out of me!"

"I'm sorry." Gregorio motioned with his hands, signaling the other man to lower his voice. "We should whisper. We don't want to attract attention."

"Oh yeah?" Legerski brushed off his phone's screen. He still didn't meet Gregorio's eyes. "And why is that?"

Gregorio shrugged. "I think that's pretty obvious. Have you seen any of the others? Do you think it got them?"

Legerski frowned. "What are you talking about?"

"The dinosaur!"

Legerski stared at him balefully. Then, shaking his head, he began to walk away, heading in the direction of the clearing.

"Wait!" Gregorio stepped out of the ferns. When Legerski

didn't stop, he reached out and grabbed his wrist. "Not that way. It might still be out there."

"Let go of me." Legerski angrily shoved him away. "I don't know what your problem is, but you'd better stay the fuck away from me. I don't have time for this!"

"You ..." Gregorio paused. "Holy shit! You don't know, do you?"

"Know what? That I trekked out here into this godforsaken jungle and I still can't find a cell phone signal?"

"Something happened." Gregorio swallowed, still out of breath. "Back at the bus. Something came out of the jungle ... it looked like a dinosaur, and it ... it ate ..."

Legerski sighed. "Back on the shuttle—you said your name was Greg?"

Gregorio nodded, swallowing hard.

"Okay," Legerski continued, "look, Greg, I don't know if you're on drugs, or if maybe you're just shook up from the crash and hallucinating, but whatever your malfunction is, keep me out of it."

Before Gregorio could stop him, Legerski turned away and marched off toward the clearing. Gregorio hurried after him, intent on tackling the man if he had to, but then the dinosaur sounded off again. The echoing growls and roaring stopped both of them in their tracks.

"What the hell is that?" Legerski asked.

"That's what I'm trying to tell you, asshole. It's a dinosaur. Or at least that's what it looked like."

Legerski shook his head. "That can't be it. Somebody is obviously fucking with us. It's a tape—an audio recording."

"Dude, I'm telling you. That thing came crashing out of the jungle and ate that injured guy. I didn't see what happened next because everybody flipped out. But it's real. We need to stay quiet and stick together."

The dinosaur cried out again, as if confirming this.

"Well, fuck this." Legerski turned around and headed back the way he'd come.

After a moment's hesitation, Gregorio followed him. He assumed that Legerski must know where he was going, and he no longer heard any of the other passengers. Gregorio reasoned again that it was better to stick with this fellow traveler, even if he was an asshole, than to be out here alone.

"Do you know of someplace up ahead where we can hide?" he asked.

Legerski shrugged, but said nothing.

After a few minutes, they came across a narrow footpath. Legerski began following the winding trail through the jungle. Gregorio hurried along behind him, glancing nervously at the surrounding foliage. He half expected at any moment for another dinosaur to emerge and snatch them up.

The path led into a wide, sun-filled clearing that was free of trees or other overhead growth. The trail continued through the center of the clearing. Both sides of it were lined with large swaths of vibrantly green grass. Legerski stopped in the middle of the trail, just at the edge of the grass, and pulled out his phone again. He tapped the screen and seemed disinterested in Gregorio.

"What are we stopped for?" Gregorio asked.

"Hmm? Oh, you can go ahead." Legerski nodded at the clearing. "There's a place to hide over on the other side. I'm just checking my signal really quick."

When he still didn't move, Gregorio stepped around him and onto the grass. He'd gone about three steps off the trail when the pain hit him. It felt like razor blades were slashing his ankles and cutting through the soles of his shoes. Gasping, he glanced down and saw that was exactly what was happening. The blades of grass, which had looked deceptively soft, were actually as sharp as knives. Each individual blade now swayed and slashed in tandem, slicing at his feet and ankles. Gregorio lifted a foot to flee, but the pain was so intense that he instead collapsed onto his knees. He screamed as the grass began flaying the flesh from his lower legs, turning his pants and the skin beneath them into tattered ribbons. His blood spurted from dozens of wounds, splattering the grass and trickling down into the dirt, which seemed to suck it up as quickly as it spilled. He cast an agonized glance back at Legerski, reaching out his hand for help.

Legerski smiled. "Interesting. I suspected there was something off about that lawn, but I wasn't sure until now. Maybe it was just a case of one killer sensing another, but I thought I'd better steer clear of it until I knew for sure. And now I do, thanks to you."

"Help me," Gregorio shrieked as his legs were sheared off at the kneecaps. "Help me, you son of a bitch. *Please!*"

"No, I don't think so. But I will stand back and admire their handiwork. I wasn't sure about this place—wherever this place actually is—but now I'm starting to think I may like it here after all."

Gregorio tried to respond, but could only scream.

"Don't you see?" Legerski asked. "This place—it's like me. It's a killer just like me."

Gregorio realized two things in that moment.

The first thing he realized was that Paul Legerski was crazy.

The second thing he realized was that he was going to die.

"Tania," he breathed. "Maricelaaaaaaa ..."

With his knees now gone, he toppled over onto his back, and the razor grass went to work on the rest of his body, slicing through his clothes and skin, and chopping up his organs as they spilled out.

The last thing he saw was the wide grin and delighted expression of rapt fascination on Paul Legerski's face.

———

DAVE SUPPORTED Jamie as they made their way through the jungle. Jamie had one arm around Dave's shoulder. He had fallen during their escape and twisted his ankle—injuring it far more than Dave had injured his own earlier. Now, both of them struggled, but while Dave seemed to be getting better, Jamie's felt worse. He hopped on his one good foot. Each step sent a twinge of pain through his leg. His face was slick with sweat, and he panted for breath.

"We should stop," Dave whispered. "Rest here and catch our breath."

"I'm fine," Jamie protested. "Let's keep going."

"You're not fine," Dave said, "and neither am I."

"We're …" Jamie gulped air and then tried again. "We're being chased by a dinosaur."

"Yes," Dave agreed. "Yes, we are."

As they collapsed to the jungle floor and hid behind some red and green ferns, Jamie studied his new friend.

"Stop worrying about me," Dave insisted. "It still hurts, but I can walk. How about you?"

Jamie grunted. "Mine hurts like hell. You don't seem in too bad of shape."

"Physically, I'm okay," Dave admitted. "But mentally? Emotionally? That's a different story."

He paused, clearly struggling over what to say next. Jamie waited patiently, not wanting to interrupt.

"Let's just say I wasn't in the best state of mind before all this happened," Dave continued. "And now? Now we've crashed God knows where, and there's a dinosaur on the loose. None of this is exactly conducive to maintaining a positive state of mind."

"No," Jamie replied, "I don't suppose it is."

"Where *do* you think we are, Mr. LaChance?"

"Call me Jamie, please."

"Okay. Jamie."

"That's better." Jamie smiled. "As for where we are, I don't know. And right now, I don't think that question should be our top priority. We'll have time to figure that out later. The first thing we need to do is find the others."

"What if that thing ate them?"

"I don't think that's possible," Jamie said. "It couldn't have eaten everyone. Yes, it was fast, or at least it seemed to be in the short time that I saw it. But it was preoccupied with that poor guy from the bus—the one with the arm injury—and the rest of us scattered in every direction. I don't think it could have caught up with everyone that quickly."

"Maybe it had friends."

Jamie frowned. "Let's hope not. But just in case it did, maybe we'd better get moving."

"To where?"

"I don't know. Like I said, let's start by finding the others. Some of them must still be alive. There's safety in numbers."

"What about your ankle?" Dave asked.

Shrugging, Jamie hiked up his pants leg, rolled down his sock, and gently touched his injured ankle. He winced at the pain. The skin was red and felt hot to the touch.

"You can't keep walking on that," Dave said. "It's swollen up like a balloon."

Gritting his teeth, Jamie pulled his pants leg back down. "I'll have to. I'm not going to just sit here and wait to be eaten."

"Okay," Dave conceded. "But let's go slow."

"I wish I had some edibles," Jaime muttered. "That would help the pain."

"Edibles?" Dave grinned. "You mean marijuana?"

"Yeah. I like the gummies."

Dave helped Jamie to his feet, and then supported him again

as they continued on their way. Jamie tried to guess which direction the shuttle bus was, but with no memorable landmarks and no sound from their fellow passengers, it was impossible to judge.

"Do you recognize any of this?"

Dave shrugged. "It looks all the same to me. But I did notice one weird thing. Some of these trees look like they belong in a forest. Others look like they're from some sort of tropical jungle. And some...I swear I've never seen anything like some of these before."

"I noticed that, too."

"What do you think it means?"

Jamie paused before answering, choosing his words carefully. "Dave, I don't think we're on Earth anymore."

"What?"

"I know, I know. It sounds crazy, but hear me out. When we were on the airport shuttle, it was night and winter. Then there were a number of weird occurrences, like your cellular service, and that watch we found. Remember?"

Dave nodded. "It ran backward."

"And then we crashed," Jamie continued. "When we did, suddenly it was daylight and the weather was more suited for the tropics. And the watch had stopped. Then that dinosaur wandered out of the jungle."

"So, you mean ... like time travel or something?"

"That's what I thought at first. But time travel doesn't explain our surroundings. At no point in Earth's history did plants co-exist like this. I mean, not only are there plants from different parts of the Earth growing side by side, but they're from different eras, too. See that oak tree? They've got them like that all over North America. Now, take a look at the palm tree over there next to it. I've seen one before—a model of one—in a museum. I'm pretty sure that tree went extinct millions of years ago."

Dave stared at the two trees. The color drained from his expression.

"But there's more than that," Jamie continued. "It's like you said. Some of these plants? I don't think they've *ever* existed on Earth. At least, not that I've ever heard of. Admittedly, I'm not a botanist, but a pine tree with red needles? I have to think if something like that had ever grown on our planet, we'd have learned about it in school. Or the orange Venus flytrap I noticed earlier, when we fled. Which brings me to the fauna. Some of the insects look normal. But others are unlike anything I've ever encountered, except for maybe in an old science fiction movie."

Dave's voice was barely a whisper. "So ... we ...?"

Jamie nodded. "We're on another planet, or in another dimension. That's my theory."

"I have to get home," Dave gasped, almost sobbing. His eyes were wide and panicked. "I can't be here! I was on my way back to Louisiana. My daughter, Autumn ... she needs me!"

"Dave." Jamie held his hands up, trying to hush him. "Calm down. Breathe. It's not going to do any good to freak out now."

"You don't understand, Jamie."

"I understand all too well. I've got kids back home, too."

"But my wife and I ... we were ..."

"Dave, stop and breathe. It's going to be okay. We'll—"

A scream interrupted him. Jamie and Dave both glanced around, trying to determine where it had come from. It sounded nearby.

Dave squeezed Jamie hard. "What was—"

Jamie held up a finger, silencing him. Then another shriek echoed through the jungle.

"Over there!" Jamie pointed. "Hurry."

They went as fast as they could, Jamie hopping on one foot and Dave assisting him, albeit slowly. Each step caused Jamie more pain, but he barely felt it. His mind was consumed instead with helping whoever was in trouble.

They pushed through a thick tangle of vines and made their way down a small hill which emerged into a grove of rainbow-colored ferns. On the other side of the foliage was a clearing lined with brilliantly-green grass. Upon spying it, Jamie's first thought was that, despite the fact that the grass hadn't been mowed, it looked like someone's lawn.

Then he realized that something was very wrong.

One of the young men from the shuttle bus was lying in the grass, bleeding from hundreds of slashes. After a moment, Jamie realized it was the grass that was cutting him, and it was doing so with horrifying speed and precision. The individual blades moved in tandem, dicing and dissecting the hapless victim into nothing more than pulp. His blood flowed over the grass and down into the soil beneath, where Jamie assumed the roots were soaking it up.

The young man—Jamie couldn't remember his name—writhed and thrashed. His mouth hung open, jaw clenching and unclenching, but he made no sound. He was beyond screaming now. Then, his movements became twitches as his abdomen was sliced open, spilling its contents out onto the grass.

"Look there," Dave whispered, aghast.

Jamie did, and saw another passenger wearing a San Jose Sharks jersey—Legerski—standing nearby, grinning with apparent amusement as the young man stopped moving.

"What the hell?" Jamie shouted. "You think this is funny?"

Legerski turned toward them, and the smile vanished from his face, replaced instead with a withering expression of hatred and disdain. Then, without saying a word, he ducked into the jungle and disappeared.

"Stay here," Dave said. "I'm going after him!"

"No, Dave. That's not going to help matters."

"But he just let that guy die! The fucker was laughing about it."

"We don't know for sure that's what happened," Jamie said. "He could have gotten here when it was too late for him to do anything, just like it was for us. And yes, he was grinning, but maybe he's just lost his mind. People express fear in different ways."

"Bullshit." Dave shook his head. "I've seen how people express fear. I saw it every day in Afghanistan. And that isn't it. That guy wasn't afraid. That guy is a psycho!"

"If you're right, then that's all the more reason for us to find the others. If he is dangerous, we need to warn them, before somebody else gets hurt or killed."

"I don't know, Jamie. What if he—ow!"

Dave let go of Jamie and slapped the back of his neck. Then he turned his hand over and looked at it. His palm was smeared with the crushed remains of some kind of bug, crushed beyond the point of recognition. The insect's blood was the color of a squished lima bean.

"Are you okay?"

"No," Dave seethed. "The damn thing stung me. Shit, that really hurts!"

"Are you allergic to bee stings?"

"I'm not sure. I mean, I'm not allergic to the ones back home, but here ...? Look at it. This thing doesn't look like any bee I've ever seen. Maybe it's a mosquito?"

Jamie sniffed. "What's that smell? Like a battery, or how the air smells in summer after a thunderstorm?"

"It's coming from my hand," Dave said. "I think it's the bug's blood. I don't think this is a bee at all."

As Dave wiped the remnants of the bug on his pants, Jamie examined the back of his neck.

"It doesn't look too bad," he said. "There's no stinger or

anything. Just a tiny little red spot. Are you having trouble breathing? Feeling dizzy? Does it itch?"

"It itches a little," Dave admitted, "but I think I'll be okay. I just ..."

He clenched his fists and closed his eyes. Jamie realized he was struggling with not breaking into tears.

"What's wrong?" Jamie's tone was concerned. "I thought it just itched?"

"My hand," Dave choked. "Where the blood was. It burns. My neck, too. I lied when I said it just itched. But that's not ... that's not what's wrong ..."

"Well, then. What is it?"

"I ..." Dave broke into deep, mournful sobs.

"Hey," Jamie whispered. "Listen, Dave ... it's going to be okay."

"I just want to get home," Dave said. "Please ... I just want to get back home. My daughter ..."

"It's going to be okay," Jamie repeated as they began to limp along once more. "You'll see. We'll get you back home. I promise."

But deep down inside, he didn't believe it.

━━━

It felt like they'd been running for hours, but Geoff knew that was impossible. Still, with their watches and phones malfunctioning, and the sun mostly hidden above the jungle canopy, there was no way to accurately judge how long it had really been. Something else puzzled him, as well. The few times he had caught sight of the sun, it had seemed to Geoff that it was immobile—still occupying the exact same place it had been when they first crashed.

He considered mentioning this to Scott and Tod, but this

frantic dash through the jungle was obviously taxing both older men. Tod, especially, was struggling to keep up. His complexion had gone from red to almost purple, and his shirt—a hideous Hawaiian print adorned with skulls—was drenched in sweat. His breathing had been reduced to a violent series of wheezing and gasps that seemed to wrack his prodigious form.

"Listen," Geoff said to Scott. "I don't hear them anymore. I think we can stop for a minute."

Scott glanced at him and tried to respond, but it was clear to Geoff that the older man, while not in as bad of shape as Tod, lacked the breath to speak. Geoff stopped. Seconds later, Scott did the same. The look of relief on his face was almost comical. Geoff was about to ask if he was okay, when Tod suddenly squawked in surprise and tumbled out of sight. There was a great commotion as he rolled down an embankment. Leaves rustled and twigs snapped in his wake. Geoff hurried to the top of the bank, and peered down at him. Tod had landed on his back atop a pile of leaves. He lay there sprawled, eyes closed, chest heaving. After a moment, Scott appeared at Geoff's side, still out of breath, and still unable to speak.

"Are you okay?" Geoff called down. "Tod?"

Tod waved his hand weakly, but didn't open his eyes. He had fallen to the bottom of what appeared to be a deep but narrow creek bed. The jungle foliage had done an excellent job of concealing it until they'd almost been on top of it. Judging by the amount of detritus and other debris at its bottom, and how dry the soil was, it had been a long time since water had flown through the ravine.

Geoff turned to Scott. "How about you? You gonna be okay?"

Swallowing, Scott nodded. "Just ... need ... to catch ... my ... breath. My head hurts ..."

"I'm going to check on him."

Crouching, Geoff scurried down the embankment. The

ravine's walls were steep, but there were thick roots jutting from the dirt that provided handholds of sorts. Again, he noticed how dry the dirt was. Clouds of dust swirled in the air, marking his descent. When he reached the bottom, he stood up. He judged the space to be a good nine feet deep, and perhaps ten feet wide. He hurried over to Tod and crouched beside him. The big man didn't seem to be injured, and both his complexion and his breathing were returning to normal. He opened his eyes, blinked twice, and stared at Geoff.

"Ouch ..."

"Are you okay?" Geoff asked again.

"Yeah." Tod sounded hoarse and stunned. "Just need a minute to catch my breath."

"Scott, too. You took a pretty good fall. Maybe I should look you over?"

"Nah." Tod patted his stomach. "I've got extra padding. Nothing's broken. Just let me stay here a minute."

"We should keep moving," Geoff disagreed. "If that dinosaur finds us here ..."

"I don't think it will," Scott said.

Both Geoff and Tod gazed up at him. Scott stood above them, hands on hips, studying the creek bed.

"You caught your breath pretty quick," Tod said.

"And if you want to keep breathing, I'd advise you to do the same," Scott replied. "I don't hear the dinosaur anymore. And the birds and insects are starting to make noise again. I have to assume it's not close."

"Good," Tod panted. "Then I can just lie here and die in peace."

"It could come back," Scott said. "Or another like it. We have to assume if there was one, then there are probably others."

"But how?" Geoff asked. "None of this makes any sense. Dinosaurs have been extinct for millions of years."

"And I agree," Scott said. "But that type of thinking isn't going to help us right now. Regardless of what makes sense, I think we can all agree that was a dinosaur. A living, breathing dinosaur. We can debate what that means later. Right now, I think we should make plans for what to do if it returns—or more likely, *when* it returns."

Geoff glanced at Tod, and then back up at Scott. "What are you thinking?"

"That the treetops would offer the best protection, but there's no way Tod or myself are going to make it to the top of them. So, we go with the next best thing."

"What's that?" Tod asked.

Scott grinned. "You're lying in it. That ravine would make a good temporary shelter. It's already got steep walls on two sides. We just need to build a roof of some kind and shore up the openings on either side of our encampment. Then we can camouflage it."

Geoff and Tod were quiet for a moment, while they considered Scott's proposal. Geoff wasn't convinced that such a structure would offer protection from the thing they'd seen at the shuttle bus, but he also had to admit this plan of action beat running aimlessly through the jungle until somebody showed up to rescue them.

"Okay," he said, shrugging. "Let's get started."

"You and me," Scott said. "We'll let Tod rest a few more minutes."

"I'm fine," the big man insisted. He sat up slowly, groaning with the effort. "We've got a lot to do. I don't know what time it is, but it will get dark eventually. Would be nice to have this thing built and have a fire going by then."

"My thoughts exactly," Scott agreed. "But it's not going to help matters if you have a heart attack. No offense, but you're looking pretty rough."

"So are you," Tod pointed out.

Scott grinned. "Touché."

The two men laughed, while Geoff gazed up at the sun. It still hadn't moved.

Despite the near-tropical heat, he shivered.

━━━

Bob, Erin, and Paula had run until they exhausted themselves. They rested for a while, crouched down between two large trees, and fearfully watched the vegetation all around them. Erin clung to her mother, eyes wide, but she was apparently too scared to speak. Indeed, she hadn't uttered a sound since their initial flight. Bob was secretly relieved by this. Remaining quiet increased their chances of staying alive.

He scanned the jungle, looking and listening for any signs of pursuit. Insects buzzed around them. A few birds chirped overhead. Something that looked like a squirrel but wasn't scampered along a tree limb, clutching a nut in its teeth. It stopped and stared at him. Bob stared back. Now that he had a chance to study it more closely, he was sure he'd never seen anything like it. It was a mammal of some kind. That much was clear. Small and furry and certainly squirrel-like. But it also seemed somehow ... alien. Its eyes were too big, and the fur around them was rimmed with gold rings. He squinted, and noticed that the creature's little black nose had four nostrils instead of two.

"Huh," he muttered.

At the sound of his voice, the squirrel-like thing scampered away.

"Sweetie," Paula whispered to Erin, "I've got to put you down for a little bit. You're hurting Mommy's arms."

Erin shook her head forcefully, but still made no sound.

"Please, Erin. It's okay. I'll be right here beside you. Nothing's going to hurt you."

The girl responded by squeezing her mother even more tightly and shaking her head once again. Paula sighed.

Bob was about to attempt to help coax Erin into relaxing when he spotted a beam of sunlight glinting off something nearby. The object was partially concealed beneath a pile of leaves, but it appeared to be metallic.

"Stay here," he whispered. "I'll be right back."

Paula's eyes grew wide. "Where are you going?"

"Just over there."

His knees popped as he stood up. Bob stretched, working out the kinks that had formed from staying crouched behind the trees for so long. Then, just as he was about to investigate the object, the leaves rustled nearby.

Bob ducked back down behind the tree and glanced at Paula. Eyes even wider now, she shook her head. Then she reached out with one hand and grabbed his arm, silently urging him to stay. Her other arm remained wrapped protectively around her daughter. The rustling sound drew closer, along with footsteps and twigs snapping. Then, they heard a hushed female voice.

"Maybe they went this way?"

"I don't know," said a second, male, voice. "Everything in this jungle looks the same."

The vegetation parted and the man and the woman appeared. Bob recognized them as fellow passengers from the shuttle bus. He jumped to his feet.

"Hey!"

Startled, the woman stepped backward and the man shrieked.

"Whoa." Bob held up his hands to show that he meant no harm. "Sorry. It's okay. It's me. You were on the airport shuttle."

"Yeah," the guy said, "and so were you. Jesus, dude. You scared the shit out of us."

"Sorry about that. I'm Bob."

"I'm Jesse."

"Colinda," the woman introduced herself.

Bob gestured behind him. "This is Paula and her daughter, Erin."

Paula nodded a greeting, while Erin clung to her leg and stared at the ground, not meeting the adults' eyes.

"Have you guys seen that thing?" Jesse asked.

"Not since we ran," Bob admitted. "How about you?"

Colinda shook her head. "No. Where do you think it's gone to?"

"I don't know," Bob admitted. "Of course, I'm not even sure where *we* are, let alone ... whatever it was."

"It was a dinosaur," Paula said. "I mean, we can all agree on that, right?"

"It looked like one to me," Colinda agreed. "But ..."

Jesse nodded. "Yeah. I don't know how that's possible, but yeah. No sense denying it."

"It chased away the butterfly," Erin complained, half-hidden behind her mother.

Paula hugged her with one arm. "I'm sure there are other butterflies here."

Bob nodded at Erin in concern, and then caught Paula's gaze. "Everything okay, you think?"

Paula nodded. "She's doing better than I am, I think."

"So," Jesse asked, "what do we do now?"

"I saw something over there." Bob pointed. "Right before you two showed up. Some kind of metal, I think."

He crept over to the pile of leaves. The others followed him. Bob saw sunlight glinting off the object again. Yes, it was definitely made of metal, whatever it was. As he started to bend down for a closer look, Paula grabbed his arm.

"Be careful," she whispered.

Swallowing, he tried to give her a reassuring grin. Bob was pretty sure that, judging by her expression and the concern in her eyes, what he'd done was more of a grimace. He turned back to the object, knelt, and brushed the leaves out of the way, revealing a machete. The others cooed their appreciation behind him, as if he had just performed an especially amazing magic trick.

Maybe I'll have to add this to my routine when I get home, he thought. *Watch the magician pull a machete from his ass.*

The machete's blade was as long as his forearm, and despite some rust and notches, still looked sharp and formidable. The handle was crafted out of hard plastic, and coated with black rubber that was worn and cracked, but still in decent shape. Bob took hold of it gently, treating it more like an improvised explosive device than a melee weapon, and picked it up. The machete was surprisingly light. More surprising was the sense of satisfaction that came over him. Just the act of hefting the weapon made him feel safer—more capable.

"Good find," Jesse said. "That ought to come in handy."

A twig snapped behind them. "I agree."

Bob and the others turned to find Paul Legerski stepping out from behind a tree. He looked disheveled. His clothes were dirty and covered in brambles, and his face shined with sweat. His chest heaved, as if he'd been running.

"Hey there," Jesse said. "You're alive."

Legerski nodded at the machete. "I'll take that."

Bob glanced at the weapon, and then back to his fellow passenger. "No offense, but I found it. I think I'll hold onto it, unless you need it for something particular?"

Legerski stepped closer, shoving past Paula and Erin, and

pushing Jesse and Colinda aside, until he stood close enough that Bob could smell his breath.

"You misunderstood me. I said I'm taking it."

"W-what ..." Bob stammered. "Look, Mr.—"

Legerski swung, punching Bob in the right side of his mouth. The pain was immediate and intense. Bob's vision blurred, and his face felt flushed and hot. He staggered backward, tasting his own blood. Legerski waded after him, both fists raised like a boxer. The others shouted, but Bob barely heard them. He was too shocked—too stunned by this seemingly unprovoked attack.

He retreated further, holding up his hand to both indicate surrender and to ward off another blow. Legerski chuckled. Bob was aware of the blood dribbling down his chin. He tried to open his mouth and tell his attacker to stop laughing at him, but doing so brought fresh agony. Instead, he could only wince.

"Hey," Colinda yelled, her tone almost panicked. "What the hell are you doing?"

Jesse stepped forward and grabbed Legerski's shoulder. Their opponent reached up, grabbed Jesse's wrist, and then spun around, yanking Jesse's arm behind his back and forcing him to the ground. Jesse wailed in pain, unable to recover his footing. Still grinning, Legerski delivered a savage kick to Jesse's side. Jesse sank to the ground, writhing and moaning.

Bob moaned, too, as Legerski turned back to him. He held up his hand again, waving the man away.

"Are you gonna give me the machete?" Legerski sneered.

Then Bob remembered. The realization cut through the pain. He glanced down at his other hand, curled into a fist around the hilt of the weapon. Sputtering, he raised his head again and spat blood.

"Yeah, fucker. I'm going to give it to you."

He raised the blade over his head, but Legerski ducked low and charged. He grasped Bob's wrists in both hands and forced him backward. Bob tried planting his feet, but his shoes slid in the soft soil and leaves.

"Kill all of you," Legerski snarled.

Bob's teeth clacked together, bringing renewed pain as his attacker slammed him into a tree trunk. His grip on the machete loosened.

"I'm going to cut you open from neck to balls," Legerski whispered, "and then string your guts in the trees."

Bob's eyes widened as Paula appeared behind them, clutching a broken tree limb about as thick as his bicep. Shrieking, she swung the length of wood, smashing it into the back of Legerski's head. He cried out, as did Jesse and Colinda. Bob felt Legerski's grip loosen, but the older man remained standing. Bob shoved him backward just as Paula swung again, bludgeoning him a second time. There was a crackling sound like shattering ice that made Bob's stomach roil. The tree branch snapped in half, and Legerski tumbled to the ground.

Paula stood over him, chest heaving. Bob glanced at her, and then toward Jesse, Colinda, and Erin. All three gaped. He turned back to Paula, and inched forward, gently taking the broken tree limb from her.

"Thanks," he said.

She nodded, breathing hard.

"Is he ...?" Colinda paused.

Bob knelt cautiously, convinced that Legerski would sit up like some supernatural slasher from a horror movie, and lunge at him. But the man lay still. He couldn't tell if Legerski was breathing or not, but the back of his head was already wet with blood. Bob pressed two fingers to his neck, but felt no pulse. He looked up at the others with wide eyes. Then he grabbed Legerski's limp arm, and felt his wrist. The injured man's flesh was warm. Bob waited a moment and then he felt a pulse—faint, but beating.

"He's alive." Bob stood up and brushed dirt and leaves from his clothes. "I think you might have cracked his skull."

"I'd say dude had it coming," Jesse muttered. "He's crazy."

"Or scared," Colinda said.

"Maybe fear drove him crazy," Jesse countered.

Paula said nothing. She remained where she was, breathing heavily, looming over Legerski's unconscious body.

"Paula?" Bob reached for her, fingertips brushing the back of her hand. "Hey, Paula?"

Hey, hey Paula. A snatch of lyrics came to him—a song he'd heard his father play on guitar. *I wanna marry you. Hey, hey Paula ...*

Bob paused, and swallowed.

What the hell is wrong with me, he thought. *You're scared, dummy. And you're in shock. Careful, or you're going to snap, just like Legerski did, and they'll find you off in the jungle somewhere, naked and eating bugs.*

He cleared his throat and spoke a little louder. "Paula?"

Her eyes flicked up to him. Judging by her expression, Paula seemed confused. She glanced toward Erin, and then seemed to relax a little. Then she turned back to Bob.

"You okay?" Bob asked.

Paula nodded. "He ..."

"I know."

Jesse stepped forward. "What do we do with him? We can't just leave him here."

Before anyone could respond, Legerski began to tremble and sputter. His body twitched, legs and arms jerking spasmodically in the dirt.

"Oh, shit," Jesse gasped.

"He's having a seizure," Colinda yelled. "What do we do?"

"Turn him over." Bob knelt beside him, frantic.

"I don't know if that's a good idea," Jesse said. "If he's got a fractured skull, I don't think you're supposed to move him."

Ignoring him, Bob struggled to turn Legerski over. He reeled back when he did. The man's eyes were rolled up white, and he'd bitten through his bottom lip. Blood and saliva dribbled down his chin. More blood pooled behind him. Bob's hands were sticky with it as well. He snatched up a stick, and tried to wedge it between Legerski's teeth, but the injured man bit through it.

"I don't know what to do," Bob wailed, pulling at his own hair.

Erin cried out for Paula.

Then, the seizure slowly passed, and Legerski lay still again. Bob checked his pulse and verified that he was still breathing.

Colinda shook her head. "Jesus ..."

Paula suddenly lurched past them, arms pinwheeling, and then collapsed to her knees in the underbrush. She leaned forward, retching. Erin ran to her side, but Paula waved her back. The smell of vomit drifted up from the ground. Erin inched forward as Paula heaved again, and gently patted her mother's back, whispering assurances that it would be okay.

Bob glanced down at his hands, grimacing at the blood on them. He bent over and wiped them on the grass, but it didn't do much good.

"You've got it in your hair, too," Colinda said.

"What do we do with him?" Jesse pointed at Legerski.

Bob shrugged. "Tie him up, I guess?"

"But what if he dies?" Colinda asked.

"He seemed pretty intent on killing me," Bob said. "I don't want him to die, but I also don't think we should take any chances. If he wakes up and decides to finish what he started ..."

Colinda nodded. "Good point."

"Okay," Jesse said, "but what do we use to tie him up?"

Bob stood back and surveyed their surroundings, wincing as

the stench of vomit wafted over them again. Then he stomped over to a nearby tree and used the machete to hack at the vines growing up its trunk. He returned with an armload and dropped them on the ground next to Legerski's prone form.

"Give me a hand?"

With Colinda and Jesse's assistance, he bound Legerski's wrists and then his ankles together. For a moment, Bob considered doing more, and perhaps hogtying all four of the man's limbs together, but decided against it. What if Legerski had another seizure? Binding him in such a way could cause more damage.

"Should we gag him?" Colinda asked.

"Better not," Jesse said. "If he starts to have trouble breathing ..."

"Hello?"

A voice echoed through the jungle. It sounded nearby—and judging by the accent, the speaker was Australian. Groaning, Paula got to her feet. All of them glanced at each other.

"I think it's that guy from the bus," Jesse whispered.

Colinda shook her head. "How can we be sure?"

"We can't," Jesse admitted, shrugging. "But it's an Australian accent."

"What if he's like him?" she pointed to Legerski.

"Hello," the voice called again. "It's Leigh, from the shuttle! Mark, H, and Chris are with me! We thought we heard you?"

Bob took a deep breath and shouted, "Here! We're here."

"Where?"

"This way. Follow my voice."

They waited for a few minutes, with Bob calling out repeatedly to guide the new arrivals. Soon, they heard footfalls and some type of motor. Then the undergrowth rustled, and Leigh, Mark, and H stepped into the clearing, followed by Chris in his motorized wheelchair.

"Hi," the Australian said. "Boy, are we glad to see you people."

Bob nodded. "And you guys, as well. Did anyone else make it?"

Leigh shrugged. "We don't know. Our friend, Paul, tried to distract the dinosaur, but we ..." His voice faded as he caught sight of Legerski. "What's this?"

Bob explained what had happened, with Jesse, Colinda, and Paula verifying the events. Leigh filled them in on what they knew of the dinosaur and its whereabouts, and related that although they'd been lucky enough to be able to go back and retrieve Chris's wheelchair, they'd had difficulty getting it through the jungle. Then introductions were made. Leigh stuck out his hand to shake with Bob, but Bob shook his head and held his palms up.

"Blood," he explained.

"Yours?" Mark asked.

"No, his. But what if he ... has a disease or something? I mean, we don't know anything about him, other than his mind seems to have snapped."

Another voice echoed through the foliage, shouting for help.

"Who's that?" H asked.

The others shrugged.

"We should go see," Bob suggested.

"Our friend Paul is still out there, too," Chris reminded them.

Before anyone could respond, another person began yelling from farther away.

"I think that's Scott," Mark said. "The guy who was delivering first aid."

"Two people shouting now ..." Colinda murmured.

"We'd better split up," Bob suggested. "Jesse, Colinda—you guys go after the first voice. Leigh, Mark, and H, you guys go after

Scott. Chris, Paula, and Erin can stay here with me, and guard him."

"I can search, too," Chris argued.

"Yeah, you can, mate," Leigh agreed, "but that chair is going to get hung up again. If they're in trouble, we need to hurry."

"I'll go with Jesse and Colinda," Paula said.

Bob frowned. "Are you sure?"

"I'm feeling better," Paula assured him. Then she knelt next to Erin. "I'm going to go help, sweetie."

"What about me?"

"I want you to stay here with Bob, where it's safe."

Erin glanced at Legerski. "He's not safe."

"He's all tied up. He can't hurt us anymore. You'll be safer here than you are out there."

Erin's bottom lip quivered. "Promise you'll come back?"

Paula hugged the little girl and kissed her forehead. "I promise."

"Okay."

The two groups hurried off into the jungle, leaving Bob, Chris, and Erin to watch over Legerski. Erin sat down cross-legged, plucked a long blade of dark green grass, and began to braid it. Chris and Bob looked at each other.

Chris grinned. "Know any good jokes?"

"Yeah," Bob replied, "but I can't think of any right now."

"Me neither," Chris agreed.

They waited.

L eigh, Mark, and H followed Scott's shouts to the edge of a ravine. When they arrived, Geoff and Tod were busy carrying dead logs and branches from the jungle floor and laying them across the top of the trench, forming a roof. The two stopped working and waved, wiping their foreheads with their shirts. Scott stood near the edge of the ravine and waved as well.

"Careful," he warned. "Don't fall in like Tod did a little while ago."

H peered over the side and whistled. "That's one hell of a drop."

"Wicked," Mark said. "Glad to see you guys are still alive."

Scott nodded. "You guys, too. Have you seen anybody else?"

Mark quickly explained everything that had transpired since the dinosaur's emergence from the jungle—Paul's rescue of H, and their encounter with Bob, Paula, Erin, Jesse, and Colinda. He also told them about how Legerski had become seemingly unhinged and violent.

Scott grunted. "And he's secured now?"

Mark nodded. "Tied up and out cold—or at least he was when we left."

"How far away are they?"

"Not far," Leigh answered. "But we'll need help. At least two people to carry Legerski, if he's still unconscious, and maybe somebody to help with Chris's wheelchair. I don't know if I can push that thing anymore."

"It's not so much the pushing," H countered. "It's motorized. The problem is, it just doesn't navigate very well in the terrain."

"I can push it," Geoff volunteered.

Scott studied the three new arrivals. "Mark, you seem the least tired."

Mark shrugged. "I'm okay."

"Why don't you lead me and Geoff back to them. Leigh and H, you stay here, and maybe give Tod a hand? He can explain what we're doing. Although, H, maybe you should take it easy, given your head."

"I'm okay now," H insisted. "I'm just worried about Paul."

"We'll find him, mate," Leigh said. "Maybe I should go look for him and you stay here and help Tod."

"No." Scott raised his voice. "Listen … we can't go running around the jungle like chickens with our heads cut off. We need to start thinking ahead. Sooner or later, the sun is going to set, and when it does, I suspect we're going to need a shelter to hide us from … well, you guys saw what it was, same as me. We need to be smart about this, and we need to stay together."

"That's easy for you to say," H countered. "Paul's our friend."

"I understand that," Scott replied, "but getting yourself lost or killed out there isn't going to help him. Stay here, and if you're feeling up to it, focus on getting the shelter built. After we get the others and bring them back here, then we'll handle finding Paul and the rest of the group. Okay?"

One by one, they nodded.

"Great." Scott turned to Mark. "Geoff and I will follow you."

Mark led them off into the jungle. Leigh, H, and Tod watched the three men go.

"What did he mean?" Leigh asked. "That bit about headless chickens? Is that some sort of American thing?"

"You don't have chickens in Australia?" Tod asked.

Leigh rolled his eyes, and Tod laughed.

"Chickens," H explained, "can live with their heads cut off."

"You grew up on a farm?" Leigh asked.

"No," H answered. "I was a biology teacher. When you slaughter a chicken for food, you cut the head off, right? But if you aim too high, the chicken can survive a beheading. There was a famous case of a chicken named Mike that lived for eighteen months without a head."

"You're kidding," Tod said. "I've heard of chickens running around the barnyard without a head, but living for eighteen months?"

"Just Google Mike the Headless Chicken if you don't believe me."

"I don't think we have Google here," Tod countered.

"Point," H admitted. "But yeah, the way a chicken's skeletal anatomy is designed, their brain is shoved upwards into their skull at a forty-five-degree angle. If you cut their head off above the eyes, you only remove their forebrain. The cerebellum and brain stem are still intact, as are their basic motor functions and ability to breathe. Provided you miss the jugular vein, the chicken will live. Sever the jugular, and it will still live for a few minutes, running around and spraying blood all over everything. That's what Scott was referring to."

Leigh shivered. His complexion paled.

"You okay?" Tod asked.

Leigh nodded. "I'm just thinking about that guy back at the

bus. Benn, I think his name was? I could ... I heard his bones, when the dinosaur bit down on him ..."

H and Tod stood silently, staring at the ground. Their expressions were haunted.

"What do we do," Leigh asked, "if that thing comes back?"

"Come on," Tod said, turning to the ravine. "We should get to work."

———

Jesse, Colinda, and Paula followed a narrow, winding game trail that was strewn with rocks and overgrown with vegetation at points. Paula took the lead, followed by Jesse, with Colinda bringing up the rear. They stayed close together, and all three glanced around nervously as they hiked. The jungle was full of sounds—birds, insects, and things unknown. Luckily, the one sound they didn't hear was that of the dinosaur. Sporadically, the male voice they'd heard previously echoed from somewhere ahead, shouting for help.

Jesse's attention shifted to the sky. He paused in the middle of the trail, head craned upward.

"What's wrong?" Colinda asked. "Do you see something?"

"The sun ..." Jesse pointed through the foliage. "How long would you two say we've been here?"

Paula shrugged. "I don't know. I've been scared shitless most of the time."

"Maybe two hours?" Colinda suggested. "Maybe three?"

Jesse nodded. "Yeah, I'm thinking two and a half or three hours. That feels right. But I don't think the sun has moved during that entire time. I've seen clouds move in front of it, but I haven't seen the sun move."

"I'm sure it has," Paula replied. "Maybe you were just preoccupied with ... well, with everything else that's happened."

Jesse turned to face her. "Maybe. But I don't think so."

They continued on their way. Occasionally, Jesse massaged his side, wincing with pain.

"Your ribs?" Colinda asked.

Jesse nodded. "Yeah, from the fight with Legerski. I don't think they're broken, though."

"They aren't," Paula assured him.

"How do you know?"

"Because if they were, you wouldn't be walking or breathing as easily as you are."

The man in the jungle called out again. His cries were closer now. The three of them hurried ahead, and after a few more twists and turns, they emerged at the top of a small hill. The game trail continued downward. At the bottom stood two men from the shuttle bus. One of them was middle-aged, with a short haircut that bespoke a military career. The other was taller, probably in his early sixties but still sporting thick hair, slowly going silver. The middle-aged man leaned against the tall one, his head nodding deliriously. Long lines of glistening drool dangled from his puffy lips. The skin on his face and arms seemed swollen. The tall man helped him along the trail, but was limping and clearly struggling.

"Hey," Paula called out.

The tall man looked up and spotted them, and shouted for help again.

Paula, Jesse, and Colinda hurried down the hill to them. Jesse eased the injured man away from the tall man, and supported his weight. As he did, they all saw an ugly red welt on the back of the man's neck. It was the size of an acorn, and its center had turned an ugly shade of blackish-purple. Pink lines ran out from it, spreading across the man's neck and shoulders like spider webs.

"What happened?" Paula asked.

The injured man tried to answer, but his words were slurred and his eyes unfocused.

"He got stung," the tall man answered. "I don't know by what. Some kind of insect. He was fine for a bit, but then ..."

"Are you allergic to bees?" Colinda asked the wounded man.

Again, his answer was unintelligible.

Jessie nodded his head at the tall man. "How about you, Mr. ...?"

"My name's Jamie. And no, I'm okay. I twisted my ankle, but I'll be fine. I wasn't stung. Just Dave. He twisted his ankle, too, but it's not as bad as mine. It's the sting I'm worried about."

"Dave," Jesse said, staring into the injured man's eyes. "We're going to get you some help, okay? Just hang in there."

"What do we do?" Colinda asked. "Is it safe to move him?"

"Let's get him back to the others," Jesse said. "Figure out what to do as a group. I'll support him. Maybe you and Paula can help Jamie walk?"

"Listen," Jamie warned. "We need to be careful. We can't just go traipsing around the jungle. One of the men from the shuttle bus ... we think he's gone crazy."

"Legerski," Paula said. "We know already."

Jamie's eyes widened. "You do?"

Paula nodded. "He's taken care of. We captured him—knocked him out."

"Well," Jesse interrupted, "technically it was Paula who knocked him out."

Paula shrugged. "The point is, he won't be hurting anybody again."

———

CHRIS COULD TELL that he made Bob nervous. Possibly the little girl—Erin—was nervous as well, although it was more likely her apprehension stemmed more from being left alone with two strange adults than it did from Chris's handicap. She sat apart from the two men, her back against a tree trunk, eyeing both men, as well as the bound and unconscious Legerski, with suspicion. Bob crouched, hunkered down on his haunches, looking at everything and nothing, not allowing himself to stare directly at Chris.

It wasn't the first time he had experienced this. Over the years, Chris had been in many situations where his condition initially made people uncomfortable. He'd learned over time that this reaction was based on their own fears and preconceived notions, rather than anything he was projecting or doing. In the vast majority of these cases, the best course of action was to just give them time to discover for themselves that he was still a human being, with an intellect and a sense of humor and all the same foibles as any other member of the human race—he just wasn't as mobile.

"Man," Bob complained, a bit too loudly, "my nose still hurts."

"Broken?" Chris asked. When Bob didn't hear him, he tried again. "Is it broken?"

"No. But it hurts like a bitch." He glanced at Erin and his ears turned red. "Sorry. I said a bad word."

"It's okay," she said quietly. "I've heard worse."

Chris and Bob both smiled at this.

"Have you now?" Bob asked. "Well, even so, I'll try to do a better job of not cussing around you."

He turned back to Chris, and then looked away, focusing on a red bird flitting about in the foliage. Then he turned his attention to Legerski, verifying the man was still unconscious. Bob picked up the machete, studied it for a moment, and then impaled the end of the blade in the dirt. He glanced around the clearing again. Chris was bemused by the fact that the younger man didn't let his gaze settle on the wheelchair. It was almost as if it was invisible to Bob. He looked at everything except Chris.

"Bob ..."

Chris was about to try reassuring him, when Legerski began to twitch and groan again.

"He's having another seizure!" Bob sprang to his feet and hurried over to the bound prisoner. Legerski rolled back and forth, stuttering and frothing at the mouth. His eyelids flickered, and his shoulder convulsed. Bob knelt beside him, his expression panicked. And then Legerski bolted upright into a sitting position. His seizures stopped, replaced with a maniacal, leering grin. With slowly dawning horror, Chris realized that the man had somehow slipped his bonds. He could tell from Bob's expression that the younger man realized it, too.

Legerski laughed. "Surprise!"

He lunged forward, knocking Bob onto his back and then straddling him. Legerski wrapped one hand around Bob's throat and balled his other into a fist. He struck the younger man three times. Chris winced at the sound of the blows. Bob shrieked, thrashing beneath the madman. Legerski delivered two more punches and Bob lay still.

Slowly, Legerski stumbled to his feet. Still grinning, he winked at Chris.

"I'll bet his nose really hurts now. Wouldn't you agree, gimp?"

Chris tried to respond, but he could barely breathe. He heard a rustling sound to his left, as Erin scampered into the jungle.

"You go ahead, little bunny," Legerski called after her. "Go ahead and run away. I'll save you for last."

On the ground, Bob groaned—a low, mournful sound. His legs twitched, but he did not rise.

"Shit ..." Legerski wiped his mouth with the back of his hand, and his grin became a grimace. "I really fucked him up, I guess."

"What ... what are you ..." Chris couldn't finish.

"Relax, Gimpy." Legerski bent at the waist and pulled the machete from the dirt. "I'll get to you soon enough."

He stalked over to Bob. The young man was struggling to sit up. His shirt was covered in blood. More blood streamed from his nose, which had swollen to the size of a grapefruit. Indeed, it didn't even resemble a nose anymore. Chris thought it looked more like a pile of mashed potatoes. Bob's eyes widened as he saw Legerski approaching. He scrambled to his feet, and tried to flee, but the killer reached out with his free hand, snatched a fistful of Bob's long hair, and yanked him backward.

"I heard you say you were a magician," Legerski said. "Want to see a magic trick, motherfucker?"

Bob screamed for help, but with his nose in ruin, the words were unintelligible squawks. He glanced at Chris, eyes wide with panic. Chris wept, sick from fear and hopelessness, and for the first time in a very long time, feeling ashamed that he could not act—embarrassed by his helplessness.

Legerski spun Bob around and plunged the machete into his abdomen, sliding it in all the way to the hilt, smiling as Bob's breath whooshed from his lungs, licking his lips as the younger man's blood spilled out over his fingers, and laughing as he twisted the blade to the right and then savagely thrust it upward. He yanked it free, and Bob's guts came out with it, splashing onto the ground.

"Ta-da!"

Legerski let go of Bob and turned to face Chris. Bob remained upright for a moment, swaying back and forth as more of his guts slipped from his abdomen like wriggling snakes. Then he toppled over, sloshing in his own gore and still-steaming entrails.

"Your turn," Legerski said, stalking towards Chris. His voice dripped with excitement. "Let's put you out of your misery. How long could you have really lasted in this place, anyway?"

Chris closed his eyes—the only act of defiance he could muster. He didn't want the killer to see his fear, to see him crying —or to see how those words rung true. Because that was the worst part of all this. Legerski had just voiced something that Chris himself had been fretting over since the dinosaur attack. Just how long could he survive here?

"And now for my next trick."

Legerski's voice was nearer. The man drew close enough that Chris could smell his cologne and his sweat, and Bob's blood, as well. Still, he refused to open his eyes.

"Look at me," Legerski growled.

"No." Chris squeezed his eyes shut tighter.

"LOOK AT M—"

From somewhere in the forest, Erin screamed for her mother. A second later, Paula shouted a response. More voices joined the fray. Curiously, they seemed to be converging on the site from multiple locations. Legerski cursed. Then Chris heard footfalls and rustling sounds. When he opened his eyes, his tormentor was gone. Paula, Jesse, and Colinda burst into the clearing, along with Erin and two other men from the shuttle. They stood gaping, mouths open, glancing from Bob to Chris and back again.

"Where is he?" Paula asked.

The undergrowth rustled and all of them screamed. Then Scott, Geoff, and Mark stepped into view. The three men stared at the scene in shock.

"Holy shit," Mark gasped. "What the hell happened here?"

Then all of them began talking at once, each one pressing Chris for answers. He tried to respond, tried to speak, but all he could do was moan.

G eoff nudged Scott's shoulder and asked, "So what's the plan, boss?"

Scott glanced around, unsure at first who Geoff was talking to. When he realized that it was him being addressed, he grinned sheepishly. Sighing, he surveyed the group, all of whom—with the exception of the still missing Legerski and Paul Goblirsch, and the three deceased passengers and bus driver—were now gathered at the edges of the ravine, rather than scattered throughout the jungle. Tod, Mark, H, Paula, Colinda, and Leigh were finishing construction of the shelter. Jamie and Dave rested in the shade beneath the trees, being attended to by the still-recuperating Jesse. Chris was parked next to them in his wheelchair. Erin sat nearby, watching the adults and braiding strands of grass together into a bracelet.

"Well," Scott pointed at the shelter, "they've got the roof finished, and they're shoring up the openings. All we've got to do yet is camouflage it."

"That's not what I mean," Geoff said. "What comes after?"

"After?"

"If somebody were coming to rescue us, they'd have done so by now. You and I both know it's not going to happen, Scott. Wherever we are—wherever *this* is—chances are good that we're not getting rescued any time soon. So, what's the plan?"

"It's a good question," Jamie called out. "We need to start making plans. It's going to get dark, sooner or later."

"I'm not so sure about that," Jesse replied. "I don't think the sun has moved since we got here."

The others stared at him for a moment, and then looked up at the sky. Scott shielded his eyes with his hand, focusing on the sun for the first time since their arrival. He ignored the throbbing this caused behind his eyes, ignored the migraine that was building, and focused on the sun. He couldn't tell if it had moved or not, but it did seem to him that the orb was smaller than the sun he knew.

When Scott turned his attention back to the ground, he saw that the rest of the group had now stopped working and were slowly gathering around him.

How the hell did I end up in charge? he thought.

"Okay." He paused, worried that he sounded timid and unsure. Everyone stared at him, waiting. Scott cleared his throat and then tried again. "So ... again, my name is Scott Berke. And, uh ... I don't remember taking a vote, so I'm not sure why everyone is looking at me."

A few people laughed at this. The others just smiled politely.

"I think we can all agree that we are ... someplace else. Now, we can discuss what that means and what our ideas might be about it later on."

"It's time travel," Mark said, ignoring the suggestion. "I mean, it has to be, right? We fell through a wormhole or something, just like in the movies."

"That's impossible," Colinda argued.

"Not so impossible," Jamie countered. "Most of us experienced weird phenomena right before the crash. Problems with our cell phones. Timepieces operating incorrectly. And we all saw that bright flash of light. Time travel is a theoretical possibility. Scientists and physicists have done the math—they just can't figure out a way to apply the math. But nature—the natural world, or perhaps the supernatural, if you like—isn't bound by the limits of human invention. We know dinosaurs existed in Earth's past. We've all seen a dinosaur today. Therefore, we need to at least consider the possibility that Mark is right—that we have, in fact, traveled to Earth's past."

"Or maybe not," H said. "I don't know about the rest of you, but the flora and fauna don't seem right to me. There are species of plants coexisting side by side here that never did that during any era in Earth's past. And Jamie, that razor grass you mentioned. What you described? I don't think that's ever existed on Earth."

Jamie's expression darkened at the mention of the grass.

"So, what are you saying?" Paula asked H.

He shrugged. "Maybe we didn't travel through time. Maybe we traveled through space."

Paula frowned. "Another dimension?"

H shrugged again. "Why not?"

"Because it sounds insane," Colinda said.

"Any more insane than a dinosaur attacking us? We all saw what happened to Benn. Or is it any more insane than the fact that our shuttle went from being on a highway in the middle of a blizzard to crashing in a tropical jungle? We all saw that. Or how about what Jamie said about a patch of grass slicing a man to death?"

Colinda didn't answer.

"Take it easy." Jesse raised his hands, palms out. "Don't take it out on her."

H's shoulders sagged. "I'm sorry. I didn't mean to."

"It's okay," Colinda whispered.

Paula pulled Erin to her side and hugged her. Seeing that the rest of the group had fallen silent again, Scott opened his mouth to continue.

"I think you're all wrong," Tod interrupted. "Time travel and other dimensions—that stuff is cool in movies and books, but real life doesn't work like that."

"Then what do you propose has happened to us?" H asked him.

"I don't know," Tod admitted. "Maybe a government experiment. Maybe somebody dosed us all with drugs or something, and we're hallucinating, or strapped into some kind of virtual reality chamber. Maybe somebody is just fucking with us."

"Look," Scott spoke up, "we can discuss all this at length later. Right now, I think we need to focus and prioritize. The one thing we all seem to agree on is that help probably isn't coming soon. We need to get this shelter finished before nightfall."

"This ravine isn't going to do much against that dinosaur," Jamie said.

"No," Scott agreed. "If the dinosaur is determined, then no, what we've built here won't be much help. But it's a start, and it beats sleeping out in the middle of the jungle. We've got injured people—yourself included—and we need a place to protect ourselves from the elements."

"I'm okay," Jamie insisted. "It's just my ankle."

"You might be, but your friend, Dave, isn't. We need to care for him. And it's not just the dinosaur or the weather that we need protection from. We have to remember that Legerski is still out there, somewhere. Some of you have encountered him since the crash. The rest of you ... well, you've heard what happened. He killed that young man, Bob, and he tried to attack several others, and he was probably responsible for Gregorio's death, as well. We're going to have to set watch—have people standing guard in shifts."

Dave groaned loudly. All of them glanced at him. He writhed on the ground, his swollen face contorted, and his body slick with sweat.

"I wish we could give him something," Colinda said.

"We might be able to," Scott continued. "There may be allergy medication or antihistamines back on the shuttle. At the very least, there has to be ibuprofen or something we can use to knock his fever down. And he's not the only one who might need meds. Are any of you here on any sort of medication?"

"I have things I need," Chris volunteered.

Scott nodded. "Me, too. I get really bad migraine headaches. In fact, I'm starting to get one now. I felt it back on the shuttle, but it disappeared for a while, after the crash. I've got suma-triptan in my carry-on bag. So, some of us need to head back to the crash site. If the coast is clear ... if the dinosaur and Legerski are gone, then we need to bring the luggage and anything else we can use back here. We should also find out if Mr. Goblirsch is still alive."

Colinda frowned. "Who?"

"The other Paul," Scott explained.

"A pal of ours," Mark said. "We haven't seen him since everyone scattered. He could be out there, wandering around lost."

"He might not be the only one out there wandering around either," Jamie proposed.

Tod clenched his fists. "Legerski better hope he doesn't cross my path first."

Jamie shook his head. "I'm not talking about Legerski. Yes, he's a concern. But he's not our only concern. We know that wherever here is, it's populated with animal life. We should assume there might be other people living here, as well."

The group fell silent, considering this.

"We'll cross that bridge when we find it," Scott said. "For now, we need to stay focused. One group to stay here and finish the shelter. Another to reconnoiter the shuttle and bring back anything salvageable and useful from the luggage."

"Why not just bring all the luggage back?" Paula asked.

"In time, we can," Scott explained. "But that's a lot of stuff to haul. For now, I think we should only retrieve things we absolutely need—medicines, food, matches. Things like that. Whoever goes to the shuttle should keep an eye out for Mr. Goblirsch, as well."

Dave moaned again. Scott pointed at him.

"We'll need somebody to keep an eye on Dave. And we're going to need food and fresh water, as well. We should probably have someone scout around nearby for that. But they'll need to stay close to this campsite. We don't want them getting lost, too."

"I can do that." Jesse got to his feet. "My ribs are feeling better now."

"Someone should go with you," Scott said.

"I will," Colinda volunteered.

"Okay. That takes care of the food and water detail. Water is our primary concern. But remember, don't stray too far. If you see Legerski or ... anything else, run."

"Maybe we should make some weapons," Mark suggested. "Spears or some shit like that. I saw some bamboo. We could make pikes?"

"Later," Scott agreed. "But for right now, we've got enough going on."

Colinda eyed the jungle suspiciously.

"You okay with this?" Scott asked her.

She nodded, but her expression said otherwise.

Jesse patted his side. "Don't worry. I've had the shit kicked out of me once today already. We won't go far."

Scott turned to Jamie. "You can't go anywhere on that ankle. How about you and Chris keep an eye on Dave?"

"Sure," Jamie replied.

"Okay," Chris agreed.

"And Mark suggested we make weapons. Jamie, if we can find you some bamboo or sticks, maybe you could make some spears while you're sitting there?"

Jamie shrugged. "I don't have a knife to sharpen them. Maybe I could use a rock or something?"

"I'll volunteer for the salvage mission," Geoff said, "but I'm going to need some help."

Mark raised his hand. "I'll go."

H nodded. "Me, too."

Leigh frowned. "Your head—"

"Is fine now," H interrupted. "It's my fault Paul is out there. I owe this to him."

"We're going to need another person," Geoff said. "That's a lot of luggage to carry back here, even if we just bring the essentials."

"I'll go," Scott said.

"No," Geoff argued. "You need to stay here and supervise. Make sure this shelter gets finished."

"Why?"

"Because you're in charge."

"I didn't volunteer for that," Scott protested.

Geoff leaned close, speaking low so that only Scott could hear him. "No, you didn't. But right now, these people are scared, and they need somebody to tell them what to do. You're it. Can you be that guy?"

Scott hesitated, and then nodded. "Yeah."

"Good." Geoff stepped away, and turned to Mark, H, and Leigh. "You want to come with us, Leigh?"

The Australian shrugged. "Sure, mate. Although I suspect you can carry a lot more weight than me."

"I don't know about that," Geoff said. "I may be big, but I'm pretty tired."

"Okay," Scott said. "Tod, Paula, her daughter, and I will stay here and finish the shelter. Everyone be careful. Be on your guard. Watch for Legerski—or anything else."

Paula cleared her throat. "There's one other thing."

"What's that?" Scott asked.

"Well, Bob ... and the bus driver, and ... what was his name? Gregorio?"

Scott nodded.

"Shouldn't we do something with their ..." She glanced down at her daughter and then back up to Scott. "It seems wrong to leave them laying out there in the jungle. Won't they attract animals?"

"They probably will," Scott replied, "which is all the more reason why we shouldn't bring their bodies back here."

"She's right though," Jesse argued. "We can't just leave them out there. It's not right. If we get rescued, their families back home are going to want closure. I don't know about you, but I'm not telling someone's kid or wife, 'Sorry. We left his corpse in the jungle where it got eaten by dinosaurs.' That's just harsh."

"We'll bury them," Scott said.

"When?" Paula asked.

"Soon. I promise. But like I said, we need to prioritize. There's nothing we can do for any of them, but there's plenty we need to do for ourselves. Let's take care of this stuff first. We'll have plenty of time to bury the dead later."

The group nodded, and began to move again. Jesse and Colinda stepped cautiously into the jungle. Paula and Tod turned back to the shelter, and began to put tree limbs and leaves over the roof.

After a moment, Erin rushed to help them. Tod gave her some long sticks, which she carried over to Jamie. The attorney picked one up and studied the tip. Then he began sharpening it with a rock. Chris sat by Dave, talking quietly to him and trying to offer comfort.

"You're right about that," Geoff said to Scott.

"What?"

"We'll have plenty of time to bury the dead later," Geoff explained. "That's the one thing we seem to have plenty of—time."

Scott turned to him, his expression grave. "I hope you're right."

Then Geoff, Mark, Leigh, and H headed off into the jungle. Scott watched until they were out of sight. The vegetation seemed to swallow them whole. He turned back to the others.

"Okay," he said. "Let's get to it."

"Are you guys sure we're going the right way?" Mark asked as they trudged through the jungle.

"Positive." H nodded.

Leigh stopped, panting for breath. "No offense, mate, but you got knocked on the head pretty hard. How can you be positive of anything?"

The others paused to rest, as well.

"H is right," Geoff said. "I recognize this area."

Leigh flailed his arms, exasperated. "Recognize what, exactly? That fern over there? This particularly pointy leaf?"

Geoff frowned. "What's your problem, man?"

"Me? I've got no problem." Leigh pointed. "Oh, look, everyone! It's Geoff's favorite fern. No worries, mate. We're fucking saved!"

Glowering, Geoff stomped toward him, hands curled into fists. Leigh flinched, but held his ground.

"Guys." Mark stepped between them. "Look, we're all freaked out. The last thing we need is to start fighting with each other. We've got to fucking work together."

"And keep your voices down," H cautioned. "We don't need Legerski or another dinosaur finding us out here."

Geoff glared at Leigh. After a moment, he shook his head and relaxed. "Whatever."

"Sorry," Leigh apologized. "Seriously, mate. I didn't mean to be an asshole. I guess I'm just ..."

"I think we all are," H agreed.

"It's no problem," Geoff said, turning away. "The crash site should be down this way. Let's go."

He led them through the jungle, until they emerged into a clearing. Sure enough, there was the shuttle bus, its front end still crumpled around a tree. The scene was quiet, save for a few birds chirping in the foliage. There was no sign of Paul Goblirsch, or the dinosaur. A bloody smear in the grass was all that remained of Benn.

"That poor bastard," Mark muttered.

"I should have gotten his address or something," Leigh whispered.

"For what?" H asked.

Leigh shrugged. "I could have contacted his family when I got back home. Let them know how he died ..."

Mark frowned. "If you showed up at my house and told my wife and son the gory details of how I got eaten by a dinosaur, I'd come back from the dead and kick your ass, Leigh."

"You've got a point, I guess." Leigh peered through the greenery. "Do you think it's still here? The dinosaur?"

Geoff shook his head and stepped out from under the trees. "I don't hear it. If it was still lurking around, the birds would be quiet. I think we're safe."

The others followed him out into the clearing, and then fanned out, searching the site.

"Paul!" Mark cupped his hands around his mouth. "Hey, Paul! Where you at, pal?"

There was no answer.

"Hey, Paul!"

"I'm going to hit you in the face with an axe," H muttered.

Geoff glanced at him, clearly startled. "W-what?"

"Sorry," H apologized. "Relax, it's a reference to *American Psycho*. He says, 'Hey, Paul,' and then whacks him with an axe."

Geoff stared at him, unblinking. After a moment, H shrugged.

Mark shook his head. "I think that knock on the head did more damage to you than we suspected."

H grinned. "At this point, it's either laugh or scream. I'll go with laughter."

"Paul," Leigh shouted. "Paul Goblirsch! Where are you?"

His voice echoed through the trees. The birds fell silent.

"Any idea which way he went?" Mark asked H.

The older man shook his head. "I don't know. It's all fuzzy. Last thing I remember was running toward where you guys were hiding. Paul pointed out Chris's wheelchair to me, and said to head toward that. Then he ran the other way, trying to get the dinosaur to chase him."

"We should look for him," Mark said.

Leigh and H nodded in agreement.

"What about the luggage?" Geoff asked.

"You go ahead and start," Mark said. "We'll help. I promise. But Paul is our friend. We were all at this convention together, along with Chris—the guy in the wheelchair. We were all on our way back to our homes when the flights got cancelled, and then ... well, you know what happened next. We can't just leave him out there."

"I get it," Geoff replied. "Go ahead. I'll get started going through the stuff. But don't go too far, and be careful. The dinosaur may not be here, but it could come back. And there's bound to be other things out there, too."

Geoff ducked low, crawled inside the wreckage, and started dragging suitcases and carry-on luggage out onto the grass. When he emerged for the third time, the others noticed he had pulled his T-shirt up over his nose and mouth.

"The bus driver," he explained. His voice was muffled. "She's starting to stink."

"Already?" Mark asked.

Geoff shrugged. "It's got to be this heat."

H, Mark, and Leigh walked over to the grisly stain marking Benn's demise, and then fanned out and began searching the crash site for signs of Paul. Within moments, they found both his footprints and those of the dinosaur. Both led away from the spot where H had last seen him. Paul's tracks made several sharp turns, veering from side to side, while those of his pursuer went in a mostly straight line, leaving a trail of crushed vegetation and deep impressions in the earth. Pink, glistening bits of Benn, which had apparently dropped from the dinosaur's open mouth, also dotted the trail at random intervals. Insects crawled over these morsels. Some of the skin showed portions of Benn's tattoos.

At the far side of the clearing, the tracks led into some tall grass and wildflowers, and then toward a nearby stand of trees. One of the trees stood out from the others. Its trunk was particularly tall and thick, and it had several low-hanging limbs.

Paul dangled from one of these branches.

Mark stopped short, and stood gaping. Leigh halted behind him, stared for a moment, and then turned away and retched.

H said what all of them were thinking. "Fuck ..."

He followed this up with, "Shit ..."

Paul's upper half hung from the tree limb. Both of his hands were wrapped around the branch, clinging tight. His lower body —everything from the waist down, was missing. Bits of shredded organs looped from his bottomless abdomen, twisting and turning in the breeze.

"Is he ..." H gasped for breath. "Is he dead?"

"He has to be," Mark whispered. "Please let him be."

Leigh bent over and retched again.

The dinosaur stood next to Paul's swaying carcass. The creature's tail and one side of its body seemed to be stuck to the tree, like an insect on flypaper. Both man and reptile appeared to be much thinner than before, almost desiccated. Their skin had turned gray in the places where it touched the bark.

"It's ... it's eating them," Mark moaned.

"How?" H asked.

Mark pointed. "If you squint, you can see little tendrils—like roots. They're growing out of the bark and into their bodies."

"Fuck me," Leigh wheezed. "We need to get him down from there. Give him a proper burial."

"I don't think so," Mark replied.

"No, he's right." H stepped closer toward the tree. "We can't just leave Paul like that."

"How are we going to get him down?" Mark gestured. "Look at it. Do either of you think we should touch that tree?"

Shaking his head, H trudged closer. When he'd gotten within a few feet of the tree, he noticed a cloud of insects hovering and flitting around Paul's lower half, crawling in and out of his body. Several of them flew toward the tree, and immediately got stuck on the bark. Choking down bile, he reached for Paul with one trembling hand. When his fingertips brushed against the bloody meat, Paul's corpse began to sway harder. Whimpering, H glanced up at his friend's arms. Sure enough, tiny little roots had grown out of the tree limb and covered Paul's hands, burrowing deep beneath his flesh. He glanced at the dinosaur, and noticed that the same thing was happening to it, but on a much larger scale. Slowly, H backed away.

"I changed my mind," he said. "Mark is right."

"He's our friend," Leigh argued. "We can't just leave him

hanging there like some holiday decoration. It's not right. What would his family say?"

"I don't like it any more than you do," H said. "But I don't see a way to do it, short of cutting Paul's arms off."

"We could burn it," Mark suggested. "Set the tree on fire. Make a funeral pyre."

H shook his head. "Too risky. We could end up setting the jungle on fire. I vote we leave him there for now."

Leigh opened his mouth to protest again, but H held up his hand.

"I know," he said. "I know. But just for now, Leigh. When we get back to the camp, we'll tell the others. Maybe Scott can think of something."

"Are we taking orders from Scott now?" Mark asked.

"We're out here on baggage claim detail, aren't we?"

"Point," Mark conceded. "But ... how well do we know the guy? I mean, he seems okay, but what if he's like Legerski?"

"Legerski didn't seem okay," Leigh said. "You guys weren't up at the front of the bus with me and Chris. Trust me, that bloke was an asshole from the beginning."

"Oh, I believe you," Mark replied. "Don't forget, I was about to beat his ass just after the crash."

Both men grinned at this.

"We should get back," H suggested. "Give Geoff a hand with the luggage. We can discuss all of this later, back at camp."

Mark and Leigh nodded. The three of them walked back to the clearing, but not before sparing one final glance over their shoulders.

Paul swayed in the breeze.

Back at the crash site, Geoff had managed to retrieve all of the luggage from the shuttle. He'd spread the bags out on the ground and now sat cross-legged, going through one of them. A laptop was on the grass next to him. The computer's power was on. He looked up as they approached.

"Any sign of your friend?" he asked.

"He's dead," H replied, his tone flat. "So is the dinosaur."

"I'm sorry," Geoff replied.

They quickly told him about the tree and Paul's condition. Geoff shook his head, bewildered.

"This place," he muttered. "I just don't understand how this can be."

"Find anything useful?" Mark asked.

Geoff nodded, pointing to a pile of random items at his left. "That's the stuff we'll take back with us. Medicine, vitamins, matches, lighters, bottled water, snack food, blankets—things like that. I was also thinking maybe a few changes of clothes for each person. The rest of the stuff, I figure we can store in the bigger suitcases and stash them inside the shuttle again. We can carry them back later, if we need them."

"Hopefully, we won't be here long enough to need the rest," Leigh said.

Mark turned to him. "Do you really think we're going to get rescued?"

"No," Leigh admitted. "Probably not. But we have to hope, right?"

"Yeah, I guess we do." Mark pointed at the powered-up laptop. "What's the deal with that?"

"None of our phones had a signal," Geoff explained, "so I got an idea to try one of the laptops instead, and see if it could pick up Wi-fi or something."

"Any luck?"

Geoff shook his head.

H nodded at the pile. "Our friend Chris, the guy in the wheelchair. Did you find his stuff?"

"Yeah," Geoff confirmed. "Dude is traveling around with his own pharmacy. Colostomy bags, Baclofen, Vicodin, Gabapentin, Vitamin D, and amitriptyline. There's not a lot of it, though."

"His wife packed enough for our trip," H explained, "plus enough for a few extra days."

"Three days," Leigh confirmed. "What the hell is he going to do if he runs out?"

"There's more Vitamin D here," Geoff said, "and Vicodin, too."

"What about the other stuff?" Mark asked. "I mean, what does he do when he runs out of colostomy bags?"

Geoff shook his head. "I found Scott's headache medicine, though."

"Fuck Scott's headaches," Leigh said. "What happens to Chris when his meds run out? What the hell do we do then?"

"I don't know," Mark admitted. "In movies and books, there's always a doctor in situations like this. Or somebody who can MacGyver some shit to save the day."

"Yeah, but this isn't a book," H reminded him. "And there are no doctors in our group."

"Speaking of which ..." Geoff leaned forward, grabbed a duffle bag, and pulled it toward him. "This thing is full of books. You guys said you were at a book convention. I figured it might belong to one of you."

All three stared at it without speaking. Their expressions were grim.

"What's wrong?" Geoff asked.

"That was Paul's bag," Mark explained.

"Shit, I'm sorry. What about this one here?" Geoff rummaged through the pile and held up a well-worn paperback copy of Agatha Christie's *And Then There Were None*. "Does this belong to any of you?"

H held out his hand and accepted the book from Geoff. He flipped it over, gave the cover a cursory glance, and then opened it to the copyright page.

"Not an original," Leigh guessed.

"Not with this title," H agreed. "And it's a fairly recent edition, too."

Geoff frowned. "It has more than one title?"

"Sure," Mark exclaimed. "This book has a long history. It's like the seminal mystery novel—one of the classics of the genre. Over two-hundred million copies sold. The seventh bestselling book of all time, worldwide."

"Indeed." H nodded. "First published in the United Kingdom in 1939 as *Ten Little Niggers*."

"What the fuck?" Geoff blanched. "Seriously?"

"I'm not kidding," H confirmed. "Don't get me wrong. I'm not making excuses for the title. It's unfortunate."

"It's problematic," Leigh agreed, "but it was a product of its time. That was a major British blackface song back then, and the rhyme played into the plot of the novel fairly heavily. When it was eventually reprinted in the United States, they changed the title to *Ten Little Indians*."

"That's not much better," Geoff said. "Was it about ... killing people of color?"

Mark, H, and Leigh laughed at this. Then H handed the book to Mark, who began flipping through it.

"Not at all," Leigh explained. "It's about a group of people who are lured to this island under different pretexts. Each of them have been responsible for the deaths of other people, but got away with it. After a lavish dinner, all of them, as well as two servants on the island, are charged with their crimes via this mysterious recording."

"A gramophone recording," H added.

Leigh nodded. "Then, one by one, somebody begins killing them."

Geoff blinked. "So, it's that episode of *Family Guy*."

Mark stomped the dirt. "No, it's not that episode of *Family Guy*. It's where that episode of *Family Guy* got the idea from!"

Geoff stared at each of them for a minute. Then he shook his head.

"I'm trapped on dinosaur island with a bunch of book geeks."

He glanced back up at them and flashed a grin, to indicate he was just teasing. H, Mark, and Leigh chuckled. Then Geoff presented another paperback novel. This one was sealed in Mylar plastic.

"That one is mine," H said. "Jeffery Lord's *The Mountains of Brega*—a Richard Blade novel."

"The Conan knock-off?"

H nodded. "Yep, sort of Conan crossed with James Bond. Always three sex scenes per book. It's a guilty pleasure."

Geoff stared at the price sticker affixed to the plastic cover. "You really paid fifty bucks for an old paperback?"

"It's in mint condition," H explained.

Shrugging, Geoff handed him the book. H and Leigh knelt down beside the luggage and began helping to sort through it. Mark continued to study the Agatha Christie novel.

"Carroll County Library, it says on the inside," Mark told them, placing the paperback on top of Paul's duffel bag. "That must be someplace here in Maryland, right?"

"Perhaps," H said, "although I don't think we're in Maryland, Mark."

"True that," Mark agreed. Then he turned to Geoff. "So, you're trapped here with us book geeks, pal. But it could be worse."

Geoff looked up at him. "How's that?"

"You could be trapped on dinosaur island with a bunch of *Twilight* readers or *Fifty Shades of Gray* fans, instead."

"Fuck you," Geoff chortled. "That sounds like Hell."

"Unless of course we're already in Hell," Leigh said.

Somewhere out in the jungle, a bird shrieked. It sounded remarkably like a human. All four of them shuddered.

"What are you humming?" Colinda asked Jesse as they tromped through the jungle, searching for water.

"You like it? It's a song my band did."

"You were in a band?"

"Not 'were' in a band. Am in a band. I'll get back to them. We're called EverSay. We—"

"Ssshhh." Colinda held a finger to her lips. "Do you hear that?"

Jesse cocked his head and listened. Then he shrugged. "I hear birds? And insects?"

"I hear water," Colinda said.

"Where?"

She pointed. "Somewhere over there."

"Are you sure?"

Colinda crept forward, pushing through the vegetation. Jesse followed along behind her. Both walked slowly, and quietly, jumping every time a twig snapped around them or a bird rustled in the trees overhead. After a few minutes, Jesse began to hum again.

"Quiet," Colinda warned.

"Sorry."

The ground sloped downward at a slight but steady angle, before eventually flattening out again. At the bottom of this slope, the sound of trickling water became clear.

"We're in some kind of hollow," Jesse whispered. "And you're right. I hear it now, too."

Nodding, Colinda pushed aside more greenery and they stepped onto the banks of a small pond, about twenty feet across. The water was black in the center, and choked with lily pads and algae. A thin, shallow stream ran from one side of the hollow and terminated into the pond. Insects flitted across the surface, and small splashing sounds were followed by ringed ripples, indicating fish striking at the bugs. Jesse and Colinda barely noticed these things at first, however, because their attention was focused on the wildflowers encircling the banks—a rainbow of reds, yellows, pinks, oranges, blues, whites, and purples.

"Oh my God," Colinda squealed. "They're beautiful!"

She started to rush forward, but Jesse grabbed her arm and pulled her back.

"Careful," he warned, shaking his head. "Remember what the others said about that grass? The stuff that cut Gregorio up?"

Colinda rolled her eyes. "This isn't grass, Jesse. They're flowers."

"Yeah, and they might be people-eating flowers."

Laughing softly, Colinda shrugged free of his grip and hurried to the bank of the pond. Jesse trailed after her, still shaking his head. Colinda splayed her arms and let her fingertips brush over the flowers. Jesse tensed, expecting a reaction from the plants, but the flowers merely swayed back and forth. Colinda turned around and smiled at him.

"See? I told you. Nothing to worry about. They're just flowers. Not poisonous or anything. They didn't try to eat me."

"How about the water?" Jesse asked. "Do you think it's safe?"

Colinda pushed through to the pond's edge. Then she knelt and peered into the pool. Jesse crouched down beside her.

"The bugs seem okay with it," Colinda observed. "And there's fish swimming around in it. I guess that means it's safe, right?"

"It doesn't look that deep," Jesse mused. "We should still be careful, though. Who knows what's lurking in there?"

"What, like an alligator?"

He shrugged. "Why not? They find alligators on golf courses and kiddie pools in Florida. Who the hell knows what we'll find here. Probably another dinosaur."

"It's not deep enough for that," Colinda replied. "You just said so yourself."

"A baby dinosaur, then."

He picked up a stick and poked the surface with it. When there was no reaction, he pushed the stick into the water, stirring up a cloud of green algae and brown mud. A few tiny, silvery fish flitted about in the gloom, and then darted away from the intrusion. The insects, which had been skimming across the pond and buzzing among the flowers, scattered. When the swirling mud began to clear, both of them peered closer into the water.

"What's that?" Colinda pointed. "Something shiny ..."

Jesse edged the stick to where she indicated, and pried something circular and silver from the mud and slime. He prodded it toward the surface, and then reached one hand into the water. It was cold. His fingers curled around the object and he brought it out. Water and mud dripped from his fist. He opened it, revealing a coin—an American quarter.

"Hey," Jesse said, surprised. "Check it out!"

Colinda plucked it from his palm and studied it closely. "Minted in 1986. But it must be a joke or something—one of those gag gifts you can buy."

"Why?"

"Because I don't believe the United States ever put Richard Nixon on their currency, did they?"

"What?"

She handed the coin to Jesse. He stared at it, incredulous.

"What the fuck? It *is* Nixon!"

"I know, right? It has to be a fake."

Jesse bounced the coin up and down in his hand. "It doesn't feel fake, though. It weighs the same as a regular quarter. And it's made from real metal, I think."

"Maybe we should take it with us and show the others."

"Where did it come from?" Jesse asked. "I mean, Nixon is on it, so it must have come from Earth. But how did it get here?"

"Maybe one of the other passengers on the shuttle dropped it here. Maybe they ran this way when the dinosaur was chasing after everyone."

"Yeah, but who? And if they discovered this pond already, why wouldn't they have mentioned it when we had that big meeting? You'd think they would have brought it up when Scott sent us for water."

Colinda frowned.

"What's wrong?" Jesse asked.

"Nothing ... it's just ... I was thinking, maybe the person who dropped it wasn't at the meeting."

"You mean one of the dead? Or that missing guy, Paul Goblirsch?"

Colinda shrugged. "Or the other Paul."

"Legerski." Jesse stood up, and nervously surveyed their surroundings. "Shit. I forgot about him. We should head back. Let everyone know what we found."

"Shouldn't we try the water first? Make sure it's safe to drink?"

"I'm guessing it's okay. There's fish swimming around in it, and they seem okay. We should probably boil it before we drink it, though, just to be safe."

Nodding, Colinda got to her feet. The two of them turned back to the forest, this time with Jesse in the lead. He stuck the Nixon quarter in his pocket.

"Do you remember how to get back to the camp?" she asked.

He nodded, then glanced skyward.

"It still hasn't moved."

"The sun? I swear, Jesse, you're becoming obsessed with it. Look around. Look how beautiful these flowers are. Focus on them for a moment." Colinda bent down and plucked a red flower from its stem, and brought it to her nose. She inhaled, and then sighed. "Oh, this is delightful. Try one."

Jesse chuckled. "No, thanks. Pollen makes me sneeze."

"Your loss," she teased. "You're really missing out."

Jesse's grin grew broader.

Colinda cocked her head. "What? Why are you looking at me like that?"

"I'm sorry. It's just ... look, I know we don't know each other very well, but it's nice to see you happy, even for a moment. There's been a lot of terrible things happening today. It's nice to have a moment like this, before more shit hits the fan."

Colinda smiled. "Are you flirting with me?"

"No!" Jesse blushed. "Well, okay, maybe a little bit."

"And what makes you think more shit will hit the fan?"

"I don't know. So far, that seems to be par for the course with this place."

Still smiling, Colinda bent down and picked more flowers, adding two reds, yellows, pinks, whites, blues, oranges, and purples to her bunch. She held the bouquet up to the sunlight, admiring the colors.

"What are you going to do with that?"

"The little girl," Colinda replied. "The one who was on the shuttle with her mother?"

"Erin," Jesse said. "I think her name is Erin. And her mother is Paula."

"I thought maybe she'd like some flowers. They might take her mind off our situation."

"You think so?"

"I know so." Colinda winked at him. "I was a little girl once."

Laughing, Jesse motioned at her. "Come on. Let's get going."

He started toward the jungle, back up the hill. When he realized that Colinda wasn't following him, he turned back again. Colinda knelt at the edge of the pond bank, staring at another flower.

"Are you coming?"

"Hang on," she said. "Look at this one. It's completely black!"

"Hooray," Jesse said sarcastically. "Dinosaur land believes in diversity, same as the rest of modern society."

"Smart-ass. No, seriously. Look. It's the only black one growing here."

Colinda reached for the flower, pinching the stem between her thumb and index finger. A second later, she stiffened and screamed, as if she were being shocked. Her blonde hair rose from her scalp, and her shrieks grew louder and more frantic.

Jesse rushed toward her. As he drew closer, he smelled something electric and burning. Then he realized that it was Colinda. The fist that was still clutching the bouquet tightened, pulping the flowers in her grip. Her other hand was still in contact with the black flower. Her movements became frenzied and blood dribbled down her chin. Jesse recoiled in horror when he saw that she'd bitten through her tongue. Still, her fingers remained on the black flower's stem. Jesse reached for her, intent on pushing Colinda away from the flower and breaking contact, but her eyes swiveled toward him and she managed to speak.

"Noooooo ... lectricccckkkkk ..."

Her eyes rolled up into her head. The skin on her hand began to turn red and flaky, and then blackened. She squealed, spittle and blood flying from her lips. Then she flopped onto the ground, and at last, released the deadly plant.

"Colinda!" Jesse fell to his knees. "Holy shit! Colinda, it's going to be okay. Hang on. Just hang on ..."

He checked her neck for a pulse. Finding none, he grabbed her arm and felt her wrist.

"Oh no ... come on, Colinda! Don't do this. Don't leave me out here by myself. Breathe!"

Panting and babbling, Jesse began cardiopulmonary resuscitation. When that didn't work, he tried mouth to mouth. Her lips tasted like a battery. After five minutes, he leaned back in the grass, gasping. Colinda lay motionless and unbreathing. The air around the pond smelled faintly of ozone.

"Your daughter," he mumbled. "And your dog ... what did you say his name was? Bender? What about them?"

He pumped her chest again, but the effort was half-hearted.

"Colinda?"

Somewhere above, a woodpecker tapped against a tree trunk.

Jesse stumbled to his feet, wiping tears from his eyes.

"Fuck ... fuck ... fuck ..."

He repeated the phrase over and over again, until it became a scream. Then, heedless of who—or what—might hear him, Jesse turned, stumbled back up the slope, and ran for the camp.

Scott, Tod, and Paula—with some assistance from Erin—were just finishing the shelter when they heard the vegetation rustling. All four of them glanced warily at each other. Erin hid behind her mother. Nearby, Jamie and Chris heard the movement, as well. Their eyes grew wide.

Paula ducked into a half crouch and stared intently at the jungle.

"Easy," Scott whispered. "We don't know what—"

The greenery parted, and Geoff stepped into view, lugging two large suitcases. Three laptop bags were draped over his shoulders. He was slick with sweat and looked exhausted. Panting, he stepped into the camp and let the luggage sag to the dirt. Geoff was followed by Mark, H, and Leigh, each of whom bore suitcases and carry-on bags, as well.

"Everything go okay?" Scott asked.

Mark and H could only nod, gasping for breath. Leigh stepped forward, easing his burdens from his shoulders.

"We got everything useful," he said, breathless. "Nearly killed ourselves bringing it back here, though."

"Shit," H said, his voice weak. "Geoff carried three times as much as we did. That guy's a workhorse."

Smiling, Geoff only shrugged.

"Well done," Scott said. "I think we all appreciate it, guys. Any sign of your friend?"

Mark, Leigh, and H glanced at each other. Their expressions darkened. Then Mark told the rest of the group about the tree, and what had happened to Paul and the dinosaur. Upon hearing this, the others expressed their condolences. After a few moments of silence, they all gathered around the pile of luggage.

"Maybe we should store it all inside the shelter," Tod suggested.

"Yeah," Scott agreed. "And we should inventory it, too. Figure out what we have, what we can use, and what we still need. And listen ... we can't just help ourselves to this stuff. We need to ration it. If everybody just takes what they want, whenever they want, we're going to quickly run out of everything.

Somebody needs to be in charge of distributing it. Any volunteers?"

"How about you?" Geoff replied.

Scott shook his head. "No way. I don't need the headache. Speaking of which, did any of you happen to find my sumatriptan?"

"Yeah." Mark held up a laptop bag. "It's in here, along with Chris's meds, and all the other medicine and vitamins and supplements we found."

"Excellent," Scott said. "Can you give Chris his stuff?"

Mark nodded.

"That still leaves the question of who's in charge of divvying the rest of the inventory out." Scott looked at each one of them. "Paula, how about you?"

She paused for a moment, before responding. "I'll do it, but I don't want to be the only one in charge."

"Okay," Scott agreed. "Fair enough. Leigh, you want to help her out?"

"Why me?"

"Because you seem like a fair-minded person."

Leigh shrugged. "Okay, sure."

"Good." Scott rubbed his temples. "Now, if you guys will excuse me for a second ... can I get my stuff, Mark?"

"Shouldn't you check with Paula and Leigh first? After all, you just put them in charge of it."

Leigh elbowed his friend in the ribs. "Don't be a whacker, mate."

Mark frowned. "What's a whacker?"

"A dickhead."

"Oh." Mark shrugged. "Here in the States, Whacker is an editor for one of the big comic book companies. He seems to spend most of his time trolling and arguing with comic book fans online."

"Except we're not in the States," H pointed out.

"Regardless," Leigh replied, "Your whacker and our whacker sound like the same thing."

Scott eagerly took his sumatriptan from the bag and walked away from the group. Tod, Geoff, H, Leigh, Paula, and Erin began lugging the baggage into the safety of the shelter. Mark carried Chris's medicine over to where Chris and Jamie watched over Dave.

"Paul?" Chris asked as Mark approached.

Mark sadly shook his head. "No ... he ... he didn't make it."

"Are you sure?"

"Yeah." Mark explained again what they had found.

"Damn it," Chris whispered. "His wife and daughters ..."

"I know," Mark replied, blinking back tears. "I know. Anyway, I found your stuff."

"Good. Although, I don't know what I'm going to do when I run out. I've only got enough for three more days or so."

"We'll be rescued by then," Mark said.

Chris stared at him, unblinking. "You don't really believe that, do you, Mark?"

Mark didn't reply. Instead, he crouched down and rummaged through the bag until he found Chris's medicine. Then he held it up so Chris could examine it.

"That's all of it," Chris confirmed. "Can you put it somewhere safe?"

Mark nodded.

"I'm sorry about your friend." Jamie shifted his back against the tree trunk. "Any sign of Legerski while you were out there?"

"No," Mark reported. Then he nodded at Dave. "How's this guy doing?"

Jamie glanced down. "Not good. Still unconscious, but at least he's still breathing. I don't know what else to do for him. You guys didn't find any allergy medicine or antihistamines, did you?"

Mark nodded. "Actually, yeah. I think I saw some Claritin and Benadryl."

"Good! That might help."

Jamie tried to stand up, but then winced in pain and collapsed back onto his butt.

"Stay there, dude." Mark got to his feet. "I'll grab him some."

"When you do," Chris suggested, "tell Scott we might want to consider moving Dave into the shelter before night comes."

Mark nodded again. "Will do."

He turned away from them, but before he could leave, the nearby foliage rustled again.

"Autumn ..." Dave wheezed. "Bryant ..."

Mark glanced down at the injured man. "What did he say?"

"I think those are his kids' names." Jamie put his hand on Dave's chest. "Easy, buddy. Just take it easy. Mark's going to get you some medicine."

"Yeah, just sit tight, pally. I'll go get it."

Dave's breath hitched in his chest. "Summer ... tell Summer ... Autumn and Bryant ... tell them ..."

Twigs snapped and branches swayed. Something charged toward them through the jungle, coming fast.

"Shit!" Mark yelled.

"Summer ..."

Dave opened his eyes, but Mark, Jamie, and Chris didn't notice. Their attention was on the foliage. The branches parted and Jesse stumbled into camp. His eyes were wide and his hair was in disarray. His clothes were torn and covered with mud. His face shone slick with sweat.

"Colinda," he gasped. "Back at the ... water ... help!"

Jesse teetered back and forth. His eyes rolled up white, and the color drained from his face. Mark rushed over, catching him before he fell, and eased him to the ground.

"Help!" Jamie shouted. "Hey, guys! We need some help out here!"

The others darted out of the shelter and ran over to them, gathering around Mark, who cradled the unconscious Jesse in his lap.

"What happened?" Paula asked. "Is he dead?"

"No," Mark replied. "He just passed out. Give him some room, guys. Everyone back up."

"What about Colinda?" Scott glanced around the campsite. "Was she with him?"

"No," Jamie reported. "He started to say something about her, but then he passed out before he could finish. Sounded like she might be in trouble."

"Guys," Chris whispered.

"Which way did he come from?" Geoff asked. "Maybe we can find her."

"That's a good idea," Tod agreed. "I'll come with you."

"Guys," Chris said again.

Jamie pointed. "He came out of the jungle over there."

"Okay," Scott said. "Geoff, Tod, and I will go look for her. The rest of you—"

"Guys!"

All of them turned to Chris.

"What's wrong?" Scott asked.

"Dave's not breathing," Chris replied. "I think he's dead."

Night never came.

Paul Legerski climbed to the top of a tree, looking for hidden cameras. He was covered in the blood of what he assumed was a wild boar. The beast had been pig-like, covered in thick, wiry hair and sporting a pair of tusks. It had grunted like a pig when he surprised it, and when the blade of his machete cleaved through its head, the thing had squealed like a pig, as well. Still, though. He couldn't be sure. It hadn't tasted like pork, because he'd eaten it raw. It was possible that the boar was just another trick, perpetrated by whomever was filming all of this.

The blood on his hands, face, and forearms felt real enough. It had dried to a hard crust on his clothes. But still ...

Legerski was convinced that he was the victim of some form of trickery. The only things to determine were who was behind it, and how he could escape. He'd checked the jungle for cameras or hidden microphones, but so far had found none. He'd wandered far in his search, and now had no idea how to find the rest of the people from the airport shuttle. Not that it mattered. They were probably in on it anyway—actors, paid to fuck with him. Maybe they'd left when he fell asleep. Maybe that was why he couldn't find them. Whoever was behind this had probably removed the crashed bus and all the other pretend survivors while he slept. They could be out there right now, in some observation studio, having a good laugh while he stumbled around this place.

He was pretty sure he'd been drugged at some point. How else to explain the fact that he'd completely slept through the night? Yes, he had suffered a head injury. Yes, they had knocked him out for a while. But he'd been fine after that. So, he must have been drugged. He'd made his bed in a grove of tall, soft ferns. When he closed his eyes, the sun had been high in the sky. When he awoke again, it was in the same position, almost as if it hadn't moved. That was impossible, of course. So were things like the razor grass and the dinosaur. The only thing that was real was that he woke refreshed. Therefore, he'd slept. But to sleep through the night like that? They must have dosed him on something.

Whoever they were.

No matter. He'd find out their identity in due time. And when he did, the bill would come due. He'd make them pay for fucking with him.

Clinging to the top of the tree, his feet spaced precariously on the branches below him, Legerski stared out at the landscape, looking for ... well, he wasn't sure. He'd climbed up here to search for cameras, but not finding any, he now looked for stage lights, or some kind of wall. If he was on a set somewhere, surely these things would be visible. Spying none, he shielded his eyes from the sun with one hand and looked instead for something—anything—different from the seemingly endless forest.

He wasn't sure at what point the topography had changed, but the jungle was now far behind him. He was perched atop one of many trees that reminded him of the redwoods and sequoias back home. They all had the same thick, fibrous bark, but they weren't nearly as tall and possessed more limbs and branches.

A butterfly flittered past. Its wings were a deep magenta color, giving way to white and pink at the ends. Scowling, he watched it hover. As it flew off, he noticed something in the distance—what appeared to be a thatched roof of some kind. It was dome shaped, and blended in with the foliage around it, but yes, he was fairly certain it was a roof. After a moment, he began to see other structures nearby—all similarly fashioned.

"Well, look at that. A fucking village."

The structures had been constructed in a circular clearing, devoid of any trees. Camouflaged as it was from his viewpoint, he suspected it would be even better concealed from the ground. He peered closer, watching for any signs of life or movement. Seeing none, Legerski debated what to do next. The settlement could be another trick or trap, but it could also provide clues as to what was going on. Maybe even food and water. At the very least, sleeping under a roof—even one as rustic as these appeared— would be better than sleeping in the middle of an open-air fern grove.

He climbed back down the tree, choosing his footing care- fully. His descent took a long time. When he was finally on solid ground again, Legerski retrieved his machete, which he'd left embedded in a rotten stump. Then he turned and marched off in the direction of the village. There was no game trail to follow, but his progress was easy, aided by the fact that very little under- growth existed beneath the trees—only clusters of ferns and some huge clover sprouted from the thick, black needle-strewn soil. It was cool beneath the canopy, and the sweat he'd worked up during his climb now dried on his skin, along with the boar blood. Insects buzzed his ears and eyes. Legerski angrily swatted them away, focusing on walking in a straight line. He didn't want to get lost again and have to climb another tree.

His head still hurt. He touched it gingerly, wincing when his fingertips brushed against the knot on his scalp. There would be hell to pay for that, sooner or later. The cripple in the wheelchair. The bitch and her little brat. He'd get even with them all, eventually. He always did.

The sunlight began to dim as he pressed on. The trees were alive with birdsongs, echoing all around him. Soon, the limbs overhead grew close enough together that only a few shafts of light penetrated them. It was the first time Legerski had experienced darkness since arriving here, and he welcomed it—even if it was more of a dusk than a true night.

He spotted plenty of multi-colored butterflies flitting about, and several salamanders. A slug, easily measuring a foot long, crawled up a tree trunk, glistening in the dim light. Its body was black, with purple spots. The creature's eyestalks were nearly as long as his pinky finger, and thick as pencils. Legerski smashed the slug with a rock, recoiling at the noxious stench that wafted up from the smeared remains.

A while later, he heard a chittering noise. Stopping, he scanned the forest. When the sound came again, Legerski spied something that looked like a furry lobster perched on top of a rotting tree stump. The creature was the size of a squirrel, and covered in brown hair. It waved two pincer arms at him. Legerski stomped the ground, and the thing scurried inside the stump.

At one point, he saw a snake, its hide the color of a lima bean, slithering up the side of a tree. The serpent was probably four feet in length and several inches round at its thickest section. It was clear from the reptile's actions that it was trying to get away from him, but Legerski didn't care. He lashed out with the machete, cleaving the snake in two. Both sections fell to the ground, curling and thrashing, dripping blood.

Grinning, he nodded at the two halves. "There you go. Don't blame me. Blame the people who put you ..."

He gaped, staring in shock as dozens of miniature snakes began to pour from the severed ends, wriggling out of the carcass and onto the jungle floor, leaving tiny, glistening trails of blood and mucous.

"Gah!"

Recoiling, Legerski gasped as more babies—because that's what he assumed they were—slithered out. There seemed to be hundreds of them, far too many to have logically fit inside the bigger snake.

"Acid," he muttered. "The cocksuckers dosed me with LSD or some kind of hallucinogen."

He stomped with both feet, mashing the tiny serpents that crawled toward him. Then he pushed ahead, fleeing from the horde. He tried to stay mindful of the direction he'd been originally traveling in. When he stopped for breath a few minutes later, he realized angrily that he was no longer sure.

"Goddamn it!"

Making sure the serpent horde hadn't followed him, Legerski climbed another tree and got his bearing again. He wasn't as off-course as he'd initially feared, and the village seemed closer now. Hurrying back down, he set off again at a determined pace.

"I know you're watching right now. You hear me? I know you're out there somewhere, watching. Getting your kicks. Well, I've got something for you." He raised the bloodstained machete. A sparse ray of sunlight glinted off the blade. "I want out of here. Right fucking now!"

The forest didn't respond. The birds grew quiet.

Eventually, he reached the edge of the village. His suspicions about its camouflage were proven correct. It was virtually indistinguishable from the surrounding landscape. He didn't realize he'd found it until he stepped into the clearing. Just like that, the gloom vanished and the sun returned, and the village became clear. Legerski inched forward, awed by the silence. Nothing moved among the buildings. Not even the wind. The structures were simple wooden huts, constructed of rough-hewn beams obviously cut from the surrounding forest, and roofed with thatch. He moved warily among them, examining the exteriors. They seemed in good shape—structurally sound and crafted with rustic expertise, but all of them were unoccupied. He peeked inside one, brushing aside a flap of tanned animal hide that served as a door, and found it empty. The dirt floor was unmarked with tracks. The furnishings were sparse. A few logs, stripped of their bark, served as seating. A sleeping area fashioned from dried ferns and leaves dominated the room, along with an open-air fire pit and assorted clay crockery. A thick layer of dust covered everything. It was obvious to him that nobody had been inside the hut in a long time.

After examining a few more huts, and finding them deserted, as well, Legerski strode to what seemed to be the center of the village. A large ring of stones had been piled up to form a fire pit, but the pit contained only a small scrap of charred wood and a few tiny animal bones, yellowed with age. Kneeling, he poked around in the dirt with the tip of his machete, but his efforts turned up nothing.

Rising to his feet, he paused to scan the rest of the structures. The buildings seemed to all be similar to the ones he had already investigated. There were no larger structures that he could see, nothing to indicate a community hall or place of worship or a medical area.

"So," he muttered, "what is this place? Some new set you constructed? Did I get here too early? Don't have your actors on standby?"

His words seemed to hang in the air. Once again, he was struck by how eerily silent the deserted village really was.

And then, someone spoke behind him.

"H-hello?"

The voice was timid, soft ... but strangely familiar. Legerski spun around, ducking into a fighting stance and clutching his machete tight. A figure stepped out from behind a hut, and gaped at him.

Legerski gaped back.

"You ..." The new arrival pointed. "But ... I'm ... how?"

Legerski's brow narrowed. He stared at a mirror image of himself. The figure was dressed differently than him. Instead of wearing a San Jose Sharks jersey, this apparent clone was clad in a T-shirt with a Cabo San Lucas logo. But they wore the same jeans, and even the same brand of sneakers, except that Paul's were black and this guy's shoes were white.

"Who are you?" Legerski asked.

"M-me? Who are you? I'm me."

"It's a pretty good trick." Legerski grinned. "What are you— one of those animatronic things? Or just a lookalike they hired to do an impression?"

The new arrival blinked. He took several deep breaths. "Please ... I don't understand. Who ... who are you? Where are we? What is this place?"

"I'm Paul Legerski."

"But that's impossible. I'm Paul Legerski."

"No, you're not. You're just another trick."

"I don't understand. We were doing clean-up at Ground Zero ... and then—"

"New York," Legerski interrupted. "I was there. My company had that contract."

"Mine did, too. I was there and then I saw a doorway in the rubble. It was just standing there, upright and undamaged. I opened it and walked through, and I came out here and when I turned around the door was gone! I don't understand what's going on. Can you tell me what's happening?"

Legerski grinned. "And that's where your narrative falls apart. I mean, I'll give you guys credit. You did your research. But I came here in 2016, and Ground Zero was 2001. I was a few pounds lighter back then, and had a little more hair. You look like me now, so you didn't come from 2001."

"What do you mean, 2001? You're talking about the 7/7 attacks, right?"

"No, I'm talking about the 9/11 attacks, when a bunch of Muslims flew airplanes into the Twin Towers."

The doppelganger frowned. "9-11? I think you're confused. The terrorist attacks on the World Trade Center and the Pentagon happened on July 7th, 2016! And don't disparage all Muslims. It was a bunch of religious extremists who did it."

"That's the other detail you guys got wrong," Legerski said. "I'm no politically correct progressive douchebag."

"I'm not either. I'm a Libertarian."

Legerski snorted at this.

His lookalike frowned. "Who are these guys you keep talking about?"

"You know who."

"No, I don't. I told you, I—"

"Whoever hired you. Whoever is in charge."

"In charge of what?"

Legerski spread his arms wide, gesturing with the machete. "Whoever's in charge of all this."

The other Legerski glanced at the weapon, and his eyes grew wide. He took a faltering step backward, and held up his hands.

Chuckling, Legerski slowly advanced.

"Listen," said the twin, backing up another step. "I don't want any trouble. I just want to get back home to Shannon, and—"

"What did you say?"

"Shannon. My girlfriend."

"Now you fucked up," Legerski snarled. "Don't bring my wife into this shit! You hear me? You don't bring Shannon into this. She's innocent!"

"What are you talking about?"

"You people abduct me. You bring me here, to this ... fucking place. Maybe you know about the real me. Maybe you don't. I'm guessing you do, since you obviously know all the other little details of my life. But you don't get to bring my wife into this. You don't fucking involve her!"

"Okay, just calm down. Maybe we can figure out together what ..."

"Don't tell me to calm down, cocksucker."

Growling, Legerski raised the machete and charged. His other self turned and fled, darting frantically between the huts. Birds squawked in the forest, taking flight, alarmed by the commotion. The doppelganger ducked inside a building. Howling with laughter, Legerski gave chase.

The village echoed with the sounds of struggle.

Then came the screams and shrieks.

Then the terrible wailing of someone dying.

Finally, silence fell once again, and a lone figure emerged from the building.

A day passed, but night never came.

At least, Chris judged it to be a day that had passed. It was hard to keep time here in ... wherever they were. Clocks and watches didn't work. Neither did their phones or tablets or other devices—at least when it came to working correctly. The devices without dead batteries still powered up and attempted to function, but behaved strangely.

Before they'd all gone to sleep, Tod, the big guy from Texas, had pulled out his Kindle, thinking he might have better luck with that, but when he'd turned it on and everyone gathered around him, the results had been perplexing. The device still worked, but Tod swore there were eBooks on his Kindle that he'd never added—or indeed heard of before. One of them was a sequel to Stephen King's seminal *Salem's Lot*, a book which Chris knew very well. The bibliophiles among the group all agreed that King had never written a sequel to that particular novel (unless you counted some of the book's characters appearing in other works), and none could account for its presence on the football coach's Kindle. Another book was titled *El*

Paso and was supposedly written by J.F Gonzalez. This had perplexed the readers in the group, as well. Most of them were familiar with the author, but none had ever heard of this particular novel. Even stranger—the books they knew Gonzalez had written now showed up as written by two other authors; Angel Garcia and Gilbert Schloss. H had wondered aloud if they were pseudonyms. Other books on the Kindle had weird titles and author names that seemed to be spelled with strange foreign letters that none of them recognized. Indeed, some of the characters were just symbols and glyphs. When Tod had tried to click on the Stephen King book and open the file, the Kindle crashed, losing all power. He'd tried to get it to turn back on, but the device appeared to be broken.

Chris based the passage of time on how long they'd slept. He'd offered to take a turn standing watch—or rather, sitting watch, since he couldn't stand. Doing so made him feel better, and gave him a sense of being useful. The group had struggled in getting his wheelchair down to the bottom of the ravine, and he'd been embarrassed by their efforts on his behalf. Guard duty was something he could do—a way for him to contribute and to show the others he was pulling his own weight, and not being a burden. When Mark had awoken him for his turn at watch, Chris felt well-rested. He was confident he'd gotten a good eight hours of sleep, and even though the sun still occupied the same position in the sky it had when he'd fallen asleep, he decided to count this as a new day.

While the rest of the castaways slept, Chris sat there in his chair, parked outside the shelter, and gazed up at the trees looming over the top of the ravine. A slight breeze rustled the leaves. Water dripped from them and glistened on the ground next to his wheels. He assumed it must have rained at some point, and was amazed he'd slept through it. But then again, he'd been exhausted and had gone through a trauma. Indeed, he was still going through a trauma.

He scanned the sky, hoping for a glimpse of an airplane, or even a contrail—something normal to latch onto, a sign that rescue was possible. He saw only clouds, a few birds, and the ever-present sun.

He wondered what Francesca was doing right now. Was she at home, worrying, or had she traveled across the country to Maryland to wait for word from rescuers? Knowing her, it was more likely that she was demanding to lead the search party herself. Chris smiled at the thought.

Out in the jungle, something roared—a deep-throated, ballooning sound, not unlike the croak of a bullfrog.

A three-hundred-pound bullfrog.

His smile faded. He held his breath, waiting for the noise to be repeated, but the jungle fell silent again. Eventually, the tension he felt passed, replaced with an overwhelming crush of depression. His breath caught in his throat, and his vision grew blurry with tears. Unable to wipe them away, Chris blinked, waiting for his eyes to clear. The sadness welled up out of him. It wasn't just that he missed Francesca—he was scared and worried and felt helpless.

When the tears stopped and he could breathe again, Chris debated whether he should take his meds. To not take them would lead to initial discomfort and sickness, followed by increasing trauma, and eventually the very real possibility of his death. But none of that would happen right away. He frowned, pondering if he should risk it and ration the medicine, rather than taking his daily dose now. Any complications from not taking the meds wouldn't present themselves immediately. They would take a few days. It was quite possible that they would be rescued before then, in which case, he wouldn't have to worry. But it was just as possible that they wouldn't be rescued, and if so, he was already looking at a dwindling supply. If he rationed, he could last longer—but he'd also be merely delaying the inevitable.

While he was still mulling it over, the rest of the encampment began to slowly wake. Jesse was the first to emerge from the shelter. His eyes were puffy and underlined with black half-circles. He nodded at Chris, but didn't speak.

"Did you get much sleep?" Chris asked.

Jesse shook his head. "No. Not really. I just kept thinking about Colinda."

"I'm sorry."

"Thanks." Jesse shrugged. "It's weird. I mean, I barely knew her. I'd never met her before we were on the shuttle together. It's not like she was a longtime friend or my girlfriend or something, and yet ..."

"And yet, what?"

"I don't know. It just sucks. She had a daughter. And a dog. I keep wondering what will happen to them."

"Was her daughter an adult?"

Jesse swallowed before replying. "I don't know. I can't remember. The only thing I remember is that her dog was named Bender."

"Like the character from *The Breakfast Club*?"

"Maybe. Or the robot on Futurama."

Paula and Erin emerged next, and said good morning to them both. Chris and Jesse returned the gesture.

"Your name is Erin, right?" Chris asked.

The little girl nodded.

"Our friend Leigh—the Australian guy with the glasses? His daughter is named Erin, too."

Paula smiled. "Well, isn't that nice?"

"Mommy," Erin whispered, "I have to pee."

"Me, too," Paula admitted, turning to Chris. "Will you excuse us?"

"Of course."

"Don't go too far," Jesse cautioned as they walked farther into the ravine. Then he turned to Chris. "I guess somebody in the group ought to dig a latrine, huh?"

"Do you think we'll be here that long?"

Jesse shrugged. "Long enough. Every one of us is going to have to piss or shit today. It would be good for all if we didn't have to step in each other's crap, right?"

"Yeah," Chris agreed. "If I get shit on my wheels, I'm going to track it all over camp."

Scott, Tod, and Geoff were the next to stir. They exited the shelter, nodded hello, and glanced up at the sky.

Scott frowned. "The sun's still there, huh?"

"Yes," Chris replied. "It hasn't moved an inch, as far as I can tell. I guess you were right last night, after all."

"How's that?" Scott's tone was puzzled.

"The debate about building a campfire, before everyone went to bed. You said if it wasn't dark, then we didn't need a fire to keep predators away."

"And it definitely wasn't cold," Geoff added.

"That's for sure." Tod nodded in agreement. "I sweated my ass off last night."

"Actually," Scott said, "I was thinking about it when I first woke up. Maybe a fire wouldn't hurt. It might help comfort everybody—give them a sense of security or normalcy. And if we manage to find food, we might need a fire to cook it."

"You're sending us out hunting?" Geoff asked.

Scott shrugged. "We need to eat."

"Legerski took off with the machete," Tod pointed out. "How are we supposed to hunt? We don't have any weapons."

"No," Scott agreed. "We don't. That's why we need to make some today."

Chris spoke up. "Jesse suggested we dig a latrine, as well. I think it's a good idea."

Scott nodded. "Agreed. Not sure what we'll use to dig one, though."

Paula and Erin returned from their walk, and the others began to file out of the shelter—first Jamie, then Mark and Leigh, and finally H. Jamie still favored one foot over the other, but his limp wasn't as pronounced. Chris smiled when he saw his friends. Mark, Leigh, and H hurried over to him.

"Made it through your watch without getting eaten by a dinosaur?" Mark grinned. "Wicked!"

"Piece of cake," Chris replied. "Listen, I hate to ask, but ..."

"Your catheter and colostomy bag?" Leigh finished for him.

Chris nodded.

"No worries, pal," Mark replied. "Like you said, piece of cake."

"Are you sure?"

"Of course!" Leigh nodded. "Just let me eat some breakfast first?"

"I could eat, too," Mark agreed.

"I'm surprised to see you awake already," Chris said. "I figured you'd sleep in."

Mark nodded at Leigh and H. "These fuckers wouldn't let me sleep. H snores like a chainsaw."

"I do not," the older man protested.

"You do, too," Leigh, Mark, Paula, and Jamie all said simultaneously.

The group broke into laughter. Even H joined in. Chris studied them all, and smiled. The sadness lifted from him.

Maybe we'll be okay, he thought. *Maybe we'll make it.*

His smile grew bigger as Mark performed an exaggerated impression of H snoring, which brought a new round of giggles from the castaways.

Yes, Chris thought, *we may be okay. I just hope Francesca is okay, too.*

When the laughter had faded, Scott crouched down on his haunches. The others gathered around him.

"Okay," he said. "First things first. The sun did not go down last night. As you can all see, it looks like it hasn't moved at all."

"It's been high noon since we got here," Jamie agreed.

"But that's just impossible," Paula said. "The sun isn't a stationary object. Neither is the Earth. They're both constantly moving."

"Yes," Scott said, "that's true. So, looking at this logically, I think we need to consider the possibility that this sun isn't our sun, and this isn't Earth. The sun maintaining its position in the sky isn't normal, but neither are any of the other things we've all experienced since the crash … or maybe even before the crash. The foliage, the … animals. And what happened to Gregorio and Dave and Colinda and Benn and the other Paul definitely weren't normal."

"He forgot Mr. Bob," Erin said to her mother.

Geoff sighed. "What happened to him can happen anywhere, kid."

Paula's shoulders stiffened. "Please don't be condescending to my daughter."

Geoff held up his hands. "Sorry."

"We're all tense," Scott said. "And we're all scared. At least, I'm scared. I don't know where we are, but I think we need to confront the fact that a rescue party probably isn't coming for us. If they're looking for us at all, it's not here. Instead of waiting to be rescued, I think we need to focus on long-term survival. Is anyone here a prepper?"

The group shook their heads.

"Well then," Scott said. "I guess we'll have to improvise."

"What are you proposing?" Jamie asked.

"I made a list in my head," Scott told them. "Jobs. I think we should focus on them today. The shelter sufficed for last night, but—"

"Can we really call it night?" Tod interrupted. "I mean, if it never got dark, then was it really night?"

"Night in that most of us were asleep," Scott explained.

"I don't know about the rest of you," Mark said, "but I don't think that qualified as sleep. I had a rock in my back."

Scott sighed. "That's what I'm trying to get to. The shelter kept us safe for the time being, but we need to work on making it sturdier—and more comfortable. Paula, I think we can all agree that Erin shouldn't venture out into the jungle."

Paula nodded. "Definitely."

"I thought you and her could stay here today and work on that," Scott said. "Mark, since you had watch in the middle of the night, you can stay and help. And Chris, I imagine you must be exhausted."

"I could sleep," Chris admitted. He turned to Leigh. "I'll need some help first though."

Scott nodded. "Why don't you stay here and do that? And when you wake up, you can give them a hand, as well. Cool?"

Chris opened his mouth to question how much help he could be, but then decided that was self-defeating. Instead, he simply nodded.

"Sure."

"Now," Scott continued. "Food, water, and defense have to be our three main priorities. I suggest we split into groups for each. We already know where the water source is. Jesse, are you comfortable leading a group back there?"

Jesse flinched. "To the pond? Yeah, I guess. We've got to bury Colinda, anyway."

Scott shook his head. "I don't know that burying the deceased should be our first priority."

"Well, we can't just leave her out there! I should have brought her back with me yesterday, but I panicked."

"I understand your feelings," Scott replied, "but Colinda is dead, and we need to focus on the living."

"Dude ..."

"I'll go with him," Geoff volunteered. "I can carry her back."

"We shouldn't bury her here at the encampment," H argued. "She ... the body ... will attract predators."

"Jesus Christ ..." Jesse balled up a fist and smacked it against his thigh. "So where are we supposed to put her, then?"

H shrugged. "How about near those flowers you mentioned?"

"The flowers are what fucking killed her!"

"Listen!" Scott shouted. He glanced at each of them, making sure he had their attention. Then he returned to speaking quietly. "Jesse, if you want to bury Colinda, then go ahead and do it. But she's your responsibility. I don't mean to sound cold or callous or disrespectful, but we've got too much else to take care of right now. And I think H is right about not burying her near the campsite, so pick another spot somewhere else."

Jesse nodded, his expression sullen. "Is farther down the ravine okay?"

Scott turned to H, who shrugged.

"As long as it's away from the camp."

"What about Dave?" Jamie asked. "Right now, his body is at the back end of the shelter, covered up with palm fronds. But if we're worried about attracting predators ..."

Scott shook his head. "Okay. Jesse. Geoff. You're on graveyard duty. Bury them both, and—"

"What about Bob?" Paula asked. "Are we going to bury him, too?

Scott groaned in exasperation. "Do any of you know how to find his body?"

One by one, they shook their heads.

"I might be able to," Paula murmured, "but I'm not sure where that spot was, exactly."

Scott nodded. "And if you go wandering off into the jungle looking for it, you might end up lost. Or worse ..."

"Good point," Paula admitted.

"Okay." Scott rubbed his forehead. "Geoff, Jesse, and Leigh. Gather up all the empty containers you can find among the stuff we salvaged from the shuttle bus—empty water bottles, canteens, thermoses, and anything else that will hold water. Let Jesse show you guys how to find the watering hole. Then he and Geoff can take care of Colinda and Dave while Leigh makes a few trips for water."

"By myself?" Leigh asked.

Scott nodded. "It's not like the containers will be heavy."

"I don't care about that," Leigh said. "I care about getting eaten by something."

"I'll give him a hand carrying water until they're done with the graves," Mark volunteered. "Then I'll come back here and help Paula and Erin and Chris."

Frowning, Scott nodded again.

"How are we supposed to dig graves?" Geoff asked. "We don't have a shovel."

"I don't know." Scott's voice was clipped and cold. "Build a cairn out of stones. Dig with a stick. You guys figure it out. Mr. H? How's that cut on your head?"

"Healing fine. No signs of infection."

"Excellent. Then I'd like you and Tod to look for food. You were a biology teacher. Can you figure out what's safe for us to eat and what's not?"

"Of course," H replied.

"Geoff brought up a good point about the shovel," Scott continued. "We have to dig a latrine later. And we'll have to try our luck at hunting. We need tools and weapons for both. Jamie, can you give me a hand making some of those? I figure we can use sticks and rocks, and maybe some of the junk we salvaged—fashion some crude spears, axes, shovels, fishing poles, and such."

"Sounds good to me," Jamie replied. "I'm sure we can rig a few things together."

"Okay." Scott stood up. "We've got the snack food stuff from the bus. Let's eat breakfast and then get to it, folks."

"I'd kill for some coffee," Paula sighed.

Most of the castaways murmured their agreement at this sentiment.

Chris watched the group as they milled around the campsite, but he paid special attention to Scott Berke. It was obvious the man had become their leader. There'd been no vote or campaign, but he was in charge, nevertheless. It was also obvious, to Chris at least, that he didn't want the job.

Then Leigh appeared with some food for Chris—potato chips, a protein bar, and some chocolate—and he turned his attention to more immediate concerns.

⬜

"I DON'T GET IT," Tod whispered. "We just saw an animal eat them. Why do we have to wait?"

H finished wiping the condensation off his eyeglasses and replaced them on his head. Then he peered through the thick copse of bushes where they crouched, concealed, eyeing another clump of nearby bushes that were bursting with berries. The fruit looked very similar in size, shape, and texture to strawberries, but these particular berries were blackish-purple in color. The branches sagged, and more berries littered the ground.

"Did you recognize that animal?"

Tod shook his head.

"Neither did I," H confirmed. "It had some of the same characteristics as a squirrel, but it clearly wasn't. Given all the other phenomena we've witnessed, I have to assume that animal isn't from our Earth. Therefore, we can't determine anything based on its dietary habits. What might be harmless to it could very well be toxic to us. So, we wait."

"They look like strawberries, though." Tod sniffed the air, inhaling deeply. "Smell like them, too."

H's stomach rumbled. "I agree. And they appear to be safe. Ninety percent of blue and black berries are usually okay to eat. It's not a hard and fast rule, though, and it might not apply here in ... this place. Also, strawberries don't grow on bushes like that."

They waited, and eventually, a crow swooped down and landed. It pecked along the ground, picked a berry up in its beak, and then took flight again. Two more birds flew down from the treetops and perched among the bushes. Then, they too hopped to the ground and began to eat.

"Okay," H whispered. "I think they're safe to try."

"Thank God."

Tod stood up and pushed through the foliage. Disturbed, the birds took flight, squawking in fright and irritation. Grinning, H followed along after him, bemused by the bigger man's impatience. Tod paused when he reached the nearest berry bush.

"So ... which one of us gets to be the guinea pig?"

"I'll do it," H volunteered. He surveyed the fruit hanging from the branches, and noticed insects flitting around them. He pointed at the bugs. "That's another good sign."

"Don't get stung," Tod warned. "You don't want to end up like that Dave guy."

H thought to himself that what had happened to Dave could happen to any of them at any time, but decided not to say it out loud. Their situation was scary enough as it was. He saw no need to add extra fear or paranoia to an already dire state. If they let fear rule them now, the group would be paralyzed into inaction, and that—most assuredly—would hasten their demise.

He plucked a berry from the branch, choosing one that looked particularly ripe, and held it in his palm, examining it in detail. Except for the coloration, it did indeed seem to be a strawberry. A dollop of juice leaked from the fruit onto his skin. It felt sticky, but ... normal. H raised his hand to his nose and smelled it. Then he looked up at Tod.

"Well, here goes nothing."

"Wait! What do I do if you ... go into convulsions or something?"

H shrugged. "Then you know the berries are poisonous. Don't eat them."

Before Tod could respond, H pinched the berry between his thumb and index finger, brought it to his lips, and nibbled off the tip. His mouth was filled with tart sweetness. Eyes-widening, he forced himself to wait for a reaction, rather than devouring the rest.

Tod shifted from foot to foot, clearly apprehensive. "Do you feel anything?"

"Yes." H nodded. "Hungry."

Then he popped the remainder of the strawberry into his mouth and chewed greedily, moaning with delight.

Tod's eyes grew wide. "Is it okay?"

"Okay?" H picked another strawberry and shoved it into his mouth. "It's fucking delicious! You've gotta try them."

"But ... shouldn't we take it slow?"

"They're fine," H said. "Trust me. They're strawberries—just a different color than the ones we have back home."

Grinning, Tod joined him. The two men spent several minutes gorging themselves, grunting and sighing with pleasure as they shoveled berry after berry into their mouths. Soon, their fingertips and lips were stained purple. Birds squawked at them from the treetops, incensed at their intrusion. Eventually, they slowed down. H took a deep breath, and Tod patted his stomach, smearing his skull-print Hawaiian shirt with juice.

"And here I thought I might lose some weight while we are stuck here."

"We won't starve," H agreed. "But eventually, we're going to need more than berries to eat. Now, how do we transport these back to camp?"

"We can get a suitcase from the shelter," Tod suggested. "There's enough fruit here to fill one."

"Good idea."

Tod picked one more berry from the bush and popped it into his mouth. Then he wiped his hands on his shirt and turned back to the jungle.

"Wait," H called, pointing. "I think camp is this way, isn't it?"

"No, I'm pretty sure it's this direction."

Frowning, H glanced over his shoulder, surveying the foliage, and then turned back to Tod. "Are you sure?"

The big man nodded. "We hid in these bushes over here."

H hesitated as Tod pushed through the greenery. He couldn't be certain, but he thought the copse of bushes they'd concealed themselves in earlier was directly behind him. He shrugged. He'd keep an eye out as they walked. If he didn't see some sign of his and Tod's previous passage, he'd suggest going in a different direction.

The vegetation closed behind Tod, and H hurried to catch up, shoving his way through. He looked up, craning his neck to catch a glimpse of the sun through the treetops, thinking he could judge their course by its position. Then he realized how futile that line of thinking was. H shrugged, deciding not to worry. The berry plot wasn't far from the shelter, so even if they did get lost, they could probably find the others by shouting. Then it occurred to him that shouting might allow the jungle's other denizens to find them, as well.

Ahead of him, Tod belched.

H laughed. "That's the sound of a happy—"

He stopped in mid-sentence as Tod came to an abrupt halt— so sudden that H nearly collided with him. Then H saw why. They had emerged into an area that seemed burned. It wasn't a large spot—maybe ten feet by twenty, H estimated, but the vegetation in that square was either dead or blackened, as if there had been a fire. The scars didn't appear fresh. The ground was covered with dried leaves and twigs, but the trees immediately above them were entirely bare of leaves, and in most cases, branches. What few limbs remained were gnarled and dry almost to the point of petrification.

"Well," H whispered, "we are definitely going the wrong way. We would have noticed this before."

"Wow," Tod wheezed. "What do you think happened here? What did this?"

"A lightning strike, maybe? That seems the most plausible explanation. If it had been a forest fire, more of the area would be burned. But it's just this spot."

They stood side-by-side, surveying the barren area. Then, H tapped Tod on the shoulder.

"We should get back to camp."

The football coach nodded. "Just let me piss first."

"Here?"

Tod blushed. "I was afraid to do it in the jungle. Everything grows so close together ... I was worried about what might be hiding in the leaves. But here? It's pretty wide open."

Tod walked toward the center of the clearing. H turned around to give him some privacy. He glanced up at the sun again, marking its presence and wondering about the orb's strange behavior, when he heard leaves rustling and sticks breaking behind him. Tod shouted in surprise. Something crashed. Then Tod's yelp turned into a frightened shriek. H spun around and was startled to see Tod sticking out of the ground from his chest upward, as if the dirt had swallowed him up. H's first thought was that the big man had fallen into quicksand, but the burned surface was hard and baked.

"Help!" Tod yelled. "I'm stuck!"

H rushed to his side. "What the hell happened?"

"I don't know!" Tod clawed at the dirt with his hands, raking through the brittle leaves and debris. "The ground just gave way beneath me."

"You're okay," H soothed, trying to calm him. "Are you standing on something?"

"No. I can't feel anything beneath my feet, and I'm kicking my legs."

"Just take it easy. Stay still."

"Take it easy? I'm stuck in a hole! Help me, man!"

Instead of responding, H studied the ground. Beneath Tod's chest, he saw flashes of silver. He brushed the dirt and leaves out of the way, revealing a steel frame buried in the earth. Its opening was flush with the ground. Obviously, it had been partially concealed by the detritus, and when Tod had stepped on it, he'd fallen in.

"What is it?" Tod wriggled, panting. "What do you see?"

"It's some kind of ... duct. Like a ventilation shaft or something."

"Oh, Jesus ..." Tod grew pale. His voice trembled. "Don't let me fall down here, H!"

"I don't think you're going to. The opening is ... well, let's just say you filled it up."

"Are you calling me fat?"

"I am," H admitted, "and I'm telling you that being fat may have just saved your life."

"Don't let me fall," Tod repeated.

He's going into shock, H thought. *I've got to get him out of there.*

"Oh, shit," Tod moaned, shuddering. "I still have to pee."

"Can you hold it?"

Tod closed his eyes and shook his head. Then he began to cry.

"Hey, hey. Come on." H stood up and clapped his hands together, brushing the dirt from his palms. "It's going to be okay."

"That's easy for you to say!"

"Here. Give me your hands."

Tod reached for him. His palms were sweaty and sticky from berry juice, and H had a difficult time grasping them. He readjusted his grip, curling his fingers around Tod's wrists, and then directed Tod to do the same with him. Once they both had a firm hold, H pulled. Tod didn't budge. H planted his feet shoulder-width apart and tugged again, grunting with the effort. The coach remained stuck.

"Shit," H panted. "Okay, listen ... I've got to go get some help."

"No! Don't leave me here by myself."

"I can't pull you free, Tod. You're too goddamned heavy for me to do it alone. We need help."

"But what if I slip through while you're gone? What if I fall?"

H glanced around hurriedly, and then ran to the edge of the clearing. He selected a tall tree that was covered in thick vines. Then he scanned the ground around it. After a moment, he snatched up a rock and struck one of the vines with it, over and over again, until he'd cut through. He yanked it along over to Tod, and then tugged on it to demonstrate how the other end was still attached to the tree.

"Can you raise your arms?"

Nodding, his face covered in snot and sweat, Tod complied.

H looped the vine around his chest, pulling it snug, and then tied it into a knot. Then he stood up again.

"You really think this is going to hold me?"

"Tod, you can't see the opening. I can. You're wedged in there really fucking tight. I don't think you're going to fall, but if I'm wrong, that vine should prevent it."

"But what if ... what if that dinosaur from the crash comes along?"

"It's dead. Remember?"

"What if it had a cousin?"

"I'll be back," H promised. "Quick as I can. Just stay calm. It's going to be okay."

He turned away, but Tod called out again. H turned, impatient, and then noticed the sheepish look on the big man's face.

"What is it?"

"Can you ... can you not tell the others I was crying? I was just scared."

Despite their predicament, H grinned. "Of course. Now stay calm. I'll be back soon and we'll get you out of there, and then you can pee."

"Too late," Tod admitted. "I already did."

"I won't tell them that, either."

H ran to the edge of the burned clearing, found his way back to the berry patch, and then started in the direction he thought their encampment lay.

⸻

Scott and Jamie were sitting on some large, flat rocks, and using stones to sharpen crude points onto the end of sticks when Mark, Geoff, Jesse, and Leigh returned to the camp. Scott looked up at their approach. All four men dripped with sweat. Their clothes clung to them. Jesse, Leigh, and Mark each carried containers of fresh water. Geoff had Colinda's corpse slung over his shoulders. Each of them had solemn expressions, particularly Jesse.

Scott nudged Jamie and nodded at the arrivals. Jamie blanched when he saw Colinda's body. The two stood up. Jamie cringed, favoring his ankle.

"Any problems?" Scott asked.

Mark shook his head. "We avoided the flower that ... killed Colinda. Saw a few more like it, but we stayed away from them, too."

"Jesse," Scott said softly, "how are you holding up?"

The younger man shrugged. "I'll be okay. I just ... once we get her buried, I'll feel better."

Geoff shifted the corpse on his back, getting a better grip. "We found a good spot some ways back. The ground is soft and sandy there. We might not even need a shovel."

Scott nodded.

"Come on." Jesse turned to Geoff. "No sense delaying, I guess."

"Can you carry her?" Geoff asked. "If so, I'll get the other guy."

Without a word, Jesse moved to accept Geoff's burden. He held out his arms and took Colinda from the bigger man. He grunted, but his expression remained stolid. Geoff ducked into the shelter and emerged a few moments later with Dave's corpse now slung over his shoulders.

"Let's do it," Jesse sighed.

The two walked back down the ravine, and disappeared from sight once more.

"We should get a fire started," Scott advised. "Just to be safe, the water should be boiled before anyone drinks it. Though I'm not sure what we can boil it in."

"Pots and pans are in short supply," Jamie agreed.

"We have a few metal canteens and travel mugs from among the luggage," Leigh said. "Maybe we can use those."

"Better than nothing," Scott agreed. "We'll just have to be careful not to melt the rubber seals and gaskets in them."

"What about a hollowed-out gourd?" Mark asked.

Jamie shifted his weight off his injured ankle. "Do you have a hollowed-out gourd?"

"No, but we're in a jungle. There have to be gourds around here somewhere."

While they were still debating, Paula and Erin approached, taking a break from working on the shelter.

"Is Chris asleep?" Mark asked Paula.

"I don't think so," she replied. "If he is, then he's not sleeping soundly. I think he might have been ... crying."

Mark sighed. "I think all of us have been doing that, at one point or another."

A rustling sound came from above them, followed by pounding footsteps. All of them glanced at the top of the ravine, tensed and ready to run. Paula protectively pushed Erin behind her.

"Bloody hell," Leigh whispered. "What now?"

"Guys!" H shouted, sounding breathless. "We need help!"

He appeared at the edge of the ravine, staring down at them. His face was pale and sheened with sweat, and seemed very small compared to the landscape around him.

"What's wrong?" Scott called.

"It's Tod ... he fell in some kind of shaft."

"A shaft?"

"Yeah, like a ventilation shaft or something."

"Is he hurt?"

H shook his head, panting for breath. "I don't think so. But he's scared, and I can't get him out by myself."

"Hang on," Scott said. "We're coming."

"I can't leave Erin here," Paula replied.

"Wouldn't ask you to," Scott said. "You stay here with her. Jamie, you stay, too. That ankle of yours will just slow us down. Mark, Leigh—you guys come with me."

He bent over and scooped up four sharpened sticks, and then handed one each to Mark and Leigh.

"Now we have spears."

Leigh stared at the weapon dubiously. "What's this going to do against a dinosaur?"

"Piss it off," Mark replied, "and give the rest of us time to run away while you get eaten."

"That's not funny, mate."

Grinning, Mark clambered up the embankment. H waved impatiently from above. Scott went next, climbing slowly. Swallowing hard, Leigh glanced at the stick. Then he hurried along after them.

THE GROUP RACED through the jungle with H in the lead. As they ran, he described what had happened, and the blasted, burned-out patch of land. Twice, the older man stopped to collect his bearings, and each time, Scott had a moment of dread, wondering if H was lost. But eventually, he led them to Tod. Sure enough, the big man jutted from the ground, visible only from the waist up. He gasped with relief when he spotted them. Tears and sweat streaked his red face. The ground around him was covered with fingermarks where he had clawed at the dirt.

"Oh God," he moaned. "I didn't think you guys were gonna come! Get me out of here."

The four men gathered around him. Scott knelt, wincing. In addition to his sometimes-crippling headaches, he also suffered from a bad back. Their current circumstances—especially sleeping on the ground—had done him no favors in that regard.

"Take it easy," he soothed. "We'll have you free in a jiffy. Just try to stay calm."

Now that he had a closer look at Tod, Scott could see just how terrified and miserable the football coach really was. His face and forearms were covered in bug bites, apparently suffered since his imprisonment. Scott pointed at a bump on Tod's arm.

"Are you feeling any effects from that?"

"You mean am I going to end up like Dave? No. I already thought of that. But from what Jamie said, the poison acted quick. I think they're just regular mosquitoes."

Scott stood slowly, wincing again. "Okay, let's grab his arms. Two men on each."

Nodding, Leigh and Mark grabbed one of Tod's arms. H and Scott took the other. Scott counted aloud to three, and then they pulled, straining. The big man didn't budge.

"Can you get any leverage?" Scott tried to ignore the new pain in his back. "Is there anything you can push off against with your feet?"

Shaking his head, Tod began to sob again. "There's nothing. Just empty air. For all I know, it might be a hundred feet down."

"Well, you're not going to fall," Mark replied. "So, there's that to be thankful for."

"Thankful? I'm stuck in here, you asshole!"

"Yeah," Mark agreed, "but if you were Leigh's size, you'd be down at the bottom, and it would be a lot tougher to get you out."

"Fuck you," Leigh said.

"I keep thinking about our horse," Tod said.

Scott motioned at the others to try again, and decided to keep Tod talking, in order to calm him.

"What horse is that?" he asked as they pulled again with similar results.

"My wife and I have a ranch near El Paso. She turned it into an animal shelter. We got this horse. I mean, she was beautiful. Just the most gentle, loving horse you've ever seen. She was abandoned on a nearby ranch. Eventually, the county brought her to us. She was nearly starved. You could see every one of her ribs through her sides. She had sores all over her. Broke my heart and made me want to kill the people who had done that to her."

"Again, guys," Scott urged.

They pulled, grunting with the strain, but Tod didn't budge.

Scott noticed the panic creeping back into Tod's expression. "So, what happened to the horse?"

"She's fine," Tod explained. "We nursed her back to health, and adopted her back out to another family eventually."

"Well, that's great," Leigh exclaimed.

"But I don't want to end up like her. She was alone, on that abandoned ranch, slowly starving to death ... I need to get back home! I need to get back to Suzin, and ..."

"Hey," Scott soothed. "Calm down, Tod. We're going to get you out of there. You've just got to keep it together, man. Can you do that for me?"

Tod nodded, sniffling. He opened his mouth to reply, and then paused.

"What's wrong?" Scott asked.

"I don't know. It's like ... I feel a warm gust of air, coming up from below me."

Frowning, Scott knelt again and felt the ground around the shaft with his palm. It felt warm, certainly, but he thought that was more from the sunlight than anything else. Then, he noticed something peculiar. The earth seemed to vibrate slightly, as if there was machinery running far below their feet.

"H," he said, "come down here a second."

H knelt beside him. "What is it?"

"It's definitely getting warmer," Tod said. "What's happening?"

"Feel the ground," Scott told H. "See how it's throbbing? Did you notice that before?"

H shook his head. "Definitely not."

"Guys," Tod gasped, "what is it? What's wrong?"

"Nothing's wrong," Scott said, keeping his tone calm. He stood up and wiped his hands on his shirt.

Something rumbled far beneath them—a deep, rhythmic thrumming.

H's eyes widened. "What the hell is that?"

"Man," Tod moaned. "That air is really getting hot. I'm sweating like a pig."

Scott glanced up at the blackened trees, and then back down at the barren dirt around the shaft.

"Oh no ..."

⌑

PAULA, Jamie, and Erin were busy entwining leafy branches into a sort of thatched wall when they became aware of a low, monotonous hum. Paula had been just about to suggest making a game of it, noticing that her daughter was getting bored, when the noise began. They paused, staring at the surrounding jungle.

"What's that sound, Mommy?"

Paula shook her head. "I don't know, baby."

The whine of a motor came from the entrance to the shelter. They turned in that direction and saw Chris wheel himself out into the ravine. He stared at them, his expression puzzled.

"Do you guys hear that?"

"I thought it was your wheelchair at first," Jamie replied, "but you've stopped and it's still going."

The mysterious hum grew louder.

"Maybe it's the guys," Paula suggested. "Mr. H said they'd found a ventilation shaft?"

"Possibly," Jamie replied. "But I don't—"

"Mommy, look!" Erin pointed down the ravine, in the direction Geoff and Jesse had gone. There was a silver glow coming from the bend where the ravine curved and vanished from their line of site. It was bright enough to be noticeable even in the sunlight.

"What is that?" Chris murmured.

"Erin," Paula said calmly, "I want you to go inside the shelter."

"But I want to—"

"Don't argue with me, sweetie. Get inside. Right now."

Jamie limped over to where he and Scott had been working earlier, and grabbed two makeshift spears. He hopped back on one foot and handed a weapon to Paula. She nodded her thanks. Holding the spear made her feel better.

"Chris, can you take Erin inside?"

"Of course," he replied. "Come on, hon."

"I want to see, too." Erin stomped her foot, scowling.

"Erin, don't argue with me. I said to ..."

Paula's voice faded as Jamie grabbed her arm and squeezed it hard.

"Look," he whispered. "Somebody's coming."

Paula's first thought was that it might be Jesse and Geoff, but as the two figures glided into view, she saw that was impossible. Neither of them were short or gray-skinned. Neither had a bulbous, pumpkin-shaped head with two large eyes, a small slit of a mouth, and an almost non-existent nose. Neither of them had elongated arms, or creepily long fingers.

But these new arrivals did.

Both of them held slender, metallic rods with blue-lighted tips. The devices reminded Paula of a magician's wand, and for one brief moment, she thought of Bob. Then the figures pointed the wands at them, and Paula felt a tingle run through her body. It felt as if her limbs were asleep. She tried to turn her head toward Erin, tried to warn her to run, but she couldn't. She was paralyzed. She desperately tried to flex her muscles, but to no avail. Her body ignored her commands. Unable to do anything but breathe—and even that barely—she simply stared in horror as the two emotionless figures approached. She fought to turn her head again, knowing that Erin was probably frantic, and hoping that she could reassure her daughter, but her body remained frozen in place.

Paula's heart pounded, one of the few remaining parts of her that seemed capable of movement. As the figures closed the distance between them and approached the shelter, she tried to scream, but couldn't. Instead, she had to let her pulse rate do it for her.

━━━

"Hey!" Tod yelped. "It's really getting hot! Get me the fuck out of here."

H, Scott, Mark, and Leigh pulled with all their strength, planting their feet in the barren, ashy soil, but the football coach remained stuck. The volume of the mechanical sound increased, changing pitch and tone. Now it reminded them all of a jet engine, building up to take off.

"H!" Tod shouted. "Listen to me ... I need you to tell Suzin that I love her, okay?"

"Don't think like that," H replied. "We're going to—"

The ground shook beneath them. Trees swayed back and forth. The noise increased. Leigh shouted something but the others couldn't hear him.

Then, Tod arched his head skyward and screamed.

His skin began to turn pink, then red. Tiny wisps of steam or smoke curled up from below him, winnowing their way between the sides of the shaft and his body. His eyes grew wide as his skin began to blister. The shaking grew severe, and all of them suddenly found it difficult to stand upright.

Mark grabbed Leigh's arm and pulled him away, pointing at the jungle. Leigh shook his head adamantly, but Mark tugged harder. Tod's mouth remained open wide, shrieking, but all they could hear was that whine from below. His shirt began to smolder. Scott stumbled backward, gaping in shock. H teetered, watching in horror. Mark and Leigh clambered aside, struggling not to fall. Then, Tod burst into flame. His clothing blackened, and his skin sizzled and smoked, before sloughing away. Something popped inside of him, spraying the ground with steaming gore. The air filled with the smell of roasting meat. A moment later, his charred remains plummeted down the shaft, and a gout of fire exploded from the opening, shooting skyward. Scott, H, Leigh, and Mark cowered, shielding their eyes and peering through their slightly-parted fingers. The flame flared like a roman candle, and the temperature in the clearing began to rise. The four men scurried back, unable to look away.

After a few minutes, the fire sputtered and then began to die down. As it did, the noise from below and the shaking subsided, as well. Finally, the flame disappeared, and the jungle fell silent. Scott, H, Mark, and Leigh stood gasping for breath, and gaping at one another. Tears stained the ash on H's face. Leigh leaned over, retched, and then vomited onto his shoes.

"Oh my God," Scott murmured. "Oh my God ..."

They all turned as one and glanced back at the shaft. The metal edges glowed with heat, and tendrils of smoke curled up from the opening. The smell of charbroiled meat hung thick in the air.

"Guys," Mark panted. "What ... the ... fuck ... just ... happened?"

———

CHRIS HAD NEVER KNOWN terror like he felt in that moment. He'd made his peace long ago with being a quadriplegic who couldn't walk and couldn't feel anything below his armpits, but now, he couldn't feel himself at all. His shoulders, neck, and head were just as paralyzed as the rest of his body. And yet, he was still aware—horribly aware. He could still think and still feel horror and despair.

It's finally happened, he thought. *I need to die. I need to die right now. I can't go on like this.*

He fought with himself, struggling to twitch his shoulders or turn his head, but they refused to obey. He tried to cry out in alarm, but his mouth wouldn't open. He couldn't even swallow. He realized then just how much he'd taken that ability for granted. Only his eyes still worked, and he wished they didn't, as he gawked at the figures approaching them.

The creatures were aliens. There was no denying it. They looked exactly like the stereotypical gray aliens he'd seen perpetuated in television, prose, and film. They wore black one-piece uniforms that ran from their feet up to their necks, leaving only their hands and heads uncovered. The garments had no discernible writing or markings on them. Chris focused on the wands in their hands. The devices reminded him of police batons, except shorter and slighter. The tips glowed with a blue light. He was certain it was these devices that had caused the paralysis.

The low, monotonous hum continued to thrum through the ravine. Chris's ears popped, as if from a change in air pressure, and his eyes began to water. He suspected the sound came from the direction of the silver glow, but he couldn't be sure. The only thing he was positive of was that Paula and Erin were just as frightened as him. He knew that, because he saw his own fear mirrored in their frozen expressions. Jamie was beyond his line of sight, but had Chris been able to turn his head, he was sure the tall man would be terrified as well.

The aliens stopped a few feet away from them, and stood still. One cocked its head to the side, studying them with those huge, black, emotionless eyes. Then, surprisingly, it spoke.

"None of you should be here."

Chris heard the voice on two different levels—aurally, but also telepathically. It had the distortion of an echo, but the words were clear and strong.

"Your arrival was by accident, but you should not be here. It is forbidden."

Chris got the sense—based on the way the statement was phrased—that the aliens were responding to something, yet he'd heard none of his companions speak.

Who are you, he thought. *Why are you doing this to us?*

"Long ago," the alien answered him, "your kind became like us, knowing good and evil. It was decreed that you must not be allowed to reach the tree of life and live forever. And yet here you are, on the outskirts of the Garden. We are simply doing His will."

I don't understand, Chris thought. *What garden? And whose will?*

"None of you should be here," the alien repeated, "but she cannot be here. She will be needed elsewhere. And thus, we have come to correct things."

The creatures turned back toward the silver light, offering no further explanation. Chris watched, helpless, unable to cry out or even blink, as Erin began to follow them. Her expression seemed dazed, but more surprised than afraid.

"No, Paula Beauchamp. We cannot do that."

Chris realized that the alien was responding to Paula's thoughts, as well.

"She will be returned safely. She will remember nothing that occurred after your arrival here. She will grow to be taller than you, and happy, and go on to do an important thing."

Hey, Chris thought, as hard as he could, trying to shout with his brain. *Hey, you fuckers. Bring her back!*

The aliens didn't reply. Nor did they turn to acknowledge him, and somehow, that was even worse than the total paralysis. Chris watched helplessly as they led the little girl along the floor of the ravine, walking swiftly toward the silver glow. Still unable to turn his head, he flicked his gaze to Paula, and what he saw in her frozen expression broke him.

Paula Beauchamp was shrieking with her eyes.

The silver light grew stronger, seeming to blot out their surroundings. Erin and the aliens disappeared into its center. Then, the glow faded and the light was gone. Their paralysis vanished with it.

Paula's distraught screams echoed through the jungle.

"Just try going a little bit longer, mate."

"Fuck you," Chris grunted through clenched teeth. He leaned to the side in his wheelchair, relieving the pressure on the back of his legs by leveraging on his elbow and raising his ass up, in an effort to prevent bedsores.

"That's not nice," Leigh countered.

"You're not my personal trainer."

"Keep that up and I won't be gentle with the catheter."

"Do we even have any left?" Chris asked.

"Catheters?" Leigh's eyes flicked to Mark, and then back to Chris. He smiled. "I'm sure we do."

"You're both lying."

Shrugging, Mark turned from the entrance to the shelter and walked over to them. "Okay, you want the truth. We're down to one spare."

"Why didn't you guys tell me?"

"Because we didn't want you to freak out," Mark admitted. "I was thinking maybe we could make you one."

Chris stared at him, incredulous. "Make me a catheter? Out of what?"

"I don't know. Reeds or some shit. Plastic straws."

"You ... you're going to stick a plastic straw in me?"

"Well, it's not like there's a medical supply company nearby, Chris. But we'll figure something out."

"Reeds? You mean, like plant reeds? Bamboo? Are you insane?"

Mark sighed. "I don't know, bro. I'm just thinking out loud."

"Well, please don't. You're freaking me out even worse."

H snuffled and coughed in his sleep at the rear of the shelter. Mumbling, he rolled over onto his side and began snoring again.

"Okay," Leigh said to Chris. "Let's try your other side for a while. You want to rest first?"

Panting, Chris nodded.

Leigh turned to Mark. "What were you looking at, mate? Standing there in the door like that?"

"Hmmm ...? Oh ..." Mark shrugged again. "I was worried about Paula. She's been out there for ... a while."

"If we're counting days by our sleep cycles," Leigh replied, "then she's been out there two days by my count."

"Has she eaten anything? Had water?"

"I don't know," Leigh admitted. "Scott tried talking to her a few times. So did Jamie and Geoff. They didn't have much luck."

"How's Jamie's ankle?" Mark asked.

"Better," Leigh said. "The swelling went down and he can put his weight on it again."

Nodding, Mark turned his attention back to Paula.

"H tried to help her, too," Chris said. "He took her some dinner yesterday. She didn't respond to him. He said she acted like he wasn't even there. She just sat, staring at that same spot."

"Did she eat?" Mark asked again.

"I don't think so."

"Are you going to try to talk to her?" Leigh asked.

"Yeah. Keep an eye on the campfire for me?"

"You've got it," Leigh replied. "Go easy with her, okay?"

Nodding, Mark grabbed a bottle of water and a plastic bag full of berries and walked outside. The campfire glowed, crackling softly, barely more than sparks. They'd constructed a ring of stones and managed to get it going, but the only cigarette lighter among them was low on fuel, so Scott had suggested they keep it going at all times. Mark added some more dead wood, and stirred up the ashes with a stick. As the flames began to grow, he walked on.

The camp was deserted. Scott, Geoff, Jamie, and Jesse had gone to further investigate the mysterious shaft that Tod had met his grisly fate in. Scott had a theory that if it was indeed intelligently designed and manufactured—and all evidence indicated that it was—then it might be a way out of their predicament, or at least provide clues as to where they were and how to get home again. By this point, Mark had pretty much conceded that the answer to one of those latter questions was fairly simple. They'd been abducted by aliens. Several of the passengers on the shuttle had reported seeing bright lights before the crash. The clock and GPS functions on their electronic devices had malfunctioned. And Erin had been kidnapped right out of the camp by two Gray beings that Chris and Jamie had described as aliens. Mark had read enough Whitley Strieber books and watched enough episodes of *The X-Files* to know an alien abduction. That's what this was. For reasons unknown to them, aliens had beamed up their shuttle bus, brought it here to this jungle, and then dropped them off. The only things that mattered now were what to do if the aliens returned, and how to get home before they did.

Dead leaves crunched under his feet as he approached Paula. If she heard, Paula gave no indication. She simply remained sitting, hunched forward, staring at the spot where—according to Chris and Jamie—the aliens had disappeared with her daughter.

"Hey, Paula? Care if I sit down for a minute?"

She didn't look at or acknowledge him.

"I'll take that as a yes. Cheers."

Sighing, Mark sat down beside her, making sure not to sit too close and violate her personal space or freak her out. When she didn't react, he relaxed a little. For a long time, they simply sat in silence. Then, Mark spoke softly.

"I'm sorry about your daughter."

Paula stiffened, but still didn't respond.

"My son ... Alex. I'd go ape-shit if something happened to him. He's twelve. Just a little older than ... Erin?"

Her posture remained tense, but Mark saw her nod an almost imperceptible affirmation.

"Yeah ... I can't ... I just can't even fucking imagine what you're going through. We don't know each other very well. Shit, I guess we don't know each other at all. But I want you to know that I'm willing to help you find her and get her back. Because if it was my little boy, I'd want someone to help me, too."

He paused for a while, and listened to the sounds of the jungle. Then he drank a sip of water and continued.

"Everyone is so worried about us. Freaking out about how we can escape from here. But you know who I'm worried about? I keep worrying about the ones back home. The people we left behind. Does that make any sense to you?"

Paula shrugged. Again, the gesture was slight, but Mark felt encouraged nevertheless.

"I don't know. What I say inside my head and what other people hear are different sometimes. It's like my son, Alex. This might not be the best story, but it's something that only me and him share. I've never told it to anyone. I mean, my wife, Lisa, not even she knows about it. Alex and I are best pals and we do a lot together. Baseball games, Legos, play video games ... shit like that. You know what I mean when I say pals? I'm not sure if that's an East Coast thing or not."

"I'm from Michigan," Paula whispered.

Mark stifled a smile, and tried to conceal his excitement at this breakthrough.

"Wicked," he replied, nodding. "I know most of my peeps say bud or friend, but I always used pal and pally in my vocabulary. But I digress. So, when he was younger, Alex suffered from a severe speech delay. When most kids are learning words and combining words, he had only a few words in his vocabulary and the rest was kid gibberish and not much eye contact. He pointed a lot and we taught him some sign language. He saw a speech therapist weekly, and me and Lisa were always teaching him."

Paula shifted slightly, turning to look at him out of the corner of her eye.

"Anyhow," Mark continued, "when I'd get home from work every day, I'd always say, 'Hey Alex, who's best pals?' and he'd answer with something like 'Gahbee-in-geeb.' It was all one long, quick, gibberish phrase. And then he'd give me a big hug. It was our own little daily ritual between everyday life shit. 'Who's best pals?' 'Gahbee-in-geeb.' Big hug."

Mark paused and wiped his eyes. When he spoke again, his voice cracked.

"It was one of my favorite parts of the day and I cherished it, and then—one day—for no reason in particular, this huge realization struck me. We said our 'Who's best pals?' 'Gahbeeingeeb.' And then I asked him, 'Alex, are you saying Gahbee and Geeb?" And he nodded yes. So, I asked who's Gahbee? And he pointed to me. And who's Geeb? And he pointed to himself. I said, 'are you saying Daddy'? And he lit up and pointed saying, 'Gahbee! Gahbee!' 'And does Geeb mean me?' And he pointed to himself with excitement saying 'geeb!' 'geeb!' All that time, Gahbeeingeeb was Daddy and me."

Paula turned to fully look at him.

"Well, just this overwhelming rush of emotions came over me. My heart was breaking, because I know in his mind he heard himself saying 'Daddy and me,' but what came out was different. And at the same time, my heart was overflowing with such love for him. That love that, well you know, that only parents can ever feel for their children. The kind that can't be measured by any means. It was a special moment with just me and him. No one else. Maybe my most special moment with him."

"Do you guys still say it?" Paula asked.

Mark smiled. "We do! That's the best part. Like I said, he's twelve now, and we still have the same mantra to this day. 'Who's best pals?' 'Gahbee and Geeb.' 'Who's Gahbee and Geeb?' 'Daddy and Me.'"

"That's some story."

"Well, it might not be the most exciting story. Lol. But it's the only one I've never told anyone until now."

"Did you really just say 'Lol'?"

"Yeah."

"Why are you telling me this?"

"Because sometimes what's in our heads and hearts doesn't come out right. And what's in mine right now is that I want to get back home to my little boy, and my wife ... but I wouldn't feel right doing that if your little girl is left behind. So, I'm going to help you find her."

Paula's lip quivered. "Erin is one of the most generous and loving people I know. She would give a total stranger her last dollar. And now she ... they took her ... and ..."

She began to shake with rage and grief. Mark reached out and gently put one arm around her shoulders.

"I know," he whispered. "I know. But we'll figure out where

they took her, and we'll get her back. I promise. But you've got to promise me you'll eat and drink something first. Can you do that?"

Sniffling, Paula sat up again and wiped her nose with her hand. She nodded. Then her expression grew dour again.

"Mark, you need to know up front ... I'm going to kill anyone who gets in my way."

"You'll get no argument from me on that." He stood up, and held out the water and berries. "I brought you these."

Paula accepted them, and smiled up at him. "Thank you, Mark. Thank you for ... everything."

"You want to come back to the shelter? Everyone is pretty worried about you."

"Tell them I'll be okay. But I want to stay here a little while longer. I'm not quite ready to be social."

Mark nodded. "Fair enough."

"Can you promise me something else?"

Mark frowned, puzzled. "Sure. What's that?"

"You've got to promise you won't say Lol ever again."

"I can do that," Mark said, laughing out loud.

G eoff's stomach grumbled as he turned his makeshift spit over the campfire, roasting a ... well, he wasn't sure what the animal was. Neither were any of the others. It was the same size and shape as a squirrel, but its eyes were bigger and its tail was a nub. H had proclaimed them safe to eat, and that was all that mattered. The aroma of cooking meat filled the air, but he was alone in appreciating it. Everyone else was asleep. Even Paula had finally returned to the shelter, and while she still wasn't talking much, at least she'd come out of her trance.

He wondered if the smell would rouse any of the others. He kind of wanted this snack just for himself, and he didn't need everyone bitching at him for not rationing. Although, in truth, he suspected some of the other castaways weren't hungry enough yet to eat the small creature. Many of them had commented on its eyes, and how thoughtful and intelligent they had appeared to be. Geoff had to admit, the thing was cute, when still alive, but the berries and the leftover junk food from the shuttle bus just weren't enough for him. He needed—craved—meat.

Geoff pulled his stick away from the fire and brought the smoking carcass toward him. The formerly pink and glistening skin was now blackened and seared. He gingerly tore off a piece, burning his fingertips in the process. Wincing, he blew on the morsel and then examined it. The meat looked well done. Without waiting for it to cool, Geoff popped it into his mouth and chewed. It was delicious. He closed his eyes and sighed. His mouth filled with saliva. Swallowing, he pulled off another piece and began to devour it.

Then, something rustled above the ravine. Geoff paused, mouth still full of half-chewed meat, and glanced up at the ridge. Branches swayed, and the rustling sound was repeated, closer this time. Startled, it occurred to him that the smell of roasted meat might attract other predators. Moving slowly, he laid his meal on the ground and picked up a spear instead. Then he stood. His knees popped, sounding very loud in the silence. He realized just how still the jungle had become. Gone were the bird songs and the drone of insects and the occasional distant roar. The only sound now was that ominous rustling.

"Shit," he whispered.

The branches parted and a figure stepped out of the foliage, peering down over the edge.

"Oh my God," the new arrival gasped.

Gaping, Geoff swallowed his mouthful. "Legerski?"

The man's eyes widened. "Do ... do you ... know me? How do you know me?"

"Don't you move, man. Don't you fucking move. Just stay right there."

"Please," Legerski replied. "I need help. I don't know what's happened to me."

"Stay there," Geoff repeated, trying to make his tone sound more forceful. He glanced at the entrance to the shelter. "Scott! Everyone! We've got company!"

"Please ..." Legerski held his hands out, palms extended. "I need help. I'm hurt ... and hungry."

"Save it, man."

Geoff heard people stirring inside the shelter, and the murmur of confused voices. Not waiting for them, he hefted his spear and began to climb up the embankment. Legerski watched his ascent, blinking. Geoff thought that the man appeared dazed —or possibly injured. His face had several ugly bruises, and dried blood crusted his lip and ear. His clothing was torn and dirty, and there was debris—seed pods, twigs, and other detritus—in his tangled hair.

Legerski wobbled on his feet. "Where am I? Can you tell me what's going on?"

Not answering, Geoff finished the climb and raised the spear with both hands, pointing it at Legerski's abdomen. The frightened man raised his arms higher, and yelped. Voices rang out from below. Geoff glanced down quickly, and saw the others emerging from the shelter. He turned his attention back to Legerski.

"Don't try anything, you sick fuck. Get down there. Slowly."

"T-try anything? Look, I don't know what's happening here, but I ..."

"Move it," Geoff demanded.

"Are you going to kill me?"

"No," Geoff replied. "I'm not going to kill you, even if you deserve it. But I'm damn sure not letting you get away, either."

"What do you—"

"Shut up." Geoff prodded him with the spear tip. "I said move it."

Legerski began to cry. Shoulders slumped, he inched forward, slinking past Geoff, and began the descent. The others had all grabbed weapons of their own now, and they ringed the bottom of

the embankment, waiting for him. Geoff saw anger on their expressions—as well as fear and uncertainty in a few. Even Paula had
joined the throng, albeit standing silently in the back, clutching a
spear with two trembling hands. Her lips were pressed tightly.

"Go on," Geoff urged as Legerski faltered. He prodded him
again with the spear. "Just keep moving."

"Please," the killer sobbed. "Please, I don't mean any of you
harm. I just ..."

"Is that what you told Bob and Gregorio?" Jamie shouted. "Is
that what you said before you killed them?"

"I don't know anyone named ..."

Jesse stepped forward. "Shut up, killer."

"Please, I didn't mean to kill him ... but he was trying to
kill me!"

Jamie snorted. "Gregorio was trying to kill you? That's not
what I saw, asshole!"

"I don't know any—"

"Enough." Geoff pushed his spear tip into Legerski's back.
"Now move, goddamn it."

Legerski stumbled to the bottom, and the others surrounded
him. Geoff noticed that the jungle was still silent. Worse, there
was no breeze down here in the ravine, and he became aware of
just how badly they all needed a shower. The hand sanitizer and
baby wipes they'd salvaged from the wreckage of the shuttle just
weren't cutting it.

"Get down on your knees," Scott ordered. "Right there in
front of that boulder. And I swear to God, if you try anything, we
will kill you."

Legerski seemed too distraught to argue. Instead, he simply
sank to the ground, moaning in terror. Geoff felt a momentary
vicarious thrill in having helped inspire that emotion in the
deranged man, and then immediately felt guilty about it.

What's happening to me? he thought. *To us? This is like* Lord of the Flies.

They used thick vines to bind Legerski's wrists together behind his back. Then they used more to secure his ankles, legs, and arms. When they were satisfied that he was tightly fastened to the boulder, they stepped back.

"Who are you people?" the prisoner groaned. "What are you going to do to me?"

"You'll be treated far better than you deserve," Scott said.

"Fuck this," Mark said. "What's with the whole amnesia act, Legerski? You gonna claim you're crazy now?"

"Obviously, he's crazy," H replied. "The real question should be, is he, in fact, responsible for his crimes?"

"Somebody help me," Legerski whined. "I want to go home. I want to be with Shannon."

Jamie scowled at him. "Bob and Gregorio wanted to be with their families, too."

"I don't know Bob or Gregorio," Legerski wailed. "I don't know any of you people! All I know is that I ended up here, and there was a guy who looked exactly like me, and he attacked me, and—"

"Shut up, asshole," Mark said.

"And he tried to kill me," Legerski shouted, ignoring the taunts. "It was self-defense. What was I supposed to do—let him kill me? I need help!"

Geoff nudged Scott. "What are we going to do with him?"

"Let's all discuss it," Scott suggested. "Over by the fire."

"He got free before," Chris said. "He could do it again."

Scott shook his head. "He's not slipping out of those knots. And even if he did, we'd catch him before he got away."

Chris frowned. "I'm not convinced. I'll watch him while you guys talk. If he starts to move, I'll call out."

Scott shrugged. "Fair enough."

Geoff followed the others over to the campfire. When they were all positioned, Scott looked at each of them.

"So ... obviously, we can't let him go. He'll just hide out there in the jungle and kill someone else. You think that's what he was doing when you spotted him, Geoff?"

"I don't know," Geoff admitted. "I wasn't really paying attention. He just sort of ... appeared. He seemed confused. And frightened."

"Probably just an act," Mark argued. "He was gonna try to lure you in."

"If he's mentally ill," H said, "which I think we can all assume is a probability, then his confusion might not be an act. He may genuinely have no memory of the crash or his crimes."

"His crimes?" Leigh cleared his throat. "Sounds like we need a court and a judge and jury."

"You need a jury to tell you that killing people is wrong?" Jamie asked.

"No," Leigh replied. "I'm just saying ..."

"We can't let him go free," Scott repeated. "And not just because of the danger he presents to the rest of us. In his condition, he'd be a danger to himself, as well."

"So, what do we do with him, then?" Leigh asked.

"Are you kidding me?" Mark thrust the end of his spear into the dirt. "We kill the motherfucker!"

"How does that make you any different from him, mate?"

"Because I'm not some crazy murdering asshole, Leigh. He admitted that he killed them. We've got witnesses, too."

"He didn't admit to killing Bob or Gregorio," Leigh argued. "He said it was someone who looked like him, and he claimed it was in self-defense."

Mark growled. "For fuck's sake, don't tell me you're siding with him?"

"I'm not siding with anyone," Leigh protested. "But I don't

think we should just start killing people, either, no matter what they've done. Haven't we lost enough people already?"

"We have," Jamie agreed. "But as long as he's around, we risk losing more."

Jesse raised his hand. Scott nodded at him.

"Anybody notice that Legerski's clothes are different?" Jesse asked.

They all glanced at the captive, and then back to Jesse.

"I didn't," Geoff admitted, "although I did notice it looks like he's been in a fight."

Jamie shrugged. "So, he changed clothes since the last time we saw him. Big deal. He could have found his suitcase at the crash site."

"Or," Jesse said slowly, "he could be telling the truth. Maybe he isn't Paul Legerski at all."

Mark snorted. "Oh, come on."

"He answered to his name," Geoff pointed out.

"Yes." Jesse nodded. "But his demeanor, personality, and actions are entirely different from the guy we all met. And like Leigh said, he claims he met and killed another version of himself. What if ... this isn't our Legerski, but a different Legerski?"

"Bullshit," Mark scoffed.

"I've got to agree," H said. "I'm not for killing him, or any of that eye for an eye crap. But I also don't believe he's some sort of mirror universe version of himself."

"Is it any more implausible than aliens or dinosaurs?" Leigh asked.

"It doesn't matter," Scott said, raising his voice. "We can debate all of this later. For now, we just need to figure out what we're going to do with him. Personally, I say we keep him captive."

"Agreed," Leigh said. "If we kill him, we're no better than he is."

"I'm with you guys," Jesse said.

"I'm not." Mark shook his head. "I vote we put him out of his misery."

Jamie nodded quietly.

Scott turned to Geoff. "What about ...?"

He trailed off, and the others all followed his gaze. Geoff turned, and saw that Paula had left their council, and had instead crossed the campsite. She clutched her spear in both hands.

"Hey," Geoff called, hurrying after her. "Hey, Paula!"

If she heard him, the redhead gave no indication. Instead, she stalked faster, pausing only to sidestep Chris's wheelchair.

"Chris!" Scott yelled, "stop her!"

Geoff broke into a run, shouting Paula's name. Instead of turning to look at him, she raised her spear and thrust it into Legerski's chest. He drew in breath to scream, but all that came out of him was a high-pitched, keening wheeze. His eyes were wide with shock and pain. Wordlessly, Paula leaned into her shaft, pushing the weapon deeper. As Geoff closed the distance between them, he heard the tip of her spear scrape against the boulder.

"Oh, shit ..." Chris gasped.

Geoff reached Paula's side. He barely heard the footfalls of the others racing up behind him. Instead, he reached out cautiously and touched Paula's elbow. Her posture was stiff, and her expression remained impassive—almost serene.

"Hey," Geoff whispered. "Easy now, Paula."

"Oh, Jesus Christ ..." Chris murmured.

Legerski's blood welled up around the stick protruding from his chest. More poured from his gaping mouth. His eyes seemed to plead with them. He coughed twice, sputtering. Then he was still.

The others reached them, and gathered around, stunned and breathless.

"Is he ..." Scott began to ask, but the rest of his question was drowned out by the sound of a second new arrival.

━━━

LEIGH FROWNED, puzzled when he heard the hydraulic whine behind them. He'd been staring in horror at Paula's act of murder, too numb and stunned to notice much else. The scariest part was the expression on her face. It was the look of a woman who had nothing left to lose.

She's lost her daughter, he thought. *Would I act any differently if somebody had stolen my Erin?*

Then the sound grew louder, and he turned around to see what was making it, and saw something far more startling than the distraught mother's expression.

A robotic vehicle of some sort cruised slowly above the ravine floor, hovering a few feet above the ground. It rounded the curve in the cliff walls and approached them, gradually slowing its speed. The thing was perhaps the size of the shuttle bus that had brought them here, but instead of wheels, it was equipped with six round thrusters of some kind. The units were affixed to its undercarriage and emitted some sort of air or energy. Leigh glimpsed leaves and dirt swirling beneath them. The metal hull was painted red, but the color had faded in spots, and there were blotches of rust and dirt all along the body, as well as a number of sizable dents. A small satellite dish rotated slowly atop the robot, nestled between two slender antennas. The unit had windows on each side as well as its rear, but although they were dirty, none of them seemed broken or cracked. Leigh wondered if they were made of something other than glass.

Mark tugged his elbow, whispering. "The fuck is that?"

Leigh shrugged. "I don't know, mate."

"There's lettering on the side." Jesse pointed. "But I'm not sure what it means."

"It's Korean," Scott told them.

"What does it say?" Geoff asked.

"I'm not sure," Scott admitted. "I've been to Korea on business many times, and I can speak a little Korean, and read a little, but not enough to know what that says. I think it might be a company name?"

The vehicle slowed to a stop in front of them and hung motionless in the air. Lights flashed along its side, as it sank lower to the ground. Finally, it hovered mere inches from the dirt. It emitted a mechanical hum and then a door slid open on its side. The interior was brightly lit, and Leigh glimpsed seats and a computer terminal.

"It's some sort of transport," he guessed, stepping toward the door.

Mark grabbed his arm again. "Better stay back, pal."

"If it was going to attack us, I think it would have done so already. I'm checking it out."

Before anyone else could protest, Leigh approached the door and peeked inside. Now he was certain, based on the interior layout and decor, that it was some type of transportation vehicle. The computer terminal flashed, but he couldn't make out what was on it from his vantage point.

Swallowing hard, he closed his eyes and stepped inside the bus.

When nothing happened, he opened his eyes and took another step. Slowly, he approached the computer terminal, which was affixed near where the driver would sit, except that he saw no seat for a driver, and no steering wheel or other navigational equipment.

Hearing footsteps behind him, Leigh turned and saw Mark

and Scott getting onboard, as well. The others clustered around the doorway. Even Paula had now turned her attention to the strange arrival. After a moment, a second door slid open near the robot's back end, and hydraulics whirred as a ramp was extended in Chris's vicinity.

Mark grinned. "Hey, look at that, Chris! It's even handicap accessible. Come on."

Chris shook his head grimly. "Fuck that. I'm not getting on that thing. You guys be careful."

"Yeah," H echoed. "Don't mess around."

"It must have some kind of sensors," Scott suggested. "How else would it have known that Chris needed a ramp?"

Mark frowned. "So, our campsite is a bus stop?"

"Maybe." Scott shrugged. "Or maybe it just sensed us standing there and stopped automatically."

"The real question," Leigh said, as he leaned toward the computer terminal, "is where did it come from, and where can it take us?"

Leigh peered over the top of his eyeglasses at the screen. It reminded him very much of an electronic bank teller machine, except the text was in Korean. Then he noticed, in small type at the bottom right corner, instructions for English, Spanish, French, and German. He pressed a corresponding button, and the text on the monitor changed to English. It said:

```
PLEASE SELECT YOUR DESTINATION
Seoul
Busan
Incheon
Daegu
Daejeon
Gwangju
```

Mark peered over Leigh's shoulder, jostling him. "What does it say?"

"It's a list of cities, mate. It says please select your destination."

"Wicked! Anywhere in Ohio? Or Boston, even?"

"Why those two?"

Mark shrugged. "I'm from Boston, originally. I live in Ohio now. Or, at least ... I did."

"Well, all of these locations are in Korea."

"Fuck it. That's okay. Korea is better than here."

Leigh turned to him. "Mark, do you really think this thing will take us to Korea?"

His friend's expression sank. "Well, we should at least try. We can't leave until we find Paula's daughter, but some of the others could get home and send back help."

Scott had wandered away, exploring the rest of the bus.

"There's a skeleton back here," he called. "I suspect this thing has been trapped in this place longer than we have."

"But there's no dust inside," Mark said. "It's fucking spotless."

"Yeah," Leigh countered, "but the outside is pretty banged up. Maybe it has some sort of interior cleaning system."

"Let's just try," Mark urged.

Leigh shook his head. "I've seen that movie, *Last Train to Busan*. I know what happens."

"It's just called *Train to Busan*," Mark corrected him. "Now, come on. Press one of the cities and see what happens."

Leigh glanced back at Scott, who shrugged.

"Might as well," he said, "although I still think the key to understanding what has happened to us is down in that shaft that Tod fell in."

Leaning forward again, Leigh selected Seoul. The screen flashed, and the text disappeared.

"What happened?" Mark asked. "Did you break it?"

Before Leigh could respond, a new message appeared.

WE ARE UNABLE TO PROCESS YOUR REQUEST AT
THIS TIME.

OUR SINCERE APOLOGIES

Sighing, Leigh tapped another button and returned to the main screen. Then he noticed another prompt, which allowed the user to switch to voice control. He pressed this, and was presented once again with a range of language options. He selected English once more, and the screen went blank.

GREETINGS, COMMUTER. WELCOME ABOARD. PLEASE
STATE YOUR DESIRED DESTINATION.

The voice was female, but undeniably mechanical. In many ways, it reminded Leigh of the Siri artificial intelligence on Apple's smart phones.

"Wicked pissah," Mark whispered.

I'M SORRY. PLEASE STATE YOUR DESIRED DESTINA-
TION AGAIN.

"S-Seoul," Leigh stammered, and then added, "Please?"

I APOLOGIZE. MY NAVIGATION EQUIPMENT IS
CURRENTLY MALFUNCTIONING. NORTH IS MISSING. MY
NAVIGATION EQUIPMENT WILL NOT FUNCTION PROPERLY
UNTIL NORTH RETURNS.

Scott hurried back up the aisle. Outside, the others crowded into the doorway, listening to the conversation.

"I'm sorry," Leigh said. "Did you just say that north is missing?"

THAT IS AFFIRMATIVE.

"I was right," Scott whispered. "It's stuck here, just like the rest of us."

THAT IS AFFIRMATIVE. PLEASE STATE YOUR DESIRED DESTINATION.

"Can you ...?" Leigh trailed off, frowning. He tried to think of a suggestion. "Can you take us to our crash site?"

I'M SORRY. THAT DESTINATION IS UNKNOWN.

"Oh!" Mark raised his hand in excitement. "Can you take us to where the aliens come from?"

"PLEASE DEFINE ALIENS."

"You know, the little gray-skinned guys with the big heads?" Leigh elbowed him in the ribs. "Be serious, mate."

AFFIRMATIVE

DESTINATION CONFIRMED. PLEASE USE CAUTION WHILE BOARDING THE TRANSPORT. MIND THE GAP.

Leigh, Scott, and Mark stared at each other, wide-eyed. Then they turned to the doorway. The other's expressions mirrored their own.

"Wait!" Leigh waved his hands back and forth at the

computer. "Um ... could you tell us a bit more about that destination? I'm not sure everyone wants to go there."

AFFIRMATIVE. REQUESTED DESTINATION WAS ...

The voice ceased, and was replaced momentarily with a whirring, static sound. Then a recording of Mark's voice piped out of the unseen speakers.

"Where the aliens come from? You know, the little gray-skinned guys with the big heads?"

The recording stopped, and the computer's voice spoke again.

DESIGNATION, ALIENS. THEIR ACCESS POINT IS THE GARDEN.

"A garden?" Scott stroked his goatee. "And where is this garden?"

THE GARDEN IS LOCATED AT THE FOUR HEADWATERS OF PISHON, GIHON, TIGRIS, AND EUPHRATES.

"Tigris and Euphrates?" Leigh frowned. "So, you can take us to the Middle East?"

NEGATIVE

"That's from the Bible," H said, pushing into the doorway. "She's talking about the Garden of Eden."

"But the Tigris and Euphrates are rivers in the Middle East," Leigh replied.

"The computer said the alien's access point was this garden," H reminded them. "What if there is some sort of dimensional doorway or rift near the Tigris and Euphrates rivers back on Earth?"

Scott shook his head. "I don't like it. How do we even know this thing is functioning properly?"

I'M SORRY. MY NAVIGATION EQUIPMENT IS CURRENTLY MALFUNCTIONING. NORTH IS MISSING. MY NAVIGATION EQUIPMENT WILL NOT FUNCTION PROPERLY UNTIL NORTH RETURNS. THEN MY ORIGINAL ROUTE WILL BE RESTORED. UNTIL THEN, I PROVIDE ALTERNATE DESTINATIONS TO THE BEST OF MY ABILITY.

"Can you give us a minute?" Leigh asked the transport.

AFFIRMATIVE.

Leigh motioned at them all to disembark. The rest of the group backed away from the door. One by one, they filed off the robotic shuttle and joined the others in a circle.

"I don't like this," Scott repeated. "This thing shows up ... supposedly from Korea, but I'd bet money it's not from any Korea we're familiar with."

"You mean like an alternate universe?" Jaime asked.

"Possibly," Scott replied. "Or maybe the future. And now it's talking about the Garden of Eden ... the whole thing is crazy."

"No crazier than anything else we've seen," Jesse argued.

"This is a different kind of crazy," Scott insisted. "If we get onboard this thing, there's no telling what could happen to us. We're better off here."

Jesse scoffed. "Tell that to Colinda and the others."

"Yes, we've lost some people here," Scott agreed, "but we've got food, water, and shelter. We leave those behind if we get on this ... robot. Not to mention you asked it to take us to the aliens.

Do we really want to encounter them again? I vote we stay here, and continue figuring out how to get down inside that shaft."

"I don't know about that." Chris eyed the robot warily. "But this thing scares me. I'm not going on it."

The others began to chime in on the debate. Leigh watched Mark glance at Paula, and then turn back to the transport. Before he could stop him, Mark walked back up the stairs.

"Hey," Leigh called. "What are you doing, mate?"

Mark waved him off and approached the computer. "My friend out there ... the aliens took her daughter. Do you know where they would have gone with her?"

NEGATIVE.

"But you said all of these aliens come from the garden?"

AFFIRMATIVE. THEIR ACCESS POINT IS THE GARDEN, LOCATED AT THE FOUR HEAD—

"Yeah, yeah. I got it. The four rivers." Mark turned back to the rest of the group. "Paula? I think this is the way to find Erin."

She nodded. "Agreed. Let's get our stuff."

"Wait a minute," Scott called. "We should all stick together, guys."

Mark clambered back down to the ground, and he and Paula strode off toward the shelter. Blanching, Leigh hurried after them.

"What are you doing, mate?"

"I promised Paula I'd help her find her daughter. This is the best way to do that."

"You don't know that, Mark!"

"He's right," H pointed out. "For all we know, that machine could be damaged—the robotic equivalent of Legerski."

Mark stopped and sighed. Ignoring them, Paula entered the shelter. Chris wheeled up to join them. The others kept their distance, letting the four friends talk alone.

"Guys," Mark said, "this is something I have to do. Not just for her or myself, but for Alex. If we get back home, how could I look at him knowing we left another little kid behind?"

"But," Leigh replied, "you don't know that you'll find her this way."

"No," Mark agreed. "I don't. But I damn sure know we're not going to find her at the bottom of that hatch."

"Scott thinks that hatch might be the way home," Chris said.

Mark shook his head. "Was it the way home for Tod? That poor fuck got cooked alive, and you guys want to climb back down inside that thing? No way. I'll take my chances on the robot. And Chris, how would you even get down inside the shaft?"

Chris's expression darkened.

"Hey." Leigh pressed his finger against Mark's chest. "You don't need to be cruel, mate."

Mark hesitated. "You're right. I'm sorry, Chris. That's not what I meant to say. It sounded different in my head."

"It's okay."

"Look ... you guys are my pals. Come with me?"

All three looked at him.

Mark pressed. "Chris, maybe we can find medical stuff for you. Hell, maybe we can find a way back home!"

"I'm not getting on that thing," Chris said.

"You don't want to get home, and back to Francesca?"

"I do," Chris said. "I want that more than anything, but goddamn it, Mark, this isn't the way. You didn't see those aliens. I did. Climbing aboard this metal taxi and letting it deliver us to them doesn't seem like the way home to me."

Mark turned to Leigh. "How about you, pal?"

Leigh sighed. When he tried to answer, a lump formed in his throat. He turned away, removed his glasses, and wiped them on his shirt. When he placed them back on his face, they were smudged worse than before.

"I'm staying with Chris. And you should, too. We started this trip together. We should stay together now."

"I can't." Mark's voice cracked. "Don't you guys understand? I just can't. I don't want to wait here to die. Helping Paula ... it's like helping myself. And my son."

Leigh, Mark, and Chris all looked at H.

"I don't know what to do," he confessed. "I'm not crazy about this plan of going to the aliens, but I also don't like the idea of you and Paula going by yourselves."

Jesse walked over to their group. "We couldn't help but overhear. I'll go with you, if you want. Watch your backs."

"You sure?" Mark asked.

Jesse nodded. "It's like you guys said earlier—if we fell through a hole in our world, maybe there's a corresponding hole around the Tigris and Euphrates. And if not ... better that than sitting around here waiting to die."

"You don't even know if it's our Tigris and Euphrates," Chris said. "That thing is definitely not from our Earth."

Jesse shrugged. "All I know for sure is that I can't sleep. Every time I close my eyes, I see what happened to Colinda over and over again. Every time a bird squawks out there in the jungle or a dinosaur roars ... it reminds me where we are and I remember everything that's happened. And then I think about her again. I can't stay here."

Mark stuck out his hand. Jesse shook it.

"Thanks for coming."

"Sure thing, man."

Blinking back tears, Leigh turned to the rest of the group.

"Hey." Mark clapped him on the shoulder and squeezed. "It's gonna be okay, pal."

Sighing, Leigh nodded.

Paula emerged from the shelter with her and Mark's luggage. Everyone gathered around.

"Jesse's coming with us," Mark told her.

"Do you want to get your stuff?" Paula asked the new recruit.

"No." Jesse shook his head. "I'm okay. Most of my stuff is still back at the crash site."

"Are you sure you guys want to do this?" Scott asked.

All three nodded.

"Okay," Scott replied. "If we get home, we'll tell people."

"We'll do the same," Mark promised. "We'll send help ... tell your families where you are."

"Good luck," Geoff said. "I hope you guys find her."

"Be careful in that shaft," Mark advised.

Paula climbed onboard the transport. Jesse said his goodbyes and followed her. Mark hesitated, staring at Leigh.

"Go on," Leigh muttered. "We don't know how long that thing will wait. Don't want to miss your flight."

He stuck out his hand to shake. Grinning, Mark pulled him close. The two hugged, fiercely. Then Mark hugged H and Chris, as well. Finished, he got into the shuttle and turned to wave.

Leigh noticed that his grin had vanished. His expression was fearful.

"Safe travels, mate."

WELCOME ABOARD. PLEASE STATE YOUR DESIRED DESTINATION.

"The Garden," Paula answered.

PLEASE STAND BACK WHILE THE DOORS CLOSE. MIND
THE GAP.

The transport's hydraulics began to whine, kicking up dirt
and leaves beneath it once again. Then, the doors slid shut and
the machine began to rise straight up into the air. It crested the
top of the ravine and floated up past the treetops, where it
hovered for a moment. The whine grew louder, and then
changed into a deep, throbbing hum. Leigh craned his neck,
trying to catch a glimpse of Mark, but all he could see was the
robot's undercarriage. Then, the transport flew away.

The group watched until it vanished from sight. Then they
looked at one another.

"I don't know about the rest of you," Geoff said, "but I'd like
to finish eating."

"Yeah," Jamie nodded. "I could eat. Maybe we should bury
Legerski first?"

They began to file back to the campfire. Leigh hesitated. H,
pushing Chris's chair, stopped and turned.

"You coming, Leigh?"

He shook his head. "I'll be along in a bit."

"Okay." H turned away and pushed Chris over to the rest of
the group.

Leigh stood alone, staring at the sky, and thinking about his
wife and daughter, and wondering if he'd made the right
decision.

J esse placed his hand against the window and watched the landscape zoom by below them. It was impossible for him to judge their speed, but he suspected it was very fast. He caught a brief glimpse of the fateful pond he and Colinda had discovered, and then it was gone. Jesse felt a strange surge of relief. Then he glimpsed the wreckage of the airport shuttle, before it, too, vanished.

"I wonder how fast we're going?" Mark asked, echoing his thoughts.

OUR CURRENT SPEED IS ONE HUNDRED AND FORTY-FOUR RI. OUR ESTIMATED TIME OF ARRIVAL IS THREE HOURS AND SEVENTEEN MINUTES.

"What's a Ri?" Mark asked.

TWO POINT FOUR FOUR MILES OR THREE POINT NINE TWO SEVEN KILOMETERS.

Jesse did some quick math in his head. "So ... we're traveling around sixty miles per hour."

"Wicked," Mark replied.

Paula stared silently out a window on the opposite side of the vehicle. Jesse wondered what was going through her head. Her fingers and clothing were spattered with brown crusts where Legerski's blood had dried.

"I'm gonna crash," Mark said, rubbing his eyes.

NEGATIVE. ALL SYSTEMS ARE FUNCTIONING PROPERLY.

"I mean I'm going to sleep, computer." Mark stretched out between two of the seats, used his luggage as a makeshift pillow, and closed his eyes.

Jesse turned his attention back to the sights below. As the transport skimmed over the dense jungle, he saw things that alternately surprised, startled, puzzled, or frightened him. A herd of long-necked dinosaurs grazed among the treetops. The rest of their massive bodies were concealed beneath the clustered foliage. He glimpsed two different villages, both set in clearings amidst the jungle. The first was seemingly deserted. The second was occupied, though he couldn't tell if the diminutive figures were human or simply humanoid. A third clearing contained what appeared to be a bubbling, smoking crater—perhaps a lava pit? A fourth clearing held a small pyramid, carved out of some type of black stone—possibly obsidian? The sunlight seemed to glance off it.

"We're not the only people here," he muttered.

Mark snuffled slightly, and Jesse realized that their companion had already fallen asleep.

"Why would we be?" Paula asked. "They've probably been pulling people in and out of here for centuries."

"Who?"

"The aliens."

"How can you be sure they're behind all of this, though?"

"I'm not," Paula admitted. "But after I get Erin back, maybe we can get them to confess to everything before I choke the living shit out of them."

She turned back to her window. After a moment, Jesse did the same.

They flew over a large lake. Birds flitted over the surface, and he saw some tiny silver flashes as fish leaped into the air and then plunged back into the water. On the bank, something that looked like a cross between a giant crab, a giant scorpion, and a giant lobster lumbered onto the shore, flashing a massive pair of serrated pincers and waving around a segmented, stinger-like tail. Jesse shuddered.

The jungle continued to flash by below. He saw a robot the size of a construction crane cutting down trees, and two smaller, dump-truck sized robots trundling along behind it. Their path seemed to originate from a massive crack in the middle of the jungle. The fissure's size reminded him of the Grand Canyon. Steam rose from the trench, drifting through the trees. A red light flashed rhythmically in the canyon's depths, but he couldn't see its source. He glimpsed a few more villages, and what looked like the ruins of a temple, but he couldn't determine if they were occupied or not.

Eventually, the jungle gave way to forest. The transition wasn't noticeable at first, but then he noticed the change in topography. The trees were different, and not as dense. The ground was still concealed, though, beneath thick undergrowth. He caught a glimpse of what looked like fighter planes, and saw several more villages, and then a series of dwellings constructed among the treetops. Hairy, ape-like figures occupied these latter structures, pointing at the transport in wonder.

"Hey," Jesse yelled, fascinated by these beings. "Can we stop? I'd like a closer look at those."

NEGATIVE. THIS IS NOT AN AUTHORIZED STOP.

"Well, where is an authorized stop, then?"

THE NEXT AUTHORIZED STOP IS THE ANUNNAKI CITY. DO YOU WISH TO CHANGE YOUR DESTINATION?

"No," Paula said. "Take us to the Garden, please."

AFFIRMATIVE.

"Anunnaki ..." Jesse frowned. He'd heard the word some-where before, but couldn't remember how.

He didn't know how much time passed, but eventually, the forest began to thin. The transport emerged above grasslands. Jesse was awestruck by the beauty. Wildflowers of every imagin-able color blossomed throughout the waving stalks. Elephants, giraffes, cattle, horses, and other wildlife were abundant, as well as animals he could have never imagined. Jesse glimpsed some-thing that looked like a cross between a horse and a centipede, and a herd of what appeared to be six-legged sheep.

"A unicorn!" Paula turned to him in excitement. "I saw a unicorn!"

"Where?" Jesse glanced below, but saw something that looked like an elephant with octopus tentacles for trunks.

"It was down there," Paula insisted.

"Oh, I believe you. I do."

"Wicked," Mark muttered, his eyes still shut, and then shifted positions.

"Erin would love this," Paula said.

"Maybe we can show it to her on the return trip," Jesse suggested.

Paula didn't respond. Her momentary excitement was gone, and her dour mood had returned. Jesse considered making some kind of joke, to try to ease her tensions, but decided against it. He turned back to the window, but not before spotting the skeleton out of the corner of his eye. He wondered just how long it had been onboard the shuttle. He cleared his throat, intending to ask the computer, but then thought better of it.

The grasslands soon ended, but not before they glimpsed a writhing mass of giant worms, coiling and flexing in the sunlight. Then the transport flew out over a vast, windswept wasteland of rocks and boulders, canyons and fissures, natural spires and craggy cavern mouths. The inhospitable terrain was completely barren. Jesse saw no bodies of water, not even a pool or stream. The only visible vegetation was an occasional stunted, scraggly, leafless tree jutting up from the hard-packed desolation.

"The geology of this place is wrong," Jesse mused. "Jungle side-by-side with forest. Then the grasslands give way to this hell-hole. It's like ... somebody put together a jigsaw with pieces of different puzzles."

"Maybe," Paula suggested, "the land came from somewhere else, too. If the aliens—or whatever force was responsible, but I think it was the aliens—brought us here, then maybe they brought different biomes, as well."

"But why?"

Paula shrugged. "Who knows? Just to mess with the prisoners here? Maybe it's a cosmic zoo, or a reality television show for people in another galaxy, or some kind of screwed up science experiment."

The barren plain stretched on all sides, seemingly endless. After watching the monotonous landscape for a while, Jesse stifled a yawn. He considered trying to follow Mark's lead and take a nap,

as well, when he finally spotted a break in the terrain. Far ahead
were a series of jagged stone spires and crags, thrusting toward the
sky like skeletal fingerbones. He wondered if they were naturally
formed or intelligently designed. Before he could study them
further, the transport changed direction. The stone structures fell
away to the rear. Jesse glanced downward again and gasped.

Far below them lay a vast, bowl-shaped depression about half
a mile deep and possibly a little less than a mile across. At first, he
thought it might be an impact crater left over from an asteroid
strike, but the walls of the depression seemed too smooth for that,
and were covered with cave mouths. Shockingly, the interior of
the basin held a small city composed of tall, spiraling towers that
appeared to be carved from stone, and sprawling buildings fashioned from bricks and rocks. These structures fringed a football-
sized courtyard, as well as a series of smaller, dome-shaped buildings. Several crude mud huts had been built on the far end of the
courtyard, away from the city. And in the center of the courtyard,
there was a massive black pit. The city bustled with activity.
Hundreds of humanoid figures scurried about.

Jesse was just about to ask the computer where they were
when Mark stirred. Yawning, he sat up and blinked sleep from
his eyes.

"Are we slowing down?" he mumbled. "It feels like we're
slowing down."

AFFIRMATIVE. WE ARE APPROACHING THE ANUNNAKI
CITY.

Jesse could feel it now. Not only were they slowing; the craft
was losing altitude. He glanced out the window again, and
yelped. He could see the figures clearly—and they weren't
human.

Paula sprang back from her window. Her expression was alarmed. "They're snake-people! We can't stop here. Keep going!"

NEGATIVE. THIS IS AN AUTHORIZED STOP ALONG THE ROUTE. I AM REQUIRED BY MY PROGRAMMING TO STOP FOR ALL PASSENGERS.

Jesse hurried over to Mark and Paula.

"We've got to do something," he whispered. "What if some of those things get onboard?"

"How do we know they're hostile?" Mark asked. "Maybe they're friendly. Hell, maybe they can help us."

"And maybe they'll eat us," Jesse countered. "They're snake-people, dude!"

CHANCE OF NEW PASSENGERS BOARDING IS MINIMAL.

Jesse glanced up at the speakers. "What? Why?"

PASSENGERS NEVER BOARD IN THE ANUNNAKI CITY. THEY ENGAGE IN VANDALISM AND ATTEMPT INTER-FERENCE.

"They ... attack you?"

AFFIRMATIVE.

Jesse slapped his palm against his forehead. "Then why do you stop, for fuck's sake?"

THIS IS AN AUTHORIZED STOP ALONG THE ROUTE. I

AM REQUIRED BY MY PROGRAMMING TO STOP FOR ALL
PASSENGERS.

The transport now hovered over one of the stone towers. The
building's roof was flat, and broad enough for the robot to land
on, but a group of snake-men stood atop it, armed with crude
bows. As Jesse watched, they fired arrows at the vehicle. He
ducked instinctively as the missiles bounced and broke harm-
lessly against the hull and windows.

EVASIVE MANEUVERS ENGAGED. PLEASE TAKE
YOUR SEATS.

"Oh, shit ..." Mark slumped back down again. "I should have
stayed asleep.

Paula sat beside him, tense and alert. Jesse took a seat on the
opposite side and glanced around helplessly.

"Doesn't this thing have seatbelts?"

EVASIVE MANEUVERS ENGAGED. WE APOLOGIZE FOR ANY
INCONVENIENCE. PLEASE STAND BY.

Jesse felt, rather than heard, a pulse of some kind, emanating
from the transport's exterior. A blue light flashed, and the snake
men fell backward, tumbling off their feet. Then, the robot took
flight again, soaring upward and once more increasing speed.

"This is fucking crazy," Mark said.

Jesse and Paula nodded.

After a while, Jesse sensed that they had leveled out again.

"Is it safe for us to move about the cabin?" he called.

AFFIRMATIVE.

Getting slowly to his feet, he walked back over to the window. Mark and Paula followed him. The three passengers stood side-by-side, watching the landscape whip by below. At last they reached the end of the wasteland, and approached a mountainous region with white, snow-covered peaks. The transport rose higher, skimming over the mountaintops. The wildlife was scarce here, save for a few birds and a group of unidentifiable, white-furred creatures. Jesse thought they looked like apes, but Mark and Paula insisted they were more bear-like.

They glimpsed another pyramid structure, half-buried in the snow. This one seemed to be carved from granite, rather than obsidian, and the top of it had broken off at some point. Snow filled the cavity, concealing the interior.

On the other side of the mountains, another series of grasslands and plains awaited them. In time, these gave way to a sand-choked desert—small, but just as unforgiving as the stone plain had been. Then, another series of mountains appeared on the horizon.

"Who built all this stuff," Jesse wondered again, "and why?"

PLEASE TAKE YOUR SEATS. EVASIVE MANEUVERS
ENGAGED AGAIN.

"What?" Jesse glanced around. "I don't see anything out there. The city is—"

A shadow fell over the transport, blocking out the sunlight. Jesse, Mark, and Paula all looked up as a monstrous pterodactyl dropped out of the sky. Talons outstretched, it veered toward the robot.

WE APOLOGIZE FOR ANY INCONVENIENCE. PLEASE
STAND BY.

Again, Jesse felt the pulse. The sky filled with bluish light, and the pterodactyl shuddered as if it had flown into an invisible wall. Its wings flapped helplessly as it careened backward and then tumbled from the air. Jesse watched in astonishment as it plummeted to the sand far below.

"Hey," Mark called. "What kind of weapons are you using?"

THIS SHUTTLE IS EQUIPPED WITH SIX PULSE CANNONS, GLOBE MANUFACTURING MODEL X V ONE V X.

"Globe?" Jesse turned to the others. "The Globe Corporation? We have them back on our world."

"Weren't they in the news last year?" Paula asked. "Something about an ecological disaster in Mauritius?"

"No," Mark replied. "That was Alpinus Biofutures. They paid a huge fine. Biggest ever levied against a company. But you're right, Jesse. Globe exists back on Earth—but unless they've kept it hidden, they don't have any technology like this."

They turned back to the window again and watched. The transport traveled on, zooming across varying biomes, and each passing mile brought more questions.

But no answers.

Jesse's thoughts wandered. He thought about home, and about what he'd be doing right now. He thought about his bandmates. Harvey and John, and wondered what they were up to. Whatever it was, it probably didn't compare to this.

"What if ..."

Mark and Paula turned to him.

"What if what?" Mark asked.

Jesse shook his head. "Never mind. It's stupid."

"No," Paula encouraged him. "Go ahead. What were you going to say?"

"Well ... what if the folks back home ... the people on Earth?

What if they don't know we're missing? What if, like, time is different here, and they don't know we're gone yet?"

For a minute, neither of them replied. Then Paula shrugged.

"Erin's missing. That's all I know. I'll deal with everything else once we get her back."

OUR CURRENT SPEED IS ONE HUNDRED AND SIXTY-FIVE RI. OUR ESTIMATED TIME OF ARRIVAL IS TWO HOURS AND FOUR MINUTES.

"Could be worse," Mark said.

"How's that?" Jesse asked.

Mark grinned. "We could be in a car that can't go a hundred and sixty-five Ri per hour. We're making great time. Plus ... pulse cannons, pal. Pulse cannons. We've got fucking pulse cannons!"

Jesse snickered, and then laughed.

After a moment, Paula did, too.

S cott sat by the crackling fire with Jamie, Geoff, H, Chris,
and Leigh. None of them had been able to fall back asleep
after the robotic transport's departure, so they'd eaten together
instead. H, Chris, and especially Leigh had seemed sullen, so
Scott had suggested they splurge on the junk food, handing out
extra rations. When that didn't lift their spirits, conversation had
turned to the worst jobs each of them had ever held—but talk of
home only seemed to increase their dejection.

A slight breeze stirred through the ravine, blowing the smoke
from the campfire directly into Scott's face. It also stirred up the
dirt and leaves on the ground. His eyes watered, and his nose
burned.

"I don't know why that wood is smoking so much," H mused.
"It's not wet."

"Maybe it's a different kind of wood," Chris suggested.
"Some type of tree that we don't have back ... home?"

H shrugged his shoulders and nodded.

Coughing, Scott turned away from the smoke, and caught
sight of Legerski's corpse, which was still tied onto the boulder,

with Paula's spear still jutting from his chest. The blood on his clothes had dried brown.

"Jamie was right earlier," he said. "We ought to bury Legerski with the others."

"Not with the others," Chris argued. "That doesn't seem right or fair. I'll be dead soon, and I damn sure don't want to be buried near that psycho."

Leigh gasped. "That's no way to talk, mate."

Chris snorted. "Why not? This place is not conducive to my condition. I'm out of the medical supplies I need. My chair is low on power. It's just a matter of time, now. I'm not happy about it, but I don't see any other outcome."

"We'll get you help," Leigh insisted. "Mark had an idea about making you some catheters."

"And now he's gone," Chris replied. "We're not going to see Mark again."

"You don't know that," H said.

"And you don't know that we will," Chris shot back.

"Well ..." Geoff swallowed a mouthful of potato chips. "You can't just give up. That robot was pretty advanced, technologically. We figure out a way to the bottom of that shaft, maybe we'll find similar things. If so, there has to be something down there you can use. Power for your chair, at the very least."

"Great," Chris scoffed. "You guys can power it up and use it for a wheelbarrow after I'm dead."

"No offense," Scott said, "but I'm already depressed enough. You're not helping. I get that you guys are worried about Mark. I get that you're worried about yourselves, and your loved ones back home. But just giving up isn't the answer."

"I'm not giving up," Chris argued. "I'm just accepting the inevitable. How many people have died since we got here? We suck at survival."

Nobody answered him. Scott found his gaze drawn back to

Legerski again. He considered Chris's tone and inflection, and what he'd said. He did indeed sound like a man who had accepted the inevitable ... but Scott thought he also sounded like he hadn't made peace with it. If they could convince Chris to tap into that anger, maybe they could spur his will to live and to fight a little while longer.

Scott opened his mouth to respond, but then stopped himself. Did it really matter? Didn't he have enough to worry about without prodding Chris to keep up the good fight, as well? If the guy wanted to die, why get in his way? After all, it wasn't like he really knew any of these people. Perhaps, he reasoned, he'd be better off without all of them—maybe striking out on his own and trying to get rescued that way.

Scott pursed his lips, deep in thought, and then decided that he was being an asshole.

His head began to throb again.

"Chris," H said, and then paused, as if reconsidering what he was about to say.

"Yeah?"

"When you ... when you first became ... paralyzed ... did ..."

"Oh, just spit it out, already, H!"

"I don't want to offend you, man."

"I know my situation. I'm not some fragile little glass thing."

H pressed on. "When you first ended up like this, did you feel the same way you do now?"

Chris glanced down at the ground and sighed. "Yeah ... yeah, I did."

"Well, what brought you around then? What gave you hope?"

"Francesca."

H nodded.

"Well," Leigh said, "we can do the same for you, mate!"

Chris snickered. "No offense, guys, but none of you are her."

"Then you need to stay alive until you get back to her," H countered.

Chris sighed again, clearly exasperated. "Haven't you been listening? Don't you think I want to get back to her? That's all I want ... but I'm running out of time here, guys. Face facts. I'm going to die."

"I'm going to live," Scott announced, slowly getting to his feet. "You guys debate all you want, but there's work to be done, starting with Legerski. Yes, he was an asshole. A murderous psychopath. Now, he's just dinosaur bait. We should get him in the ground. Somebody want to give me a hand?"

Geoff nodded. "Sure. Just let me piss first."

Jamie stood up. "I'll help, too."

"It's funny," H murmured, staring into the crackling flames. "We sit around this fire, despite the heat of the jungle and despite the fact that it's never dark here."

"And despite the smoke," Leigh added.

"That, too." H nodded. "I guess we do it for comfort. But what is it about fire that's so comforting?"

Scott opened his mouth to respond, but before he could, something snorted in the jungle. All of them glanced at each other, startled, and then looked up at the top of the ravine. The leaves and undergrowth rustled as something crashed through them. Then it snorted again.

"An animal," Scott whispered. "Get your weapons ready."

The snorting changed to a series of soft sniffing and grunting sounds. Then, slowly, a figure emerged at the top of the ravine.

H moaned. "Son of a bitch ..."

Scott gripped his spear and stared in wonder.

It was a baby dinosaur—possibly a *Tyrannosaurus Rex*, although he couldn't be sure. Despite their peril, and the danger

of the situation, Scott couldn't help but be fascinated by the creature. The infant stood about eight feet tall, and he estimated it
probably weighed a little over three hundred pounds. Walking on
its hind legs, the juvenile sniffed along the edge of the ravine,
obviously attracted by either their food or the scent of Legerski's
blood. It snorted in surprise when it saw them. Then, cocking its
head to one side, the creature made a loud, excited croaking
noise. It edged closer, standing on the very rim of the chasm.

"It can't get down here," Leigh said. "Right?"

"No," Chris agreed. "There's no way it could climb
down the—"

The soil at the top of the ridge gave way. With a frightened
squawk, the dinosaur tumbled down into the ravine, followed by
a small avalanche of dirt, rocks, and leaves. It crashed to the
bottom and rolled three times. Then it cried out.

And was answered from above.

"Oh fuck," H gasped. "That sounds like mommy dinosaur."

The ground shook. They heard trees splintering and
toppling. Another mighty roar echoed through the forest. Scott
was stunned by how loud it was. The baby answered, croaking
and mewling in alarm. Footsteps pounded, coming closer. Each
thud sent more dirt and rocks hurtling to the bottom of the ravine.
The juvenile clambered to its feet, shook its head, and called out
again, swiping its tail back and forth in agitation.

Then, its mother appeared at the top of the ravine. Her
massive, towering frame blocked out the sun, and a shadow fell
over the campsite.

"She definitely can't get down here," Leigh said, breathless.

The *Tyrannosaurus* cocked her massive head and hissed. She
looked at her offspring, and then at them. Grunting, she waved
her tiny forearms in agitation. Then, she leaped.

"Goddamn it, Leigh," Chris squealed. "Stop jinxing us!"

The adult hit the ground like a bomb, and Scott struggled to maintain his balance. A huge cloud of dirt swirled around her. She bent her head, snuffling her baby. The infant mewled, nuzzling her. Snorting, the Tyrannosaurus turned back to them and glared balefully. It made a low rumbling noise in its throat that made Scott's skin prickle.

"Get in the shelter!" Jamie screamed.

"No!" Scott yelled. "That's a dead end! We'd be trapped."

"Everybody just stand still," Geoff whispered. "It's like Jurassic Park. Their vision is based on movement. Right?"

They each froze, trembling, as the dinosaur continued to stare at them. Then, it swished its massive tail back and forth, raised its head, and roared.

"I don't think she's seen Jurassic Park," Chris said.

"Up the side of the ravine!" Scott shouted. "Move your asses!"

H, Leigh, and Jamie fled toward the embankment. Chris motored along behind them. Scott and Geoff remained where they were, spears raised.

"You're not thinking about fighting this thing?" Geoff asked.

Scott shook his head. "No. I'm just too scared to move."

Geoff pushed him hard. Scott staggered, stumbling back and forth.

"Go!" Geoff shouted.

For one terrifying moment, Scott thought he might fall over, but he recovered his balance, and they ran. The sides of the ravine shook, and rocks rained down on them. Scott glanced over his shoulder and screamed. The Tyrannosaurus was in pursuit. He was shocked by the dinosaur's speed. The creature's bulk was deceptive. Its powerful leg muscles writhed as it charged after them.

Scott and Geoff reached the embankment on the other side.

Jamie was already at the top, shouting at the others to hurry. H and Leigh struggled valiantly to get Chris's wheelchair up the slope. Chris yelled at them to leave him behind.

"I'll carry him," Geoff panted. "Just climb, goddamn it!"

Scott glanced over his shoulder again. The dinosaurs had paused in their pursuit. The juvenile sniffed curiously at Legerski's corpse, while the adult paced, looking at them and then back to its offspring. The behemoth snapped its jaws, hissing. Talons clawed at the dirt.

As Leigh and H scrambled to the top, Geoff bent over to pick up Chris.

"Can you grab around my neck?" Geoff asked.

"This is pointless," Chris said. "I can't go anywhere without my chair. Somebody would have to carry me around the jungle from now on."

"Now's not the time to argue about it," Scott urged. "Just do what Geoff says."

Behind them, the Tyrannosaurus growled, low and throaty. Then it plodded forward, moving slowly, stalking, seeming to relish the chase.

"Leigh," Chris cried. "H! Tell Francesca that I love her. That she was the best thing that ever happened to me."

"What?" Leigh lunged toward the slope, but H grabbed his arm and yanked him back.

"She taught me how to live," Chris said. "Remind her of that!"

"Come on, Chris," Scott pleaded. "You don't have to do this."

"Yes, I do. I'm out of meds. Sooner or later, a pressure sore or a bladder infection is going to do me in. I don't want to suffer or be a burden. Francesca taught me how to live. This place has taught me how to die."

"Fuck this," Geoff said.

The big man reached for Chris again, clearly intending to

pick the quadriplegic up and throw him over his shoulder, but despite his condition, Chris was faster. He reversed the chair, backing up out of Geoff's reach. Then he spun it around and drove directly toward the oncoming dinosaur. Pausing, the Tyrannosaurus cocked her head and stared at him in bewilderment.

Leigh and H screamed, distraught.

Scott felt a hand grip his arm. He turned and saw Geoff, grabbing him.

"Come on, Scott. Let's go. If he wants to die, let's make sure it's not for nothing."

Shaking his head, Scott allowed Geoff to lead him up the embankment. He slipped and stumbled amidst the loose soil, and was wet with sweat and tears by the time they reached the top. He heard the dinosaur roar below him, but he didn't turn to look. He didn't need to.

His companion's expressions were horror enough.

Then came the awful sounds.

Chris shrieked once—a high-pitched warbling gurgle—but it was cut mercifully short.

"Please," Jamie sobbed. "Let's go. Let's just go!"

They ran, fleeing back into a forest they'd sought shelter from only days before.

▭

"It's still back there," Leigh gasped.

H tried to answer him, but he lacked the breath. His lungs felt like they were on fire, and his pulse hammered in his throat and head.

I'm going to have a stroke, he thought. *Right here, on this spot. This is where I die. Stroke or heart attack. Fuck me ...*

Images of Chris's death flashed through his mind—his friend

holding up his one good arm in a futile effort to ward off the predator, the Tyrannosaurus ducking its head and the massive jaws enclosing both the wheelchair and its occupant, Chris's muffled shriek, that came from inside the beast ... and then that awful moment of silence before the chewing sounds began.

"We should split up," Jamie panted. "Maybe we can confuse it."

Scott shook his head. "No ... stick ... together ..."

I can't, H thought. He wanted desperately to say it out loud, but he didn't have the strength. *I can't keep going. I'll sacrifice myself next.*

He forced himself onward, realizing with sudden surprise that he'd fallen to the rear of the procession. The dinosaur's roars had faded somewhat, but it was still back there, plodding along in determined pursuit. He heard saplings snapping and breaking as it pushed through the foliage. His head felt like it had when they'd first arrived in this place, and his ears began to ring as they had after the crash. Except that this time, he hadn't banged his head. Maybe he just reacted badly to being chased by dinosaurs? H started to laugh at his own gallows humor, and then doubled over in pain as a cramp squeezed his abdomen.

Leigh glanced back at him, panicked. "You okay, mate?"

H shrugged, mouth agape, and blinked sweat from his eyes. Then he nodded.

They raced on, and the dinosaur relentlessly pursued them. The ground began to slope downward, and the trees thinned out, becoming shorter and slenderer. H spotted a grove of lush multi-colored ferns, and imagined what it would be like to simply collapse in them. Then he remembered where they were, and decided that the ferns were probably poison or carnivorous.

Soon, they reached a clearing and their descent grew steeper. The trees disappeared completely, replaced with thick stands of shrubbery and undergrowth.

"There's a valley up ahead," Scott called.

Geoff, now in the lead, darted toward a narrow game trail that winnowed between two boulders.

"This might throw it off," he called.

"I hope so," Jamie breathed. "Because there's no trees here to slow it down."

They ran single file down the steep and narrow path. After a short descent, the undergrowth cleared and they emerged into the valley. All five men stopped, desperately gasping for breath. H sank to his knees, groaning. It occurred to him that the ground felt odd. When he glanced down, he saw why.

"What ... the fuck ...?"

A mind-boggling assortment of socks—gym socks, dress socks, footy socks, children's and baby socks—blanketed the valley floor from one side to the other. Some of them looked brand new. Others were obviously weather-beaten and worn. Weeds jutted through in some sparse places, but most of the vegetation was buried beneath the pile.

The dinosaur roared, single-minded.

"Jesus," Geoff muttered. "Give up already, and go eat Legerski."

Leigh boggled at the ground. "What is this place?"

"No ... time ... to figure it out." Scott straightened up and pointed. "The forest continues on the other side. Come on. Maybe we can lose it there."

Groaning, he trotted off across the valley. Jamie, Geoff, and Leigh followed. H struggled to raise his head, and watched as they waded through the multi-colored landscape. The socks came up to Leigh's knees, deep enough to ...

H's eyes grew wide, as an idea struck him. He couldn't keep going. It was pointless. But maybe he didn't have to.

He burrowed through the socks, digging like a dog burying a bone, and then lay flat on his back. Then, he used his arms to scoop the socks overtop himself, not stopping until he was completely covered and could no longer see the sun. It was hot, and musty, and hard to breathe, but he stayed still, and focused on staying conscious.

I'll just catch my breath. Just wait here and rest a bit. After it passes me by, I'll come out and circle around. Find the others. If the dinosaur doesn't get them ...

"H!"

The voice was Leigh's, but it was muffled and distorted beneath the layers of cloth.

Go, H thought. *Just keep going, damn it ...*

"He fucking disappeared?" H thought that might be Jamie, but it was difficult to be certain.

He heard them frantically yelling for him.

He heard the determined dinosaur, drawing closer now.

Then, he heard them shout at each other to run.

H waited, biting his lip and struggling not to cry. The Tyrannosaurus plodded into the valley. He couldn't see it, but he could hear it—the stuttering, staccato growls, and the steam-kettle wheezing. The plodding footfalls. The scrape of its tail against the ground. The way the socks seemed to collectively shudder as it plunged into their midst, stomping and gnashing.

He took a deep, shuddering breath, and held it.

His pulse quickened, throbbing in his throat.

He suspected the socks might have confused the Tyrannosaurus. He heard it grunting and snuffling, but quieter now.

H waited, lips quivering, eyes scrunched into slits, paralyzed with fear, but grateful that he couldn't see the beast, and that it couldn't see him.

Unfortunately, he didn't see the dinosaur's foot, either, until it crushed both him and the socks into a leaking, jellied mess of flesh and fabric.

His next vantage point was from between the monster's

clawed toes, but what he saw confused him. H realized that he was staring down at the pulped remains of his own body, but his head was missing.

He wondered where it was.

Then he saw and thought no more.

WE ARE NOW APPROACHING YOUR FINAL DESTINATION. WE THANK YOU FOR YOUR PATRONAGE. PLEASE USE CAUTION UNTIL WE HAVE COME TO A COMPLETE STOP, AS CARGO MAY HAVE SHIFTED.

Paula stared, speechless as a dazzling bright light filled the horizon. It flashed, reflecting off the windows, and she held up a hand to shield her eyes. The radiance was almost physically painful. Spots danced in her vision. Paula blinked, then squeezed her eyes tightly shut, but the disturbance remained.

"Jesus," Mark yelled. "What's making that light? I can't see shit. What is it?"

The computer did not respond. Paula wondered if it was just as clueless as they were, or if it was electing not to tell them.

"It's brighter than the sun," Jesse mused. "But I can't tell what ..."

Paula parted her fingers slightly, and cautiously peered through them. The landscape below was breathtakingly lush and colorful, and more beautiful than anything she had ever seen. For one brief moment, she forgot all about Erin, all about her husband and the rest of her family, and just stared, overcome with wonder. Slowly, she raised her head, trying to find the source of the light. It was a structure of some kind, looming over the garden—indeed, over the entire biome—but it was too bright to discern clearly.

"I can't see," she said. "It hurts! Make it stop!"

THIS TRANSPORT IS EQUIPPED WITH PYROFLEX BRAND WINDOW TINTING CAPABILITIES. DO YOU WISH ME TO ENGAGE?

"Yes," Paula gasped. "Please. Engage!"

AFFIRMATIVE.

The windows darkened slowly, and the light—while still dominant—became bearable. She lowered her hand and looked outside. Jesse and Mark shuffled to either side of her and did the same.

"It's a sword," Jesse said, his voice awestruck.

"If that's a sword," Mark muttered, "then it belongs to King Kong. Or maybe God."

"It's not a sword," Paula said. "It's a cross."

"It's a sword," Jesse replied, "shaped like a cross ..."

In the center of the greenery was a massive, towering construct, bigger than any skyscraper she'd ever seen back on Earth. Paula realized that all three of them were correct. It resembled both a sword and a cross. If it was the former, then the point was thrust into the ground, and the hilt formed the top. Clouds drifted around this, breaking apart on its glimmering silver-white surface. Hovering above the sword was a second large structure—a shining trapezohedron. The latter seemed to levitate, having no support beams to hold it in place. The sun sat perfectly above both, shining directly down on them. This was the source of the light, Paula realized. The giant trapezohedron, bigger than any aircraft, seemed to absorb the sunlight and then blast it out all sides, as well as down into the sword itself.

"What is it?" Jesse asked. "Computer, what is this place?"

THIS IS YOUR FINAL DESTINATION, AS REQUESTED. THIS IS THE GARDEN.

The robot began to decrease speed and drift down toward the surface. Paula was about to prod it for more information, but before she could, Mark grabbed her arm and squeezed.

"Look!" His tone was harsh.

Paula turned to where he was pointing, and gasped. A small, wedge-shaped craft seemed to soar out of the sun and zoomed toward the gleaming trapezohedron. It slowed, and then hovered alongside the structure.

"Is that ...?" Jesse wobbled unsteadily on his feet. "Is that a flying saucer?"

"More like a flying triangle," Mark said, "but yeah, I don't think there's humans flying it."

"How do you know?"

Mark shrugged. "I don't, I guess. Just a hunch ..."

"They have her," Paula murmured. "Erin! She could be onboard that thing right now."

"Easy," Mark said. "We'll be on the ground soon. We'll find her."

The suspected alien craft continued to hover. Then, it eased forward and the trapezohedron shone brighter. Paula was reminded of a car pulling into a parking space. The light flashed, momentarily blinding them. All three gasped. When it faded again, spots danced in front of Paula's eyes. She searched the sky, but the unidentified ship was gone.

"It's some kind of portal," Mark guessed. "That diamond. It's a dimensional doorway or some shit. Maybe a wormhole?"

"I don't remember anything like this from science class," Jesse said.

"It's not a diamond," Paula corrected him. "It's a trape-zohedron."

"Whatever it is, it's a portal of some kind. I'd bet on it."

AFFIRMATIVE.

Paula turned to the computer. "You're confirming that ... that thing is a doorway?"

AFFIRMATIVE.

"Can you take us through it?"

NEGATIVE. I AM REQUIRED TO STOP ONLY AT AUTHO-RIZED LOCATIONS.

"Do you know if they took my daughter through there?"

THIS IS THE GARDEN, YOUR FINAL DESTINATION. WOULD YOU LIKE TO CHOOSE A DIFFERENT LOCATION?

Paula rushed forward, and pounded her fist against the moni-tor. "Answer me, you fucking thing! Where did they take my daughter? Where's Erin?"

YOU HAVE BEEN MY ONLY COMMUTERS ON THIS TRIP. I DO NOT KNOW THE LOCATION OF OTHER COMMUTERS.

"Can you fly us through that doorway?"

NEGATIVE. AUTHORIZATION DENIED.

"Is Earth on the other side of that portal?"
The computer paused.

AFFIRMATIVE.

Paula couldn't be sure, but she thought she detected a hint of uncertainty in the computerized voice—if such a thing was even possible.

"Hey," Jesse said. "We've landed."

AFFIRMATIVE.

Yes, Paula decided. That confirmation was much more confident than the previous.

The doors slid open with a hiss, and a wave of heat and humidity roiled into the shuttle. Mark's eyeglasses fogged over, and Paula felt herself begin to perspire.

"Why can't you fly us through that doorway?" she demanded. "What if we overrode your programming?"

NEGATIVE. THIS UNIT IS NOT EQUIPPED FOR COMBAT.

Paula frowned. "Combat? What do you mean? Does that thing have defenses?"

"We've got pulse cannons," Mark said.

"The structure," Paula said, gritting her teeth. "Can it defend itself, computer?"

AFFIRMATIVE. WE HAVE REACHED YOUR FINAL DESTI-

NATION. PLEASE USE CAUTION WHILE DISEMBARKING.
MIND THE GAP. HAVE A PLEASANT DAY.

"Fuck you!" Paula struck the monitor with her fist again.
"We're not done here. Tell me everything you know about
this place."

THIS TRANSPORT HAS A DESIGNATED ROUTE AND MUST
KEEP TO SCHEDULE. DEPARTURE CANNOT BE DELAYED.
THIS IS YOUR FINAL DESTINATION. ALL PASSENGERS
MUST EXIT AT THIS TIME. PLEASE USE CAUTION
WHILE DISEMBARKING.

Even in her rage, Paula noticed that this time, the computer
didn't tell them to mind the gap or wish them a pleasant day.

Shaking his head, Mark motioned to Paula. "Come on. This
thing's useless."

Paula hesitated. "It might know something about Erin ..."

"I think any answers we're gonna find are out there." He
cocked his thumb at the window. "Come on. Let's go find your
daughter."

He grabbed their luggage, grunting with the effort. Jesse
hurried over and gave him a hand. Then, the three of them
stepped down out of the shuttle and back onto solid ground. The
doors hissed shut behind them, and the transport began to slowly
rise back into the air again, with its lone, skeletal occupant. They
watched as it turned around, and then zoomed off in the direction
they'd just come from.

Paula noticed that here at ground level, standing amidst the
lush greenery, the light wasn't so overwhelming anymore. While
this area was certainly brighter than the jungle and ravine had
been, it wasn't unbearably so. She shielded her eyes again and
peered straight upward, craning her head back. The sun was

directly over them, as if the garden was its focal point. The shining trapezohedron floated beneath it, hovering in the atmosphere. And below that stood the sword, towering over the landscape. It occurred to Paula that the massive structure cast no shadow. She wondered how that was possible.

Jesse waved as the transport faded from view. "Next stop Anunnaki City, I guess. I'd hate to see what climbs onboard there. Glad we didn't get any closer to them than we did."

"So long, Blaine," Mark said. "You were a frigging pain."

"Blaine?" Paula asked.

He nodded. "Yeah. It's from Stephen King's *Dark Tower* books. Blaine is this robotic monorail—an artificial intelligence, but totally ape-shit insane. His tracks go through this post-apoca-lyptic landscape with monsters and shit. He takes the characters on a ride through Hell, basically."

Paula glanced around, surveying the greenery and smelling the various wildflowers and other aromatic plants.

"I don't think this is Hell," she said. "But maybe that shining trapezohedron can take us there."

"We'll find your daughter," Mark said gently.

Paula reached out, took his hand, and squeezed it.

"Gahbee and Geeb," she replied. "We'll find them both."

"What are you two talking about?" Jesse asked.

"About going home," Paula replied. "Let's do that."

She let go of Mark's hand and started off, pushing through the thick foliage, heading in the direction of the portal. Mark and Jesse followed.

SLAUGHTER OF THE SNAKE MEN

J amie sat with his back against a tree trunk, fighting a losing battle with panic. They'd stopped to rest—a decision forced upon them when Leigh suddenly collapsed, unconscious. That was when the panic began to well up inside him. Before that, he'd been operating on fear-driven instinct. Run from the dinosaur, hide from the dinosaur, run from the dinosaur again. But now that he had time to catch his breath and seriously consider their situation, that raw, primal terror had been replaced with a deep sense of dread.

"We've got no shelter." Jamie dug his fingernails into the tree bark. "No food. No water. We're lost. Hell, we're back to square one. Everything we did—all that we accomplished. We're no better off now than we were when we first got here."

"Calm down," Geoff insisted. "We'll be okay. We did it before. We can do it all again."

"How?"

Geoff shrugged, and then glanced at Scott, who knelt over Leigh, gently patting his face. The Australian's complexion was the color of cheesecloth, but his breathing—while shallow—was steady. Scott looked up at them. His expression was grave.

"Is he okay?" Jamie asked.

Scott nodded. "He just passed out. Fatigue or maybe shock, is my guess. His eyelids are flickering. He should come around in a minute. How are *you*, Jamie?"

"Scared shitless."

"We all are. But like Geoff said, we'll get through somehow."

"How?" Jamie scoffed. "You're the leader! What's your plan?"

Scott stood up. "I'm not the goddamn leader, okay? I don't even like people that much in general."

"You could have fooled me," Jamie said. "You've been the one caring for everybody else since we got to this fucking place. Have you taken any time for yourself?"

"No," Scott admitted. "I've been too busy trying to help us survive."

"Exactly! So, I'll ask again ... what's the plan? What do we do now?"

"I don't know!" Scott waved his hands in the air, stomping about in frustration. "I don't know what we do, other than try to stay alive and find a way back home. That's all I've got, man. That's it. If you want somebody to come flying down like Superman and save us all, it's not me. All I can do is what I've been doing, and try not to get any more of us killed in the process."

Jamie turned away from them, and focused on his breathing, trying to calm himself. He looked back when he heard Leigh begin to stir. Scott and Geoff knelt over him again, and helped the Australian sit up.

"Take it easy," Scott said.

Leigh blinked. "What happened?"

"You passed out," Geoff told him.

"Where's H and Chris and ..." Leigh trailed off, his expression changing. "Oh, that's right."

"You might be in shock," Scott said gently. "Just sit here for a bit."

"Is there any water?" Leigh asked. "I'm parched."

Scott stood up and shook his head. "It's all back at the camp. And I don't know where that is anymore."

Leigh began to quietly weep, his shoulders shaking with grief and frustration.

Geoff clambered to his feet. His expression was sour.

"You okay?" Scott asked him.

"Just feeling guilty," Geoff muttered.

"About what?"

"About Chris. We let him die. We just let it happen. We're no better than Legerski."

"Stop that," Scott said. "That's not helping. You heard what Chris said, before that baby Tyrannosaurus fell into camp. He was prepared to die."

"Well, Geoff is right," Leigh said. "You guys shouldn't have let it happen."

"Us?" Scott's complexion turned red. "Geoff was the one who tried to grab him. Maybe if the suicidal prick hadn't motored away—"

Leigh exploded. "That's my friend you're talking about, mate."

Jamie watched as the slight-framed Australian squared off against the bigger Floridian. Neither man was backing down. Geoff got between them, trying to push the two men away from each other before the situation grew any more heated.

Sighing, Jamie closed his eyes and turned away again. He was sick of fighting, sick of running. Sick of being scared. He wanted to go home. Wanted to see Lisa and Leslie and Travis.

Still turned away from the argument, he opened his eyes

again and stared off into the forest. For a moment, it didn't register with him what he was seeing. Then, blinking away tears and sweat, his vision cleared. Through a break in the trees, Jamie spotted foothills in the distance. They surrounded a small mountain range, whose peaks were encircled with clouds.

"Hey," he said.

The others ignored him, still focused on yelling at each other.

"Hey!" Jamie waited until they turned to him. When he was sure he had their attention, he pointed at the horizon. "Look. A mountain range. Maybe there's a cave or something we can take shelter in."

"Yeah," Geoff scoffed, "and no telling what will be lurking inside that cave."

Scott rubbed his goatee. "It might offer some protection against the Tyrannosaurus."

"I don't think she's following us anymore," Leigh said.

"Maybe not," Scott agreed, "but we saw a mommy and a baby. It stands to reason that Daddy is around here somewhere. Looking at their legs and those tiny foreclaws, and the way they navigated the ravine ... I don't think they're very good climbers. The mountains would offer us some protection from them, at least."

Leigh snorted. "You thought the bloody ravine would offer protection, too, and look how that turned out."

Scott bristled again. "I don't want to fight with you, Leigh, but I've had just about enough of—"

A sense of calm came over Jamie. No, he decided. Not calm. Indifference. If they wanted to stay here and squabble, he figured he would let them. Standing up, he started off toward the foothills.

"Hey," Geoff called, "where are you going?"

"There." Jamie pointed. "If you're coming with me, then let's go, because I'm not waiting around here to get eaten."

The forest merged with jungle topiary again. With Jamie now in the lead, they pushed through the underbrush. Birds and wildlife sang and chittered overhead, but there were no more dinosaur sounds. When they came across a winding, narrow game trail, he decided to follow it. The ground began to rise, and the foliage thinned. Eventually, the vegetation gave way to the sparsely forested foothills Jamie had spotted earlier. They paused for another quick break, and then pressed on, continuing to follow the game trail until it terminated at the top of a shallow gorge. They stood side-by-side at the edge, peering down. An animal skeleton lay scattered and broken among the rocks at the bottom. The body looked like that of a panther or a tiger, but the skull was similar to an elephant, and it had three eye sockets instead of two.

"What kind of skeleton is that?" Geoff wondered.

"Another castaway," Jamie murmured. "Just like us."

He turned to Scott and noticed that he was stroking his goatee and surveying the rest of the gorge.

"You're not thinking we should make a new camp down there, are you?" Jamie asked.

Scott shook his head. "No ... I was looking for water. But it's dry."

"Should we keep going up?" Jamie asked.

The others nodded. They continued on their way, navigating around the gorge and hiking farther up into the hills. Jamie found himself still in the lead, followed by Geoff, and then Scott, with Leigh lagging behind. Jamie considered asking him if he was okay, but decided instead to just give the Australian some space. Unlike the rest of them, he had arrived here with friends—people he'd known from the real world. Now, three of those friends—H, Paul, and Chris—were dead, and another was gone.

The real world, Jamie thought. *Why did I think of it in those terms?*

Gravel crunched beneath his feet, and sweat dripped from the tip of his nose. The vegetation thinned even more, reduced to a few scraggly trees and dry, brittle grass. Moss and lichen were abundant, covering the larger stones and boulders in a blanket of green, brown, grey, orange, red, and yellow. Jamie spotted several small animal tracks in the dirt. They also came across another skeleton, but the yellowed, moldering bones were so scattered that it was impossible for them to identify what they had belonged to. Birds circled overhead. Spiders, small lizards, ants, and centipedes scurried through the dirt, skittering beneath rocks at their approach.

"Watch for scorpions and snakes," Scott advised them. "This is the kind of territory they like."

"The animal tracks are all tiny," Jamie replied. "That's a good sign, right? No Tyrannosaurus footprints."

"We can hope," Geoff agreed.

Soon, the foothills gave way to a series of cliffs, ledges, and looming rock walls. More moss covered the latter, but all four of them instinctively avoided touching it.

Look at us, Jamie thought. Finally learning to adapt to our environment.

The sun, still perpetually frozen at high noon, glinted off something further ahead. Jamie stopped, shielding his eyes with his hands, and craned his head upward. The others halted behind him and did the same.

Scott gaped. "Is that ..."

Jamie nodded. "Looks like we're not the only ones who crashed here."

High above them, near the top of the range, was a treacherous outcropping of jagged, grey, lichen-covered rock, teetering above a steep, vertical cliff face. Jutting from the center of this cliff was the front half of a bright red Jeep, rigged for off-roading. It had oversized tires, a roll cage, and a black canvas top attached to the roll bars. The rear of the vehicle wasn't visible, as if it had fused with the rock, materializing half in and half out of the cliff.

"It looks new," Leigh surmised. "Could there be somebody inside?"

"If so," Jamie said, "I'm not sure how they would get down ... or how we could reach them. That's a pretty dangerous climb."

"Yeah," Scott agreed, "but maybe we should risk it. At least one of us. Even if the driver isn't inside, there might be things we can use."

They stood quietly for a few moments, staring at the Jeep. Jamie looked at the sheer cliff face, the dizzying drop, and weighed whether or not he could make the climb. Ultimately, he decided that he couldn't—not at his age. He was still in relatively good physical shape, but scaling something so precipitous was a job for a younger man, or better still, a professional mountain climber.

Leigh sniffed.

Jamie considered whether they'd find anything useful in the Jeep should one of them succeed in reaching it. Maybe some junk food, or water, or a travel mug with cold coffee inside. Matches or a lighter, possibly. A blanket, perhaps. But would there really be anything worth one of them risking their lives?

Leigh sniffed again. Jamie turned to him.

"You're not getting sick, are you?"

"Do you guys smell that?" Leigh asked.

Jamie inhaled, and caught a whiff of ...

"Moth balls?" he replied.

"I was thinking cucumbers," Leigh said.

"It's a reptile," Scott told them, his posture stiffening. "I'd know that smell anywh—"

Five figures emerged from behind a large, oval-shaped boulder. At first glance, they appeared similar to humans, with two arms, two legs, and a head, but that was where the likeness stopped. Instead of being human, they were reptilian, possessing scaly, greenish-grey skin and serpent heads. Forked tongues flickered from their mouths, and their lips pulled back in snarls, revealing pointed fangs. Their hands had three fingers and a thumb. Their weight and shape varied, but overall, they seemed to be slender and wiry, and stood an average of seven feet tall.

Jamie held up his hands, palms extended. "We mean you no harm."

The reptilians stared at him in silence.

"Careful," Scott cautioned. "Don't anybody do anything to spook them. No sudden moves."

"They're horrible," Leigh whispered.

Jamie shushed him.

The snake men carried a variety of weapons—everything from crude swords and crossbows to futuristic rifles—and wore a bizarre assortment of armor and gear. One wore chainmail. Another was dressed in sturdy police riot armor, complete with a mirrored-visor helmet that didn't quite fit over its serpentine head. A third wore the rusted armor of a Roman centurion. The last two—one of which had an olive-colored backpack—were clad in leather armor. Jamie frowned, staring at the strange patchwork on the latter. Slowly, it dawned on him that the leather was human skin, and the patchwork designs were faces, tattoos, and surgery scars. One of the tattoos, stretched across the humanoid's chest, was a cartoonish, Big Daddy Roth-styled four-wheel drive truck with four demonic looking characters behind the wheel.

Jamie tried again. "We mean you no harm. Can you understand us?"

"I doubt they speak English," Geoff said under his breath.

If the creatures did, they gave no indication, and yet Jamie was certain they were, in fact, communicating with each other, although no visible speech or hand movements were apparent. There was something in their eyes—something besides malevolence and intelligence—that indicated a conversation. They seemed particularly focused on Geoff. Perhaps, given that he was the biggest among the four men, the reptilians found his size intimidating?

Twitching nervously, Jamie licked his lips. "Um, Geoff?"

"Yeah?"

"I think you'd better—"

One of the rifle-wielding snake men pulled the trigger of his weapon. Jamie felt rather than heard the blast, for the report was soundless. He cringed as a wave of heat rushed past him. He smelled burning hair, and realized it was Geoff's. The hair atop the man's head, face, and arms had singed. Jamie watched in horror as the air around Geoff grew wavy and distorted, like a shimmering desert heat mirage. Geoff's eyes and mouth went wide, reminding Jamie of a fish. Then, the big man's skin blackened and smoked. Within seconds, he was reduced to a smoldering ash pile—incinerated without time to scream or probably even feel the pain.

"Holy shit," Jamie gasped.

"Run!" Scott screamed, and dodged to the side.

The snake people spread out, rushing them. They moved silently, for the most part, hissing but not making any other sounds. Jamie heard no speech, and he saw no hand gestures or other visible signals, yet the creatures moved and fought as a team, seemingly anticipating each other's actions.

A crossbow bolt thudded off a rock directly over Jamie's head. Leigh screamed his name, but Jamie barely noticed. He watched as Scott slipped over the side of a rock outcropping and dropped from view. Two of the creatures scrambled after him.

"Jamie, run!"

Jamie turned to him, and saw that Leigh had managed to flank their attackers, and was barreling back down the mountain. Two more of the reptilians gave pursuit, leaving Jamie to face off against the remaining opponent. He thought of his makeshift spear, dropped and abandoned back in that strange valley full of socks. Then it occurred to him that such a weapon wouldn't do much good against this snake-man's armor.

Hissing, it took a step toward him. Its chainmail clinked. The creature's forked tongue flicked at the air. It notched another crossbow bolt with seemingly unhurried precision. Jamie giggled in terror.

"There's no need for that," he said. "We can talk this over. Look, I just want to get back home, okay?"

Finished, his opponent raised its weapon and took another step, forcing Jamie to do the same. He retreated backward, hands still in the air, and stepped in a smoking pile of ashes that, until a few moments ago, had been Geoff. The heat seared through the sole of his shoe, melting the rubber. Howling with pain, Jamie hopped on one foot.

"Goddamn it!" he yelled. "It's not like I can buy another pair of shoes in this—"

Something punched him in the chest, pushing the air from his lungs. Jamie glanced down and saw a crossbow bolt protruding from his breast. He glanced back up at the snake.

"Hey ... you ..."

Then he collapsed, striking his head hard against the ground. Jamie barely noticed. His eyes felt heavy, and it hurt to breathe, so he decided to stop breathing for a while, and close his eyes instead.

[17]
BLOOP

Scott fled, chased by two snake men armed with swords. Heedless of which direction he was going, Scott ignored the burning in his lungs and the throbbing in his temples, and focused only on not toppling over one of the cliffs or outcroppings, and breaking his leg. He didn't glance behind him to check on his pursuers. He simply stared straight ahead, concentrating on not stopping or stumbling. Concentrating on putting one foot in front of the other. Concentrating on staying alive.

Earlier, he'd heard Leigh shout for Jamie, but there had been nothing since. More unnerving was the silence in which the reptilians engaged while in pursuit. The only clue they were still behind him was an occasional shuffling footstep or the sound of rocks sliding down a hill or their armor brushing against a boulder. Sometimes, he didn't even hear those things.

He came to a fissure in the rocks and jumped across without pausing. He happened to glance down and saw that, while narrow, it was dizzyingly deep. Then he landed on the other side. The soles of his feet stung as he hit the hard surface, and Scott tumbled, losing his balance. He fell, sprawling in the gravel and dirt, and only then did he risk a glance behind him.

The snake men were gone.

He lay there on his back, propped up on his elbows, panting and tensed, waiting for them to appear from behind a boulder. When they didn't, he tottered to his feet and wiped the sweat from his brow. Gasping for breath, he finally studied his surroundings. The cliffs and the Jeep were gone now. He realized that he was back in the foothills, although at a different spot than the one they had traversed before. The mingled biomes of jungle and forest stretched out below him. Scott glanced behind him, debating whether or not he should go back for the others. Geoff was most certainly dead, but Leigh and Jamie might still be alive. It was possible that they'd been incinerated just like Geoff—but it was equally possible that they had been captured. Perhaps Geoff's execution had been meant to serve as a warning to the rest of them not to flee or fight back. If so, that hadn't worked out so well for anyone, including the snake men.

He resolved to return to the lowlands. If Jamie and Leigh were dead, then there was no point in risking the same fate. And if they had indeed been captured, then ...

It was time he started to look out for himself.

LEIGH COWERED in a crevice between two boulders, curled into an almost fetal position to better hide himself, and waited for the sun to go down. He'd have better luck moving about at night.

Then he remembered that the sun didn't set in this place, and he started to cry again in frustration.

He felt something tickle his rib cage. Startled, he saw a large gray spider, about the size of his thumb, crawling on him. With a yelp, he lashed out, smashing it with his hand. The arachnid squirted across his palm, wet and sticky. Disgusted, he wiped his hand on his shirt and cursed beneath his breath.

Although he didn't know how much time had passed, he hadn't seen the snake men for quite a while. They'd pursued him doggedly, charging after him in silence. At one point, he'd gained the higher ground and tried to dislodge a boulder, burying them in an avalanche, but he'd lacked the physical strength to do it, and had instead only sent a few small pebbles hurtling down toward them. Although his pursuers didn't speak, Leigh thought they'd laughed at him.

He waited in the crevice until the cramps in his legs, thighs, and back became unbearable. Then he slowly crawled out. Wincing, he clambered to his feet and stretched, working out the kinks in his muscles. He scanned the countryside, looking for any sign of danger, but the snake men were gone.

Leigh walked to the edge of a rock ledge and stared down at the landscape below. He was surprised to see that he was right above the foothills. He hadn't realized he'd descended so far. The relative safety of the jungle was just a short distance away.

"Hooray," he muttered. "I'm saved! I can go back there and get eaten by a dinosaur rather than melted by snake men with heat rifles."

Then he spotted a small figure emerging from the base of the foothills and crossing the plain, heading for the tree line. Gasping, Leigh squinted, peering first through his glasses and then overtop them. It was Scott! He stopped himself from calling out for the man, in case their attackers were still within ear shot. Instead, he hurried down the slope, intent on catching up with him. There was safety in numbers, after all, and the two of them would have a much easier time rescuing Jamie together than alone.

If Jamie was even still alive, that was.

He jumped from rock to rock and then ran down the slope,

dislodging gravel and small stones on the way. Picking up speed, Leigh made great time until a small red and white serpent with two tails slithered across his path. Yelping, he skittered out of the way and tried to stop, but instead, he tripped and fell, sprawling. His glasses flew from his face and his palms were cut by numerous small stones. Hissing with pain, he sat up quickly and glanced around for the snake. He spotted its tails slinking beneath a boulder, but they were blurry, as were the rest of his surroundings.

"Shit ..."

Warm blood trickled from his hands as he felt around, searching for his glasses. His fingers brushed against the frames and he snatched them up, only to groan in dismay when he realized that the eyeglasses were now useless. One lens had completely shattered. The other was spider webbed with cracks and chips.

Not knowing what else to do, he shoved the bent frames into his pocket, and continued slowly down the hill, goggling at the blurry shapes around him.

SCOTT STOPPED for a brief rest when he reached the jungle. Then he plunged into the tree line and pushed through the undergrowth. He found a thick, sturdy stick about five feet in length and used it as a walking stick. When the vegetation grew too thick and impeded his progress, he began hacking at it with the staff. At one point, a vine latched on to his makeshift scythe, coiling around it and trying to wrest the stick from his grasp, but Scott fought back, wrenching it free. Then he hacked and slashed at the vine until his weapon was covered in green pulp.

"Jesus," he groaned. "I really want a cigar ..."

As he headed deeper into the jungle, the undergrowth

cleared, and his passage became easier. Scott spotted something that looked like a cross between a carrot and a pineapple growing in clusters atop a group of trees. A few birds pecked at them, so he assumed the strange fruit was safe to eat. Unfortunately, they grew high up in the branches, far beyond his reach, and he was too exhausted to climb a tree. He kept his eyes on the ground as he walked, hoping to spot any fruit that had fallen from above. Instead, he discovered a patch of what looked like watermelons growing wild across the jungle floor. They were the same size as the ones on Earth, and possessed the same green and white rind. Kneeling, Scott poked a hole in one with the end of his stick not covered in vine goo. The inside of the melon was pink and red, and dotted with black, teardrop-shaped seeds. He inhaled and sighed. It even smelled like watermelon.

"Fuck it," he grumbled. "Only one way to find out."

He sat cross-legged on the ground and cracked the melon apart, digging out a pink chunk. He stared at it, glistening in the sunlight. His fingers dripped with juice. Scott's mouth watered. He popped the morsel in and bit down. It squirted, filling his mouth with sweet relief. Groaning, he tore into the rest of the melon, ravenous, eating with both fists, happily gorging himself. He chomped and moaned, blissfully unaware.

Which was why he didn't hear the intruder until the tiny creature surprised him.

There was the sound of soft, padding footfalls and then an alarmed yowl, like a cat might make. Scott looked up, so startled that he dropped his melon rind. A two-foot tall, blue-furred animal stood on the other side of the watermelon patch, staring at him with wide, frightened yellow eyes. The creature was covered in downy, blackish-blue fur, and had pointed ears. It stood on two legs, and its fingers and toes sported tiny black talons. It also had a thin prehensile tail that twitched and coiled.

"H-hello ..."

The small blue-furred thing started at the sound of Scott's voice. Its nostrils flared and its tiny black lips curled back, revealing whitish nubs that would presumably develop into fangs eventually. Its tail twitched faster. Then it growled, sounding less like a cat and more like a cornered dog.

"Easy," Scott said, slowly reaching for his stick. "Just take it easy now. I'm not going to hurt you."

He stood cautiously, and the things agitation grew more pronounced. Chattering, it raised its head and howled.

"Git!" Scott pounded the end of his stick against the ground. "Go on, get out of here!"

Scott heard a rustling sound behind him, but he didn't want to take his eyes off the creature. Then, the leaves rustled in front of him, and an adult female, identical in appearance to the smaller creature, emerged from the foliage.

"Oh, shit," he whispered. "You must be Mommy. Take it easy. I didn't hurt your little guy, okay? I'm leaving."

The small creature didn't respond, but a voice from behind him did. It said one word, deep and sonorous.

"Bloop ..."

Before Scott could turn, the toddler charged forward, snarling, and sank its tiny claws into his thigh. Shrieking, Scott lashed out, striking it with his stick and then kicking it away from him. The youngling landed on all fours in the midst of the melons.

Whatever was behind him—and Scott was pretty sure it was Daddy—growled, clearly enraged. He spun around to face this new threat, but there was no time. He saw a flash of blackish-blue fur and bared fangs. Then, black talons—much bigger than the ones on the cub—slashed through the air and struck his jawline. There was an instant of incredible, burning pain. Scott saw a flap of meat fly through the air and slap against a tree trunk. With horror, he realized that it was his own face.

"Bloop," the creature snarled, and lunged at him.

⊏⊐

LEIGH WAS FUMBLING through the jungle, alternating between sobbing and hyperventilating, when a scream echoed through the trees. He dropped to the ground on his hands and knees and glanced around in confusion. Everything was blurry. He heard birds and insects, but he couldn't see them. The trees were abstract geometric shapes, and the undergrowth was a bewildering mix of multi-colored blobs.

A second scream followed, made all the more horrific by the sound quality of the jungle. The echoes bounced off the trees, sending the birds fleeing into the sky, and adding their own cacophony of squawks and cries.

Leigh's fist closed over a rock. He pulled it from the dirt and held it tightly. A crude weapon, yes, but it made him feel better. Then he noticed something shimmering just a few feet away.

"W-water ...?"

He crawled toward it. Yes, it was a puddle of water, spread out along the jungle floor. Forgetting his fear, he gasped with gratitude, and inched closer, pulling himself along the ground. If he could have a drink, he'd feel better about facing whatever was making that scream—or whatever was making it scream.

He reached for the puddle, but before he could dip his hands in, something came charging through the underbrush. Realizing it was too late to hide, Leigh hurriedly decided to dive into the puddle, hoping it was deep enough to conceal him. He took a deep breath ...

... and let it out with a shriek as a screaming, red-faced thing plunged out of the jungle and rocketed toward him. At first, Leigh didn't understand what he was seeing. Without his eyeglasses, he glimpsed just a running human figure, but the person's face appeared to be glistening and wet in addition to red. Then, something else erupted out of the jungle in pursuit—a furry, blackish-blue ape?

"Leigh," the red-faced thing cried. "Help me!"

"S-Scott ...?"

Leigh tried to jump to his feet, but the fleeing figure crashed into him, knocking them both into the puddle. Yes, he saw that it was indeed Scott. He wore the same clothes, and was the same height. But something was wrong with his face ...

The water flowed over them both, twisting and coiling, and Leigh realized too late that it wasn't a puddle at all. It was some sort of large amoeba. The ape-like creature skidded to a halt and watched them as tendrils of fluid flowed upward and over them. Leigh gaped at it in astonishment, before the pain set in. It felt like his skin had been doused in acid. He heard a hissing, bubbling sound that reminded him of bacon grease in a frying pan. He thrashed, turning toward Scott, and saw that whatever had happened to the man's face was now happening to the rest of him, as well. Leigh glanced down at himself and realized in horror that the skin on his hands had been stripped away. What he saw now was a red and white blur rather than a flesh-colored blur. He opened his mouth to scream, and the liquid flowed inside of him.

The last thing he saw before the pain rendered him unconscious was the blurry shape of the blue-furred creature, watching his and Scott's demise. Then, the amoeba slithered over his eyes and the blurriness turned to black.

"It's beautiful here," Jesse murmured.

"Yeah," Mark agreed. "It is."

Paula didn't respond, focused instead on saving her breath as she led them toward the sword, looming over the garden like some sort of watchtower. Yet she couldn't deny that the two men were right. It was beautiful here—more beautiful than anything she'd ever seen on Earth. It felt primal and lush. Even the air seemed different. Were it not for Erin's abduction, she thought she probably would have been okay staying here for a bit. They'd seen no signs of dinosaurs or any other dangers. The abundant insects and wildlife seemed non-threatening. Granted, many of them were strange and bizarre, and unlike anything she had ever encountered. But so far, the bugs and birds here in the garden weren't trying to kill them. Indeed, the wildlife seemed ... happy. Even joyous. The trees and bushes echoed with their chorus. For a moment, Paula lost herself in their song, and her spirits began to lift.

Then it occurred to her just how much Erin would like this spot, and her anger and fear and resolve returned.

"Come on," she said. "We can sightsee later."

She led them forward, pushing through the foliage. Jesse and Mark asked to stop briefly when they came across some raspberry bushes. Paula reluctantly agreed, and soon joined the two in gorging herself on the ripened fruit. Soon, their lips and fingertips were stained red. Sated, they pressed on.

They crossed a trickling brook and saw tiny, silver fish darting beneath the surface. On the other side was an orchard. It appeared to be well-tended. The grass was cut short and the space between the trees was cleared of any undergrowth. The limbs held a myriad of different colored fruits. Paula recognized the peaches and plums and bananas, but there were many others that—just like the birds and insects—she was sure had never originated on Earth.

"Wow," Jesse said. "We should have set up camp here instead of that ravine."

"We still can," Mark replied. "Soon as we rescue Erin, we can come back here and—"

"Mommy!"

All three of them turned. Paula gasped. Erin ran across the orchard, arms outstretched, squealing with delight.

"Erin! Oh my God, baby! Are you okay?"

The girl ran to her, and Paula knelt, scooping her up in an embrace. She sobbed tears of joy and relief into her daughter's hair.

"I missed you, Mommy. I'm okay. We can go back now."

"Back where?" Mark asked. "Erin, do you know how to get us home?"

"No," she answered, her voice muffled against Paula's breast. "Don't be silly, Mark. I meant back to our camp."

Paula stiffened. She put Erin on the ground and slowly pushed her away.

The little girl cocked her head. "What's wrong, Mommy?"

"You're not Erin. You're not my daughter."

"Now you're being silly, Mommy. Of course I'm Erin."

"Paula ..." Jesse stepped forward and put a hand on her shoulder. "You've been through a lot. Maybe—"

"No!" She pushed his hand away and lunged to her feet. "This isn't Erin. She doesn't smell like her. I know the smell of my daughter's hair. It's always on her pillow, even after I do the wash. This isn't her."

Mark and Jesse glanced from Paula to Erin. The little girl stood, hands clasped behind her back, smiling sweetly.

"And she wouldn't have called you Mark. She would have called you Mr. Sylva. But I don't even think she knew your name before they took her."

Mark's expression grew darker. "I think you're right. I don't remember telling her ..."

"Mommy," Erin said. "Come now. Stop this."

"Shut up!"

Paula wheeled around and slapped the little girl across the face. The sound echoed through the orchard. Jesse gasped.

Still smiling, Erin sighed. "Oh well. No fooling you, I guess. A mother's love, eh?"

As they watched, Erin began to change shape, transforming into a tall, shimmering angel. Golden-tipped wings spread out behind it. The being looked down upon them and smiled, sadly.

"I apologize for the—"

"That's fucked up, pal," Mark interrupted. "That's some fucking bullshit."

"My name is Uriel."

"Your name is Fucknuts," Mark countered. "And I don't believe in angels."

Uriel spread his hands. "And yet, here I stand before you."

"It's another trick," Paula guessed. "You're a shapeshifter. Show us your true form."

Sighing again, Uriel began to change once more, shrinking in size until a short grey alien stood before them, naked and withered.

"Your kind used to like that other form," he complained, his tone sullen.

"Where's my daughter? You took her!"

"I did no such thing. I rarely leave my post." He pointed up at the shining trapezohedron. "Indeed, I have not set foot here in the garden since we planted the apple tree."

Mark frowned. "Apple tree?"

"Yes. It symbolized what happened to one of our brothers ... now fallen. Fallen a long time ago, actually."

"Your people took my daughter," Paula snarled. "I want her back! Where is she?"

"She is back on Earth," Uriel replied, "returned exactly where she was when you first arrived here. She is safe. No harm befell her. Indeed, that was why we removed her from this place."

"Why?" Jesse challenged. "Why just the little girl? Why not all of us?"

"Because she was not supposed to be here. Erin has things to accomplish. Her arrival here was a mistake."

"But we're supposed to be here?" Mark asked.

"No. None of you are supposed to be here. It was decreed long ago, and it is my honorable task to keep that command. Your arrival was an accident—the result of a momentary hole in the fabric of space and time. A door was opened that should have been left closed. But now that you are here, you may not leave."

"Why not?" Paula asked.

"Because that is how He decreed it."

"Who?"

"The Creator."

"Oh yeah? Well, then take me to see this creator. I want my daughter back. If you took her home, you can take us home, too."

Uriel gestured at the sword. "None may pass. Indeed, if you go further, you will be struck down."

Mark balled his fists. "You threatening us, pal? Because I've gotta tell you, right now, you and your friends are all that stand in the way of me getting back to my own son, and I will cut through each and every one of you."

"I am not threatening you, Mark Sylva. I am merely informing you of what will happen. No, I will not destroy you. But nevertheless, you will die if you continue this crusade. And this is not a place that you humans want to die in."

"Why not?" Paula asked.

"Because you have souls. Have you not been listening? Once here, nothing is allowed to leave. That includes your spirits."

Paula glared at the alien for a long moment. Then she turned back to Mark and Jesse.

"Come on. Let's keep going."

"Take care, Paula Beauchamp. I have warned you what will occur should you continue. I pray you heed me."

Paula strode forward and poked Uriel in the chest with her finger. "You claim to know us humans?"

"Indeed. I was there when your ancestors first—"

"You don't know us," she interrupted. "You don't know us at all. If you did, you'd know to never get between a mother and her daughter. Now get the fuck out of our way."

Uriel held up his hands. "So be it."

Then he disappeared.

Paula blinked, and then glanced around the orchard.

"Fuck him," Mark said. "Obviously, we're on the right track. He doesn't want us getting any closer to that cross-sword thing, right? That's gotta be the way home."

Paula bit her lip, blinking back tears. "Do you guys think he could have been lying? About Erin? Do you think she's really back in Baltimore?"

Mark took her hand. "Let's go find out."

Paula smiled. "Gahbee and Geeb?"

"You're goddamned right, Gahbee and Geeb."

"There you guys go with that again," Jesse said. "Is somebody going to let me in on this little private joke?"

They continued on their way, with Paula once again leading, and Mark explained the story of him and his son Alex to Jesse as they went along. Paula teared up, hearing it again.

"I'm coming, baby," she whispered. "Mommy's coming. Just hang on."

The orchard terminated into a vast field of wildflowers. Beyond those, beneath the sword and the trapezohedron, was a circular area devoid of any growth. Far above them, the alien spacecraft continued to buzz around, darting up to the sun and then back down again. As they watched, several of the craft seemed to blink out of existence near the trapezohedron, as if they had teleported elsewhere.

"That thing is the key," Mark guessed. "The portal is probably inside of it."

Jesse shielded his eyes and gazed skyward. "So, how do we get up there?"

"The sword can't just be a sword. I mean, that's ridiculous."

"As ridiculous as a moody mass-transit robot trying to drop us off in a city full of snake people?"

"I mean," Mark continued, "that it's a building of some kind. I mean, it has to be. These aliens have to live somewhere. Other than Fucknuts—"

"Uriel?" Jesse said.

"Fucknuts," Mark insisted. "Other than him, we haven't seen any of them here in this ... garden. And I doubt they're living out there in the jungle or the desert with the dinosaurs and all that other shit. Where else would they go?"

"The sun?" Jesse guessed.

"How would they live on the sun? No, Fucknuts pointed up when he was talking about his post. I'm betting that at the base of that sword, we'll find a door, and stairs or elevators or teleporters or some shit."

"What makes you so sure?" Paula asked.

"Because what other purpose would it serve?"

Nodding, she shrugged. "Okay. Let's try it."

They walked into the clearing, side by side, and walked toward the looming structure. The full light of the sun bore down on them, and Paula found herself squinting.

"Wow," she gasped. "It's hard to see."

"Hold hands," Jesse suggested. "That way we don't lose each other."

They clasped hands—Mark on the left, Jesse on the right, and Paula in the middle, and then they started forward again.

As they drew closer, the sword began to glow. Waves of reddish-orange energy crackled along its surface.

"Gahbee and Geeb," Mark said.

"Gahbee and Geeb," Jesse agreed.

"Gahbee and Geeb." Paula nodded, swallowing. "I'm coming, Erin."

Then, without warning, flames flickered out from the sword and shot across the field, engulfing them where they stood.

They were swallowed by the light.

———

SILENCE RETURNED TO THE GARDEN. Then, after a while, the birds and insects began to sing again.

E xcerpt from *The Baltimore Sun*

... but authorities still have no comment on the status of the investigation into the missing shuttle. The vehicle, operated by Globe Transport, disappeared in last week's blizzard, with nineteen people onboard, including the driver. Only one of those passengers, Erin Beauchamp of Michigan, has been located. She was found wandering the highway just moments after witnesses reported seeing the shuttle vanish, and has since been reunited with her father. A source who spoke on condition of anonymity says the girl is in good health, but has no memory of what happened, and has been unable to help in the ongoing investigation ...

TRACK YOUR PACKAGE ONLINE
TRACKING NUMBER 1672 8724 0085 7777
SENDER:

Benn Martin ADDRESSEE:
Benn Martin
XXXXX XXX XXXX
Dunalley, Tasmania, Australia
STATUS: Package Arrived Safely

AFTERWORD

Hole in the World serves as a prequel of sorts to my novel, *The Lost Level*, and as such, should be considered a part of that series (even though the main protagonist, Aaron Pace, is missing from the novel you just read). The events in this book take place a short time before Aaron's arrival in the pocket dimension known as the Lost Level, and explain a few of the mysteries from later in the series (such as the scene when Aaron, Kasheena, and Bloop find a wheelchair in a pile of dinosaur feces).

This novel is a bit different than your standard tale, in that— while it is a work of fiction—all of the characters featured in the book (with the exception of bus driver Lucinda Hawkins) are real people, who paid for the opportunity to be a character in the book via Kickstarter and several other programs. I've done this before, most notably with the two short story collections *The Rising: Selected Scenes from the End of the World* and *Earthworm Gods: Selected Scenes from the End of the World*.

In those two examples, each individual person starred in their own short story, and thus, they didn't have to share the page with anyone else. In the case of *Hole in the World*, they were each a small part of a much larger ensemble cast. This proved challenging to me, as a writer. After all, these folks paid good money for this opportunity, and I wanted to make sure they saw a value for that. But at the same time, I also knew that in such a fictional setting, somebody would have to die. Otherwise, there's no suspense for the reader.

I struggled with that for a long time, and as a result, the book missed its deadline. (My thanks to the publishers—Tony and Kim at Camelot Books and Jason and Lesley at Apex Book Company —for their infinite patience and understanding).

So, with the deadline slipping more and more, I decided the only fair thing to do was to kill everybody.

I scrapped a half-written, earlier draft of the novel and started completely over from scratch (which just delayed things further). Then, I wrote each person's name down on a slip of paper, and put them into a mason jar. After that, I pulled out the names one by one, thus determining the order in which I'd kill them. I decided that to make things even fairer, I'd kill Lucinda first, since she was the only fictional character. Benn had the honor of being the first name drawn from the jar, so I think it's only fitting that his books are the last scene of this novel. Benn never made it home, but his books did.

The only person I didn't kill was Paula's daughter, Erin. There are a couple of reasons for that. One, Erin hadn't actually paid to be in the book. Her father (who purchased Paula's placement) requested that I include her, as well. Secondly, I've met Erin. Her parents have brought her to numerous signings and conventions over the years, and I've watched her grow up, and she's a remarkable young woman. Every time I see her, she gives me a gift—a picture she's drawn for me or a craft that she's made. So, there was just no way I could bring myself to pull that particular trigger. Believe me, I tried. There are several earlier drafts of this novel that fell apart because I tried. Ultimately, I decided to let her live, and thus, the gray aliens (which readers of my novel *The Seven: The Labyrinth Book 1* know are really angels) provided me an out. I'd already established them as part of the Lost Level's lore, so it was a pretty easy fix.

So, yes. I couldn't kill the little girl. But I had no problem killing all the grown-ups, and indeed, it was a lot of fun inventing their various demises. I only hope that they—and you—had as much fun reading it as I did writing it.

If this was your first introduction to the world of the Lost Level, the story continues in *The Lost Level* and *Return to the Lost Level* (both currently available) and the forthcoming *Beneath the Lost Level* (and possibly more after that, if the universe allows it).

As always, thanks for reading.

Brian Keene
Somewhere along the Susquehanna River
July 2017

ACKNOWLEDGMENTS

Thanks, first and foremost to Tony and Kim of Camelot Books, and Jason and Lesley at Apex Book Company, for their infinite patience when this novel inexcusably got lost in the space between time and reality, and thus was turned in way past deadline.

Thanks also to my pre-readers Tod Clark, Mark Sylva, and Stephen McDornell.

Thanks, as well, to Mary SanGiovanni, and my sons.

And finally, extra special thanks to Paula Beauchamp, Erin Beauchamp, Scott Berke, Colinda Carroll, Jesse Carroll, H Michael Casper, Tod Clark, Paul Goblirsch, Geoff Guthrie, Leigh B. Haig, Chris Hansen, Jamie LaChance, Paul Legerski, Bob Lewis, Gregorio Lopez, Benn Martin, Dave Rodeheaver, and Mark Sylva for allowing me to put them in this situation.

The Seven

ABOUT THE AUTHOR

BRIAN KEENE writes novels, comic books, short fiction, and occasional journalism for money. He is the author of over fifty books, mostly in the horror, crime, and dark fantasy genres. His 2003 novel, *The Rising*, is often credited (along with Robert Kirkman's *The Walking Dead* comic and Danny Boyle's *28 Days Later* film) with inspiring pop culture's current interest in zombies. Keene's novels have been translated into German, Spanish, Polish, Italian, French, Taiwanese, and many more. In addition to his own original work, Keene has written for media properties such as *Doctor Who, The X-Files, Hellboy, Masters of the Universe*, and *Aliens*.

Several of Keene's novels have been developed for film, including *Ghoul, The Ties That Bind*, and *Fast Zombies Suck*. Keene's work has been praised in such diverse places as *The New York Times, The History Channel, The Howard Stern Show, CNN.com, Publisher's Weekly, Media Bistro, Fangoria Magazine*, and *Rue Morgue Magazine*.

He has won numerous awards and honors, including the 2014 World Horror Grandmaster Award, 2016 Imadjinn Award for Best Fantasy Novel, 2001 Bram Stoker Award for Nonfiction, 2003 Bram Stoker Award for First Novel, 2004 Shocker Award for Book of the Year, and Honors from United States Army International Security Assistance Force in Afghanistan and Whiteman A.F.B. (home of the B-2 Stealth Bomber) 509th Logistics Fuels Flight.

A prolific public speaker, Keene has delivered talks at conventions, college campuses, theaters, and inside Central Intelligence Agency headquarters in Langley, VA.

The father of two sons, Keene lives in rural Pennsylvania.

For more information:
www.briankeene.com

 twitter.com/briankeene

The first book in Grand Master Award winner Brian Keene's
Lost Level new series is a loving ode to lost world classics like
Burroughs's PELLUCIDAR, Howard's ALMURIC, and
Lansdale's THE DRIVE-IN, but with a thoroughly modern twist
that only Brian Keene could conceive.

Available from Apex Book Company
ApexBookCompany.com

Can Aaron Pace and his small band lay siege to the Anunnaki city and rescue their friends, or will they suffer the same cruel fate so many others have before them?

Available from Apex Book Company
ApexBookCompany.com

CPSIA information can be obtained
at www.ICGtesting.com
Printed in the USA
LVHW091329050419
613117LV00001B/64/P

9 781937 009724